Reign of Viscus

(Special Edition: John Bradford memorial edition)

By Kevin C. Davison

© 2013 by Kevin C. Davison.
All rights reserved.

Special Edition: John Bradford Memorial Edition.

All characters in this book are fictitious, and any resemblance to real persons, living or dead, is coincidental.

Cover art design by Amy Wenzel.

ISBN-13: 978-1484001783
ISBN-10: 1484001788

Dedication:

This special edition release of Reign of Viscus is dedicated to the memory of John Bradford who passed on from this world to the next on the fifth day of October in the year of 2012. He will be missed.

Acknowledgements:

    This book was made possible through the inspiration of my dear friends as well as my passion for writing. Without their influence and support the Athyxian Chronicles series would possibly never have been possible. Special thanks to my dear friends, John Bradford, Paul and Joseph Punley, Casey Moyer, Aaron Roark, Josh Pruitt, and everyone else who I had the pleasure of gaming with those years ago. Without the support of my wife Amy I don't think I would have succeeded at publishing my work.

Prologue:

The creation and balance of a new world sometimes go hand in hand. During the creation of Athyx, there were only two gods. They were each other's opposition and kept balance among the endless universe they had dominion over. They united once to begin the creation of Athyx. During the time, it took to create Athyx, other gods emerged and assisted in its creation, taking on rolls necessary to form the world and keep things balanced. Over the thousand years of its formation, Athyx was forged with power from every deity in its growing pantheon and that power was supposed to bring life to the world in many different ways. What they did not know right away, was the power also united to create a relic that served as a balance point for their created world. It was an apocalypse stone; a stone of power. It was the Marble of Godly Doom. The relic was a small smoky marble of red, black, and purple with the power to put order into a pantheon that had none. No god could wield its power. It was discovered by the elder gods that only a mortal could wield its seemingly limitless power. With that possibility threatening the pantheon, the gods created a temple that touched both the material world of Athyx and the Ethereal Plane, the plane of ghosts and spirits. It was created within a swampland deep in the Great Forest near its southern borders and was dubbed the Ethereal Temple on the world of Athyx, but on the Ethereal Plane, it was known as the Eye of the Gods because all gods watched this temple on the Ethereal Plane with great caution. Some of the gods felt that a hero should be forged from the world to destroy the relic that could bring the gods to their knees. Other gods plotted for their most devoted servants to seek out the relic and use it to destroy their enemy gods. The gods created a great guardian that watched over the temple on the Ethereal Plane and was powerful enough to at least maim a god and remind whoever dared to steal the relic that the gods would curse them forever. On the world of Athyx, a sacred cult was forged that served no god. They used the Ethereal Temple as their sacred place for meditation and prayer to themselves. The priests of the atheist religion hired an evil man called Shang Tao from the Far East continent of the Orient to protect the temple in the swamplands. Shang Tao was an outcast from the foreign realm of the Orient, but he was one of the greatest swordsmen of his time. The evil samurai slaughtered many just for coming too close to a temple that they did not know existed. No one but the cult even was aware of its existence among mortals. When the gods first created the temple that touched two planes, they created a gate to the Ethereal Plane within the temple for the one worthy to wield the relic to pass through if ever it was decided that a mortal was worthy to wield the relic. Over the many years, the gods had placed their attentions elsewhere and forgot about the relic they could not touch nor destroy. Undead were created by the atheist priests to help Shang Tao. They were skilled warrior undead known as the swaiths. Unlike the commonly known undead in the realms, swaiths were a corporeal embodiment of atheism. They were non believers that had no home to go to after they passed on. Most swaiths roamed the lands mindlessly killing worshippers of gods. They sapped physical strength from anyone they touched in battle, and were capable of vanquishing the mightiest of heroes. Shang Tao had done such a good job over his many years of service that the atheist priests wanted him to continue his service after his death. The high priest offered Shang Tao immortal life so long as he agreed to guard the temple and allow no one access to it. The samurai agreed. The priests instructed the evil samurai to kill himself with his own sword in front of all of them to prove his devotion and loyalty. The evil samurai was in his prime when he committed the act. He impaled himself, driving his own curved short samurai sword known as a wakazashi in the Orient, through his heart. The priests called upon the dark forces to animate the body and Shang Tao arose as a swaith. Unlike the common swaith he remembered who he was in life and his promise to the priests, his promise to allow no one access to the temple. He was the warden, the chosen guardian of the temple. Shang Tao kept his promise and to the surprise of the atheistic priests Shang-Tao slaughtered them all for dwelling within the sacred temple he was told that no one was allowed inside. They eventually arose as mindless swaiths that Shang Tao gave a purpose to. He directed them to stay with him as guards of the temple. They were his extending arm beyond his limits. Part of his creation bound him to the temple and a small area around the temple. They could leave, however and would make protecting the temple much easier.

*****

A vile god known as Viscus sent his most powerful minions into play so that he might achieve his ultimate goal, the extinction of life. The man known only as the Servant of Viscus walked the realms using his divine and arcane knowledge to find a way for his master to achieve his goals. The man was pale like a vampire and wheezed with sickness, but he was not undead as were most of the minions of Viscus. He was among the living. The life sapping energy he wielded over the years had taken its toll on his body and seemed to have fed upon it. The Servant of

Viscus felt as though he had disappointed his god and researched by every means to find his answer. Armco knew that Viscus planned on trying to destroy Enamor and take control of the pantheon as a Supreme God of the realms. He transported himself to the castle of the Servant of Viscus and his mere presence brought the Servant of Viscus to his knees.

"I am Armco," the devil god claimed. "I know secrets that others have chosen to forget and hide." The Servant of Viscus felt the power dim enough to allow him to look upon the devil god.

"I seek the means to help my god reach his goal to vanquish all life," the Servant of Viscus claimed.

"You do realize that you are among the living, do you not?" Armco asked curiously.

"For now I am, but eventfully I will become one with Viscus and he will devour my soul," the Servant of Viscus replied. The total devotion was surprising to Armco. Armco saw purpose in this walking contradiction. He wanted to extinguish life and yet he was among the living. Armco wanted to increase his power. He saw devotion in the dark heart of the kneeling man. He had enough devotion to die for his god if he had to. He was truly worthy to wield the power of the forgotten relic if he could defeat the guardian of the temple. No god would dare try and stop him. They all feared the power of the relic so much that none of them ever went to its hidden location. The temple was a shared temple with shrines to all gods of the pantheon on the ethereal plane, but not on the material realm. No shrines existed on the material realm to keep any such followers from using the temple as a place of worship. The atheists that had taken it as a place of self worship discovered that in using the temple they had become cursed by the gods for more than just their blasphemous ways.

"There is a powerful relic on the Ethereal Plane hidden within a place called the Eye of the Gods. It holds power that makes the gods cower in fear. There is a great guardian that protects the relic. No one but a mortal can wield its power or even touch it. With the Marble of Godly Doom you can fulfill your deity's wishes. Use it to empower your master." Armco cackled before vanishing. The Servant of Viscus remembered the name Armco and that was all that the deity wanted. When Viscus was empowered, his name would be remembered for guiding the mortal servant to the relic. Viscus would reward him with great power and a higher status among the pantheon. He would not have to live among the mortal world anymore. The Servant of Viscus wasted little time and used his divining magic to scry the relic's location. The location was protected by the power of the gods and the Servant of

Viscus had failed in finding its location. He devoted his life to discovering the relic and traveled to the ethereal plane with the relic in mind as he searched for its hidden temple over the course of ten years. With the guidance of his god, the vile servant found the temple upon the Ethereal Plane. Before him stood the temple, and the powerful guardian that watched over it. The great guardian was unlike anything he had ever seen before. It stood like a man, but its body was made of pure darkness. It had no solid mass to it, but was not a ghost or a wraith. Whatever it was called, the guardian was powerful. It was like a void of nothingness had taken the shape of a man. The Eye of the Gods was right in front of him but the guardian blocked his path. A great battle began between the Servant of Viscus and the guardian of the temple. The guardian of the temple proved to be very devastating to the Servant of Viscus, wreathing him in a strange black fire. Flames of cold blackness wracked his body and sapped more of his health as it burned with cold rather than heat. The Servant of Viscus managed to dissipate the effects of the cold-fire and turned an arsenal of spells upon the guardian. The guardian was more surprised than the Servant of Viscus as it was vanquished. The Servant of Viscus crawled into the temple, beaten and badly hurt. He climbed up two flights of stairs to the top terrace where a gate shimmered and led to some unknown place. A pedestal rested with a small marble of black, red, and purple swirls and the Servant of Viscus knew he had found the relic. Without any patience or caution, the Servant of Viscus took the relic and evoked its power.

"Make my god the supreme ruler and give him all of the power of the universe," the Servant of Viscus shouted as he held the relic over his head. The relic was created to maintain balance among the gods and the world of Athyx and could do nothing but that. Viscus was empowered in a way that he could not have foreseen.

All other gods that had dominion over Athyx were stripped of their divinity except for Enamor. This was how the balance was maintained by the power evoked by the relic. Armco was a part of the story and the one named as the instigator of the cataclysm by name and reputation. To his surprise he was affected as well, being stripped of his divine status and power. All of the stolen power was absorbed through the body of the Servant of Viscus and into the relic, vaporizing the once powerful man that devoted his services to a god that would have him killed without a second thought because he was among the living. Nothing but a fine dust remained of the Servant of Viscus. The relic fell to the floor pulsing with the stolen power of all gods except Viscus and Enamor. The Servant of Viscus arose from the ashes of his vaporized body as a wraith. He shrieked in pain as he felt nothing but the coldness and loss of his soul. He still wielded great power, but he was without a body and now among his allies the undead. Like his deity, he was now a wraith and though most would have been angered, he was not. The servant of Viscus was a fanatic and wanted to be one with his god. Now he was that much closer to his goal. He had become a wraith during the service of his god.

Viscus and his forces hunted down the former gods and imprisoned them one by one. Even though he was without his divine power, Armco helped Viscus and for his aid, the mighty god of darkness and destruction did not imprison the former god of devils. He was left in control of his dominion on the world of Athyx. Devils were not among the living. They collected the souls of the living for personal gain and power. That only aided Viscus further his plans to reach his ultimate goal of total lifelessness. It took a great effort, but Viscus with the aid of his faithful servant was able to defeat Enamor and imprison him as well. He would have rather killed the deity, but there had to be balance and the power of the relic protected him from being slain. He had to live. Viscus had created a special cell to hold his nemesis. Over the next fifty years, Viscus had hunting parties of undead slaughter the living. He put out the sun and wreathed it in black flames of life sapping energy. It was as if the gates of Oblivion were opened inside the sun. Balance was in accordance to the relic at first, but not any longer. The relic called out for the first time to someone who was worthy to restore balance. The relic had stolen the power of many gods and with it some of their characteristics and personalities. The first to surface was Tevlos the god of a nature. A thought from a mind of the dwarven god, Brom aided its plan. It was a simple thought and rather a point of philosophy more than anything. The thought of Brom the dwarf god was that heroes are forged, not born.

*****

One of the many daughters of Aphrodite and Armco named Villisca became a powerful devil that roamed the world of Athyx, destroying mankind and preying on the most noble of knights. She desired more than anything to join her parents among the pantheon. Her father wanted to guide her, but she would not listen to his instructions and rebelled against his wishes whenever he instructed her to do something that she did not desire to do. After a thousand year reign as the nemesis of knights, Villisca became the hunted along with the evil dragons of the world that had overrun the lands of mortals rather than the lands of their ruling god or goddess. Villisca sought refuge from her hunters and left her kingdom as it was brought to ruins. Because she had not obeyed her father, she had caused the destruction of her devil kingdom in the world. She took on a humanoid form of an elf maiden and took refuge among the elves in the Golden City. The Golden City was one of the Great Cities known in the world. She eventually listened to the voice of her father beckoning to her and obeyed. Villisca met an elf named Soel and became his bride. She conceived and gave birth to a mortal child. The child was to be the next legacy of Armco. He was the key to his mother's ascension and Armco's usurping the greatest of the gods. The half-devil offspring was mortal and therefore could wield the power of the Marble of Godly Doom. Villisca was told to leave the elf to begin the next phase of her father's plan. Soel was instructed by Villisca to raise the elf boy in the arcane arts of the elves that he practiced. Soel saw no problem with teaching his son the arcane arts. What he did not know was that the mother of his child was a devil and not an elf.

  The child was named Gilthanus, and when he reached the proper age, Soel began his teachings. Gilthanus did not learn as Soel did, and seemed more naturally innate at his practice learning magic in the manner of a sorcerer. The sorcerer was a rare being in which magic ran through the very blood of its existence. Soel continued to teach his son even with the suspicion of his wife. She had been gone for many years and he believed that she had died somewhere during her journey to wherever it was she had to go so abruptly. Gilthanus was seventy-four years old when the sun turned black with life sapping energy feeding upon the living of the world. He fought the urge to leave for nearly fifty years after the black sun appeared in the sky. Soel awoke one day to find that Gilthanus had gone. His son had run away to seek out his missing mother and live out his dreams. He did not know his purpose just yet but he did not want to fulfill the dreams of his mother and father. They had their own lives to live out. This was his life and not theirs to control. Gilthanus had no idea where to begin his search for his mother and walked from the west from the great city. The wraiths found the great city days later and consumed the life within. Some invisible force had directed Gilthanus out of the city to keep him safe. Villisca returned to check on her son's development and learned of the city's destruction when she found in its place a great city of wraiths. Villisca was furious. Armco was angered as well. He had power that his daughter only dreamed of and knew that his grandson had left, but he did not know why. He told his daughter that Gilthanus still lived. Groups of devil minions were sent in search of the missing grandson of Armco. Even Villisca was sent in search of her son to redirect him.

Chapter One:

Deep in the subterranean realm of Athyx, the vermin-kissed elves were at war. An uprising of their own kin-creations had turned on them. Unfaithful vermin-kissed elves were tortured until they submitted to serving Na-Dene. Those who had unbreakable wills were sacrificed to Na-Dene in a vile ritual before all within their house and were transformed into embodiments of mindless madness and pure chaos. They were no longer humanoid creations, but an oozing and ever-changing specimen of madness called chaos minions. All chaos minions were magically transported out into an area of the wilds that was designated to distribute them safely away from the city where they could roam mindlessly through the darkness. The vermin-kissed elves that had their wills broken were also publicly displayed before their house and through a second known ritual; they were transformed into vermin-kissed horrors. The vermin-kissed elves screamed during the magical process as their bodies merged with their totem vermin and augmented both of their features, as they became one vessel of chaos. They became giant-sized vermin with the lower bodies of a giant rat, spider, centipede or some other vermin type and the upper body of the vermin-kissed elf similar to a centaur. Vermin-kissed elves were the wicked offspring of good elves and Na-Dene the Vermin Queen and Mistress of Chaos. They had dark skin and wielded venomous magic that could maim or kill their foes. The wicked elves could also summon a minion of their goddess to aid them in battle. Each vermin-kissed elf was part of a house governed by a monarch house queen. Among those house queens, there was a council and one ruling queen over all other houses. Each individual vermin-kissed elf bonded with a specific vermin, and that became the totem of that vermin-kissed elf. The totem bond decided what kind of vermin that particular vermin-kissed elf summoned.

The faithful subdued vermin-kissed horrors believed that it was their responsibility to free their goddess if possible. The vermin-kissed elves refused to listen to once unfaithful abominations. The vermin-kissed horrors were divided. Many served their house queens loyally, believing that whatever the house queen ordered was the will of Na-Dene. Others that had taken up the devotion of priestesses of Na-Dene believed that it was their duty to rescue their goddess or die trying. The vermin-kissed elves were also divided. Some believed that it was necessary to switch their devotion to the dark god Viscus in order for their race to survive. Because of this blasphemous debate, the faithful vermin-kissed horrors turned on the elves and left the city of Maovolence to form an army of their own and first punish the vermin-kissed elves for not even trying to rescue their goddess and secondly make the attempt their selves. Each house sent their soldiers into battle against the traitorous vermin-kissed horrors that believed it was the will of Na-Dene to punish the vermin-kissed elves for their failure to rescue their imprisoned deity. Priestesses' had little power due to the absence of their goddess from her domain. The minions of Na-Dene took over duties and upkeep of her realm during the absence of the goddess and were divided. They did not war between one another, but they did act, as they believed their goddess would and sent a representative from the chosen faithful called Mo'Reens to each side and supported both decisions of either rescuing their goddess or remaining diligent for her to return. Both hated the unfaithful path chosen by many of the vermin-kissed elves to leave the city to serve Viscus. They at least agreed that those traitors would be the first to be killed for their blasphemy. The vermin-kissed horrors believed that they were superior in their devotion to Na-Dene and the Mo'Reen that visited them enforced the idea. The chosen faithful was a vermin-kissed horror as all chosen faithful that visited the devoted of Na-Dene were. That fact stirred the issue even more and fueled the fire, enforcing the war between the vermin-kissed elves and the vermin-kissed horrors. The words of the Mo'Reen echoed in the devoted minds of the vermin-kissed horrors.

"Vermin-Kissed Horrors are superior. We should rule the city and not the elves. After all, we were once the unfaithful and through our cleansing of torture from the elves we became even more devoted to Na-Dene than them." The Mo'Reen was cheered. She chose a high priestess to become the empress to lead them before leaving them to their war. The vermin-kissed horrors wanted to rule over the vermin-kissed elves and punish them for not acting and attempting to save their goddess. The house queen that ruled over all other houses in the city of Maovolence was slain by a Mo'Reen, but they believed it was a vermin-kissed horror and not a chosen faithful of Na-Dene. The message of the empress called out to all of the vermin-kissed horrors and a large group left the city and went out into the wilds of the subterranean realm of Athyx to take refuge. Without a ruling high priestess, the vermin-kissed elves were divided and took time debating as to what actions should be taken. Many loyal subjects to the former high priestess house queen, of house Lirvir believed that it was the duty of all vermin-kissed elf houses to avenge their fallen queen and hunt down the rebellious vermin-kissed horrors. House Lirvir's new house queen was not given the title of ruling queen and in her anger; she declared that all vermin-kissed horrors in their house should be executed as an example. House Lirvir carried out this order and hung the mutilated corpses outside the house gates for all to see. This act inspired the other houses to follow in their example. Many more vermin-kissed horrors abandoned their houses and fled into the wilds before their houses had given the order to kill them as well. Soon there was no such thing as a vermin-kissed horror in any house and the uprising had begun. Minor demons were summoned by arcane spell casters to help raise an army.

Within months, the vermin-kissed horrors had a mighty army of demons and the war began. The vermin-kissed elves chose only to defend their borders and had not gone after the vermin-kissed horrors in the wilds. They would regret that choice for a long time. The Mo'Reens' were pleased with their actions and knew that their goddess would be as well if she were to return. It was chaos among the servants of Na-Dene above and beyond the expectations of the goddess. Without a single ruler to guide the vermin-kissed elf houses and keep control, it was every house for itself. Something had to be done fast. Without their goddess, they were at a loss. House queens from all houses gathered and argued about what needed to be done, until at long last they decided that the only thing they could do without too much debate, was place the eldest daughter of the slain queen into power. Fein'Rauvarra Lirvir was voted as the new queen over the vermin-kissed elf houses. She took action immediately. Every house that remained loyal to Na-Dene was again united and formed a mighty army that was able to at least hold off the demon forces and the vermin-kissed horrors from invading their city and destroying them. It was a chapter in the life of the vermin-kissed elves that they could have surely done without. The war lasted a long time and it seemed as though it would never come to an end.

Forty-five years passed since the war had begun and House Alvraloth suffered the most, having been constructed so close to the borders of the wilds on the outskirts of the vermin-kissed elf city, Maovolence. The eldest son of the weapon master and the house queen was lost along with a large group of house soldiers during an expedition into the wilds. It was a great loss for House Alvraloth. Only one other than the weapon master himself mourned the loss of the eldest son, Aleiz Alvraloth. The second to share in the mourning along with the weapon master was his younger brother and also the son of the weapon master and house queen of house Alvraloth, Indigo Alvraloth. Aleiz had been a promising vermin-kissed elf ninja in training under the house weapon master while Indigo had followed the path of a house thief and spy. He was among the most skilled spies that made discoveries of other houses that schemed against them. Only news of houses plotting against theirs had ever been taken seriously. Other houses were not their concern. No houses plotted against them as far as they could find out, but no one really aided them in defending their house borders either. Only the borders of the city itself, had been defended by the great vermin-kissed elf army, but when a small group of demons managed to infiltrate the borders and assault a houses gates, the army was not called back to help. The queen claimed that if a house could not defend their own gates that it was a sign Na-Dene no longer felt that house was worthy to remain among them. The army was only to guard the borders of the city until a course of action that did not send thousands of soldiers to their deaths and thus steal the only chance at saving the vermin-kissed elf city Maovolence could be devised. Even the ruling house of Lirvir was not above that decision. Soldiers would not be called back to defend their gates, but every house knew that was because a third of the mighty army was already within the gates and housed there in case they were needed to defend the gates of House Lirvir. Other houses had obeyed the queen and sent their soldiers to form the great army under a general of House Lirvir's command to defend the borders. The ruling vermin-kissed elf queen, Queen Fein'Rauvarra Lirvir was smart and had taken a third of that mighty army without any other house queen's notice and housed them inside her gates. If not for the efforts of Indigo Alvraloth, no one would have ever known. For now only House Alvraloth knew of this. It was not wise to start another uprising while they were already at war. The queen had united them and if the news of her hiding a large chunk of their vermin-kissed elf army inside her gates got out, all other houses might turn on House Lirvir and forget that an army of demons still assaulted their borders. Chaos ran through their veins and more often than not, a vermin-kissed elf's worst enemy was another vermin-kissed elf. Five more years passed and House Alvraloth survived the assault. Through the skills of Sabal and Indigo under the house weapon master, the army was turned away and retreated from the house gates.

*****

Protected from the harmful black sun rays within the Great Forest, a small group of druids trained their fellow members so that one day they can restore nature to its prominent and healthier status. Vegetation of all kinds had lost color from the sapping energy of the sun and some vegetation had evolved into monsters that stole life from living beings they entangled. A circle of druids that dwelled within the Great Forest that called themselves Nature's Allies. They had sworn to restore nature to its glory at any cost and trained as well as studied the possibilities of defeating the forces of Viscus. For the druids belonging to this circle, everyday was difficult whether something bad happened or not. For a disciple druid that had not yet earned the title of druid, days were very difficult indeed.

"Today you will learn to call out to nature and find what ally Tevlos has sent to be your companion," the great druid instructed to his amateur group. "This is a pet that you need to befriend and bond with spiritually and magically. It will serve and aid you in your life. Now picture a local animal you have seen in the woods and call to it." The great druid watched his group attempt to call out to whatever animals would hear them. The sounds they mimicked were almost entertaining to hear. He fought back a laugh or two. Within moments of the chanting, animals began to arrive. Denizens of the forest came to see who it was that was magically calling to them. The great druid watched as hawks that had taken refuge below the canopies of the trees arrived and landed on outstretched arms. He stood proud when he saw his half-elf daughter rolling and playing with a wolf like it was her best friend. He was a full blooded elf and his wife had been human. Humans matured sooner than elves, but elves lived longer lives. His daughter would outlive any human husband, but not an elf. She had to go through life as a half-breed that had pros and cons from both of her heritages.

"Gilthiam," one of the human students called to the great druid in charge of their group and the elf turned to see that the boy had summoned and befriended a hawk. He smiled for a moment at his student's excitement from his accomplishment, but only a moment.

"Slay it now!" Gilthiam ordered frantically as he noticed what the boy had not. The boy did not understand until he felt a coldness drain the life from his body and darkness took him as his life energy was drained from his body, leaving it to collapse on the ground as an empty gray husk. The hawk was undead and in disguise. It was an enchanted pet of a sorcerer that must have been nearby. They were like a druid's animal friend in many ways. In addition, that meant that their days of training were now going to be put to the test. The undead hawk took off from the lifeless body and flew away through the branches of the trees until it arose above the forest into the life sapping energy-filled sky. Skeletons emerged with outstretched claws as they approached the druid class. Gilthiam was not sure if they could escape. Most of the students were human and a few were elves, but they were all so young. His elven mind took over. Life was as it was meant to be and they would make the best of it.

"Defend our forest!" Gilthiam shouted as he drew out his scimitar and charged at the skeletons. His class followed his lead. Their companions looked panicked and confused, but the druids coached them into battle with them.

"Dillveign," Gilthiam called and a large bear charged out of the trees to assist the elf it had befriended many years ago. Gilthiam watched his students and their companions struggle in battle against the skeleton warriors. They were fleshless and difficult to bring down. Gilthiam waded through shattered and chipped bones defying the forces of Viscus to keep his students alive so that they might become full-fledged druids. He heard screams and shouts coming from their hidden village in the trees. The smell of smoke began to distract him as the thought of a forest fire burning down their shelter and homes enhanced their panic. Another student fell, but Gilthiam mourned him not. The sadness would only bring him down more, weakening his spirit. Dillveign the bear roared as it crushed several skeleton warriors with his body and ending the skirmish. Gilthiam saw that they had stood strong and defended against the skeleton warriors, but who sent them and why was their so few?

"Quickly, those of you who can still fight follow me back to the village. The rest of you take refuge in the forest. May, Tevlos bring you light." Gilthiam and Dillveign led the charge back to the village. The village was built within the trees as the elves that dwelled in the woods often constructed. That was where the primary forces were and that was where the darkness prevailed over the light.

"Wraiths," Gilthiam whispered in panic.

"Father where is mother?" The half-elf daughter he had raised for twenty-eight years asked. Gilthiam looked around in panic as he counted nine wraiths in all flying about within the tree village and sucking the life from the living before they could hit the ground. Gilthiam covered his daughter's eyes as he watched their fellow druids diving from their homes in the trees in an attempt to die naturally without the sapping energy devouring their souls, but the wraiths did not allow it for many.

"Do not look my daughter," Gilthiam whispered as he saw his beloved wife dive from their home and plummet towards the earth below. He smiled when he saw that she had successfully killed herself before a wraith could drain her. The half-elf pulled her father's hand away from her face in time to see her mother impact with the ground.

"Mother," she gasped.

"Sametria, your mother will live again because the wraiths did not feed on her soul." Gilthiam said in an attempt to comfort his daughter. Sametria looked to her father speechless.

"Our people are dying. Do we not fight?" Sametria asked. She was confused with her uncontrollable emotions on the issue. Gilthiam looked to his half-human daughter.

"I know your human side would have you rush into battle, but listen to your elven heritage and live to fight another day. Come quickly. There is nothing we can do here but die with our fellow druids." Gilthiam whispered to his remaining students and daughter as he led them away from the death and destruction without being seen.

"But father, won't they hunt us down and kill us anyway?" Sametria protested.

"Yes they will Sametria, but they will have to find us first and when they do, we will fight back. I promise you." Gilthiam responded with sincerity. The few druids that remained moved swiftly through the forest in search of a new shelter to call home while they trained. Gilthiam knew of another village in the trees three days travel from the place they once called home. It was home to the last remnants of the cat people. The cat people were elf-like humanoids crossed with feline blood and resembling cats of all kinds. Some looked like lions, others looked like leopards and some resembled domestic cats with their features. They were Gilthiam's only option that he knew. For now, they had to keep moving beneath the cover of the trees and hope that a scout or wraith on their way to the cat people's village did not spot them. The screams of their people diminished fast as they put their ruined village behind them. Screams diminished for all but Sametria. She remembered her mother's scream and the vision of her impacting the ground from her great fall. Her head hit first and folded over to one side breaking her neck instantly. She could almost hear it snap in her mind as it replayed repeatedly. Her mother's body slumped over to one side folded over her head and neck bones protruded from her broken flesh.

"Father, we cannot hide our tracks as you do. Won't we lead the wraiths to wherever we go?" Sametria dared to ask. Gilthiam realized that she was right and stopped in his tracks.

"We must split up," Gilthiam said suddenly. "One day we will rise up against the wraiths and the rest of the minions of Viscus. For now, we must survive and go our separate ways. You all must lead them away from me."

"But I want to go with you where it is safe," several of the young apprentice druids protested.

"Nowhere is safe my fellow druids," Gilthiam said regrettably but the fact he had called them fellow druids was enough to raise the lowest of morale. "We must do what we have to survive and put nature back into order. Some of you will choose to run and hide while others," Gilthiam paused as he looked to his daughter, "will choose another and more dangerous path. Whatever path you choose, no, that it will be the right one for you and that there is no shame. Now go." The druids all obeyed and left alone or in pairs in directions away from where Gilthiam was heading. A few brave druids turned back towards their ruined village.

"I know what you would want me to do father, but it is not in me to run for the rest of my life." Sametria said boldness to her father.

"Then your life will be a short one my daughter," Gilthiam claimed. Sametria huffed in defiance.

"I love you father and I love mother still. I will find a way to decimate the wraiths that slaughtered our village." Sametria declared.

"And will you stop there or will your vengeance take you farther up the ladder to Viscus himself?" Gilthiam asked without any hint of expression or emotion. Sametria almost despised her father at times. Because of an elf's long life span, they perceived things differently than races with shorter time in the world.

"I do see it as vengeance father. I see it as what we vowed to do when we became members of druid circle Nature's Allies." Sametria shared her honest opinion and for the first time in a long while she saw emotion suddenly flow across her father's face like the rush of water flowing through a broken damn and spilling out over everything in its path. He smiled proudly and wept.

"That is why you are so special. You see things in both eyes elf and human alike. You will be someone very great." Gilthiam said with so very much pride that Sametria was overwhelmed and did not hear the screams of another fallen druid nearby as her father did. She just saw as he drew his scimitar, an enchanted blade filled with magic. Fear overtook her as she thought her father jealous and trying to kill her. She drew her clan crafted scimitar in response and raised it to defend herself as Dillveign charged passed her and her father chanted a spell. Sametria turned as she realized something was wrong and saw a wraith circling Dillveign and several skeletons emerging from the brush.

"Go Sametria now. Head South to the cat people." Gilthiam barked as he moved in and touched the hide of Dillveign, discharging his spell and enchanting the bear's natural attacks with temporary magic so that it might defend itself against the wraiths. Sametria noted the number of skeletons and looked to her finely crafted blade. It was no match for a wraith and she was not about to become that which she hated. Sametria obeyed her father reluctantly and ran to the south all-the-while wishing she could fight beside her father. She had not gone far away when she heard a cry of her father's voice behind her and she knew it would be his last. He shouted a single name that would forever be imprinted into her mind. He shouted, "Tevlos."

Sametria knew that she was not being followed by the way her wolf acted. Animals could sense the undead when they drew near. They had an unnatural aura about them that made animals cringe if they were not trained to do otherwise. Sametria looked to her wolf in sadness.

"I guess it's just us now. You should have a name. In honor of my mother, your name will be Sadie." Sametria declared and the wolf barked acceptingly as they continued their trek through the Great Forest. "How about some light?" Sametria asked Sadie as she chanted a minor spell upon her drawn scimitar that made the blade shed light like it was a torch. Sametria and Sadie moved through the difficult underbrush knowing that the skeletons would have great difficulty following them, but not the wraiths that could pass through solid mass.

"Who is this Tevlos that my father called out to? Do you know?" Sametria asked Sadie as though she could honestly answer. She had not learned about the dogma of the god of nature, as she should have. The wolf barked, happy to hear her companion speaking to her again, like when they first met earlier that day. "I think the first thing I will teach you is to heel. You understand heel?" Sametria commanded more than asked. The wolf just walked beside her. The wolf suddenly stopped in its tracks and began sniffing the air.

"What do you smell? Is there undead around us?" Sametria asked as the wolf continued to smell the air and growl.

"Not for miles," a voice answered from the trees and Sadie began to bark as a cat-like humanoid with white fur covered in black tiger stripes dropped down from a high branch. "I am Taegrid Prowler a ranger of the cat people village and all that remains of my people. I was on my way to warn your village but I was apparently too late."

"You came to warn us?" Sametria asked as she lowered her scimitar to appear not so threatening towards the cat man.

"My village was attacked and my father apparently knew Gilthiam a great druid of your people. I made a promise I would warn him but I fear I failed my father." Taegrid said sadly, as he knelt low to the ground and picked up a handful of dirt.

"Gilthiam was my father and he was on his way to warn your village." Sametria said in shock. Taegrid dropped the dirt and dusted it from his white fur covered hands. He looked up to the half elf druid.

"Our fathers knew each other that would appear to be an omen then that we found each other." Taegrid claimed as he stood back up.

"An omen, what do you mean?" Sametria asked in confusion. Taegrid seemed to talk as if he was a high-ranking druid.

"Our villages are not so different. Many of my people were a part of your circle of druids having their own sect within our village. I chose the path of a ranger, but my father was as your father a druid that passed on the knowledge of all things natural to the next of kin. The fact that we must have been destined to meet is an omen to me because our fathers knew each other and did great things. Now it is our time and our turn to follow in their steps." Taegrid Prowler explained.

"I would have to agree with you my new friend. I am Sametria." Sametria responded as she absorbed the explanation and silenced Sadie.

"Well met Sametria."

"If your people and my people have been slain, then I guess there is nowhere left to go but to Castle Fallen." Sametria suggested as she looked back behind her. Taegrid shrugged as he slung his longbow into hand.

"We will be exposed to the black sun's rays and the snow of the Frozen Wastes up north will magnify their effects from what I hear."

"I have heard this as well."

"Well as long as you already know what you are getting us into. Let's go." Taegrid took the lead and Sametria smiled as she watched the five and a half foot tall white tiger man lead them to what may be their dooms. He was brave and like herself an orphan. Whatever forces had brought them together seemed to be directing their paths to a higher purpose. Now they ventured to the far north where forest turned into plains and plains into mountains and then mountains into frozen wastes. The great trek could take months for them on foot. The issue at hand was not the journey itself, but the obstacles along the way. Terrain, weather, the black sun and undead minions would all play factors in their journey. They both were well aware of the great dangers and risks they faced ahead, but they did not falter. Sametria truly believed that it was her destiny to restore balance to Athyx and return her precious world to the way it once was before she was even born. Taegrid did not know if it was destiny or just a path that he chose. Whatever the case, he followed the course with Sametria and her wolf Sadie that barely tolerated the fact that he was a feline descendant. Unknown to them, the essence of Tevlos absorbed within the great relic guided them on their path. It was only able to guide them at the moment, but if they were to ever succeed in finding the relic, it could help protect them. It was not Tevlos or any other god, but it acted and reacted as any of the gods would when their personalities surfaced. Tevlos was only the first personality to surface, but if any other were to surface before the heroes could find the relic, they might not be as helpful. The relic tried to empower the essence of Tevlos to keep it dominant over all other swirling personalities it contained.

*****

Gilthanus wandered the Great Plains, encountering the drain of the black sun that weakened the living creatures that walked beneath its life sapping brilliance. With his past behind him, the elf sorcerer sought out adventure and riches, even in a dark world such as this one he wandered through. He was not afraid to face the wilds and dangers before him. Gilthanus had his fine long sword strapped to his belt and his crossbow on his back. He was young and arrogant to the ways of the world even at the age of a hundred and twenty-four, but he learned fast. His keen elven eyes spotted what could very easily been mistaken for his own shadow if not trained what to look for. The hair on the back of his neck stood up as he saw the incorporeal and vile undead known as a wraith begin to swoop towards him through the eerie light cast by the black sun. He knew that his sword and crossbow could not even begin to harm such a creature. They would pass harmlessly through such a being without the proper enchantment. Even his magic had a chance of passing harmlessly through the ghostly being, but it was the best chance he had against such a foe. Gilthanus had something to prove to himself and to his father. He wanted to become the greatest sorcerer in the world, but he wanted to do it his way and if possible get rich during the process.

"I've got a spell or two that might cause you a little pain," Gilthanus warned as he began pulling back his left hand and reaching into the open air as though, he was picking up some invisible element. As he finished chanting the sacred words of his spell he through forward a beam pure light. It was the essence of life and the opposition of what created undead beings. The beam struck the wraith as it swooped in and knocked it backwards. The wraith hissed with anger in response to the sorcerers attack and began cautiously circling the elf.

"You are prolonging the inevitable," it hissed.

"You are accurate in that statement for I am mortal and I am in fact preventing my death." Gilthanus responded trying to be sarcastic but sounding more like a bookworm stating facts from an arsenal of knowledge. The wraith came in suddenly and with blinding speed reaching at the heart of the elf to sap his life essence from his physical body and devour it. Coldness surged through his frail elven body as the wraith tried to drain him of his life energy. He felt as though his chest had been scratched beneath the very clothing he wore. Though the wraiths were incorporeal, they still caused physical harm along with their spiritual drain.

"That felt good." The wraith fed on the life force of Gilthanus. The elf sorcerer felt sickened by the combination of the black sun and the touch of the wraith. He summoned a second beam of the life giving energy, and again it struck the wraith dead on. The wraith felt the anguish and pain of the beam and ducked into the shadows hoping to make the elf sorcerer think that it had given up. The power that created undead and the power that healed were like polar opposites. They were like magnets that pushed one another away. Gilthanus knew better and cast another spell that created an illumination of magical light upon his sword as he drew it from its sheath and exposed the wraith within its hiding place. The black light cast from the sun was an eerie shadowy light that aided creatures that hid or dwelled within the shadows.

"I will not be your meal wraith. I am Gilthanus. You would be wise to remember the name and leave me be, for I am the son of a great elf wizard." Gilthanus warned the wraith as it took flight above.

"You are foolish and you are an abomination to Viscus," the wraith cursed as it launched towards Gilthanus again with blinding speed. Gilthanus sent a beam at the wraith each time the wraith made a pass at him and each time the effort distracted the wraith enough so that its draining touch would fall short of the elf sorcerer. Whether or not the spell harmed the wraith was beside the point. Gilthanus proved he could hold his own against even the most feared of undead beings, the wraiths. The wraith had finally given up. It left the wounded elf drained of magic and sickened from its touch. Gilthanus refused to give up and continued forward. He needed to find shelter to regain his strength. He staggered for hours across the Great Plains. His vision began to blur, but he was certain that ahead of him he could see a wild wolf guarding what appeared to be a cave den before he collapsed from exhaustion. His final thought was one of fear that the wolf was going to eat him. He heard the heavy paws as it came upon him. His consciousness left him at that moment and he would not know the pain of the wolf's bite as it latched upon him.

Chapter Two:

The orc tribe known as Bloody-Knucks was once a great force that pillaged and slaughtered all surface dwellings they came across. Since the great cataclysm and the blackening of the sun, they have not been as prosperous. A master vampire has since taken control over them, using the orcs as a food source like cattle. Among the tribe Bloody-Knucks the orcs had taken human and elven women to have their way with over the years. Through these acts of rape half-orcs were born. The orcs looked down upon them but they were still a part of the tribe. They were just treated as servants to the orcs. One such half-orc was named and cared for most of his life by his human mother until she was taken by his father and never seen again. She had called him Morglum. Morglum remembered when she was taken just a year ago to be fed to the vampires in place of the orcs who pledged themselves to the vampires that protected them from the forces of Viscus. Morglum was treated like a servant having to tend to the slaves, clean their pins, and feed them. One such slave a vermin-kissed elf always tried talking to him. Over the last year since the loss of his mother, Morglum had been having conversations with the vermin-kissed elf and they had bonded in some degree. He had been a prisoner now for nearly five years.

"I bet they turned your mum," the vermin-kissed elf pondered as Morglum entered the pin to bring him food and water.

"Into a vampire, they had best hope not for their sakes." Morglum gasped at the thought and shook the possibility away.

"Whoa! For their sakes, do you mean to defy the orc chief and Master Vampire?"

"I'll have you know that I have gotten quite good with weapons and my axes would do well to be covered in blood some time soon." Morglum boasted.

"Your father, the chief of the tribe treats you worse than any other orc because you are his son. You have seen him do things to your mum that would make a vermin-kissed elf gasp and perhaps even the denizens of the Oblivion."

"I am one and they are many Aleiz. I would gladly slaughter the whole lot of them if I could." Morglum said as he slumped against the wall feeling defeated more and more each day.

"Help me escape and together we can go far away from here and one day you can return and lay them all to waste." Aleiz suggested as he always had since the half-orc began speaking with him.

"You are a vermin-kissed elf. Why have you not simply killed the orc guard and take his keys with your vermin powers?" Morglum asked curiously.

"I did not want to offend you," Aleiz lied. Unlike his brethren, he had turned away from the religious beliefs of his people when they decided to abandon him after their enemy had ambushed his battalion. Aleiz managed to sneak away before he could be killed as well. His escape from certain death led him closer to the surface. In his wounded condition, he was discovered by a group of slaver orcs and could not defend himself successfully. He wound up a slave of the orcs and waited for rescue from his people, but they never came. He eventually turned away from them and now hated all vermin akin to his former deity. He did not possess the same innate abilities as his vermin loving people anymore. Na-Dene removed the blessing when he became a vermin hater. Now he instead specialized in killing any vermin he stumbled upon. He feared that the orcs may not hold as much fear towards him if he admitted that he did not possess the powers of his people and kept that a secret from them. He did not even tell the half-orc he trusted of his secret.

"Morglum, you are not to speak to the slaves," an orc shouted as it entered the dark tunnel of the slave pits. Morglum felt a heavy fist hit him in the back of the head and topple him over. He was already leaning against the wall and the orc had easily knocked him to the filth covered cave floor. The filth did not bother Morglum and neither did the disrespect. He was use to it after fifteen years. Still something inside him snapped and he found himself drawing his great axe as he stood to his feet. The orc laughed for just a short moment when he saw the slave feces falling from the half-orc's face, but stopped when he saw the long handle swinging around with a massive double blade coming right at its body. The orc silenced his laughter as he tried to block the powerful swing with a gauntlet. Morglum severed the arm with his axe. The force behind the swing was so powerful, that the great axe continued through to dig deep into the left side of the orc. The orc watched as its own arm fell to the cave floor and gasped for air as his left lung collapsed. It growled through the pain and swung its other gauntlet-wearing fist at the half-orc, but Morglum let go of the heavy hafted great axe to duck beneath the swing. He moved under the swing and back up on the other side with a battle-axe now in hand that found a home within the forehead of the orc. The orc fell to its knees missing its left arm with a great axe stuck deep within its side and a battle-axe sticking out of its skull before falling to the left and crashing to the floor. Its blood pooled and painted the stone floor.

"You're in trouble now! I never knew that you had it in you." Aleiz gasped. Morglum had finally tasted blood and he liked it. He felt a rush that he never thought he would have from a kill and it was exhilarating to him.

"I told you I was no one to be messed with," Morglum boasted again but this time he had proven the matter.

"I still don't think you can take the entire tribe and the vampires. You might want to get me out of here."

"I think you're right," Morglum laughed as he pulled free his axes and kicked the door wide open allowing Aleiz to leave his cell.

"How do we get out of here?"

"Well I don't plan on becoming a vermin-kissed elf's slave so you are on your own if you want to return to your city. I'm going outside where the orcs would not dare to follow." Morglum replied.

"We are friends. I will go wherever you go. Where are my things?" Morglum led the vermin-kissed elf to a nearby cave where they stored unwanted gear such as the equipment of their slaves. They had to search through the storage room for a while, but they eventually found the gear of the vermin-kissed elf covered in dust and cobwebs. Aleiz strapped on his weapons and slung his backpack over his shoulders.

"How many will we have to kill to get out of here?" Aleiz asked Morglum as he looked about for more orc guards to show up.

"Possibly ten or so orcs and maybe a vampire or two." Morglum replied.

"Is that all?" Aleiz asked sarcastically. Morglum turned to meet the vermin-kissed elf's gaze.

"You asked," Morglum reminded him.

"Indeed I did," Aleiz grumbled as he drew out his kukri. The two fugitives moved as quietly as they could. Morglum had to check and make sure Aleiz was still with him from time to time because he moved so quietly. Morglum knew the way to the surface, but he had never before been outside and rumors that the black sun would suck his life force from his body kept all orcs within the caves. Only the vampires were allowed to leave the caves. That made the orcs board so they often ventured into the depths of the world to acquire slaves or ransack a settlement. Morglum strapped his great axe to his back as he noticed the caves fluctuating in width and height. They moved up to the caves leading to the living quarters of the orcs. A massive cavern was home to thousands of orcs. Passing through it was the only way to the surface. Morglum looked back to the vermin-kissed elf when they reached the entrance to the great cavern.

"There is always someone awake in here," Morglum warned.

"I will keep out of sight," Aleiz whispered. Morglum nodded and turned to enter the great cavern. Morglum strapped his battle-axe next to his great axe upon his back. He paced himself as he walked through the vast cavern large enough to house a great dragon. He looked from side to side absorbing the sights as he looked upon his people for what he hoped would be the last time. Mothers nestled their young, but not like his mother did. His mother was human. These were orcs and they were not as loving to their young as humans apparently were. Ahead of him, he saw two orc guards standing by the entrance to the upper levels. There were always at least two orcs on duty in case the vampires decided they wanted to feed suddenly. Only the chief could decide who would be food and who would remain a member of the tribe. Those that were drained rose as vampires under the command of the Master Vampire or his minions. Depending on who turned the victim decided whether the vampire was a pure blood, a spawn or a fledgling.

Morglum stopped in his tracks as he saw the one orc he hated most. The chief lay sprawled out naked and barely covered by a fur and three female orc consorts that he would discard in the morning. One was the wife of one of the chief's captains. The chief had privileges that no orc could challenge without facing the chief's wrath. A challenge meant that the chief had to face off against the challenger for reign of the title as chief. The current chief was challenged five times ten years ago and no one has since dared to challenge him after what he had done to the five that did. He was Morglum's father and the half-orc understood where he got some of his behavior from now. He was passionate like his mother and savage like his father. He wanted to kill his father where he slept, but he had seen too many orcs try to sneak up on his father in his sleep only to wind up missing an eye. It was claimed that for his service to Bolnarg, even after their gods fall to Viscus that the chief was still blessed having the orc disciples of Bolnarg watching over him while he rested and that was why he always plucked an eye from whomever tried to attack him in his sleep to honor their fallen god. Morglum did not dare to try to kill the sleeping chief. He sighed and moved towards the orcs standing guard and wondered if Aleiz would be able to sneak passed them without a distraction. The dark cavern needed no light source because the orcs could see in the darkness.

"Half-breed," one of the orcs barked as Morglum approached. Morglum growled.

"You are lucky that Chief Gaji Bloody-Knucks is your father," the other orc warned.

"Or else what," Morglum dared growl in response. He saw the opportunity for distraction. If only Aleiz was close by he could sneak passed while Morglum had the guards distracted. The two guards looked to one another before shrugging and then looking back to Morglum.

"Chief may be your father, but we still have rights to honor." One of the orcs barked. Orc honor was simply put, meant that any orc daring to talk down to another was a challenge.

"As do I," Morglum claimed reminding them that it was them that first spat the rude remarks.

"Do you challenge us then?" one orc asked sounding excited.

"I would love a good match against the both of you, but I dare not wake my father or he would surely beat all three of us." Morglum did not have to lie for the truth was far more effective at times.

"What do you suggest?" the orc asked.

"I suggest we take our fight to the upper levels, maybe even outside where my father can not intervene if you two happen to get lucky enough to overpower me." Morglum dared to insult the two orcs and it worked. Blinded by their rage, the two orcs actually agreed to leave their posts.

"We are full blooded orcs and much stronger than a half breed such as yourself," the orc guards taunted.

"I guess you'll have to prove that you are superior to me outside," Morglum challenged the orcs as he pushed between them to lead the way out. One of the guards began to follow, but the other stopped suddenly.

"What about the vampires and the black sun?" the orc asked. Morglum was relieved that it was not a question about his father and turned to face the orc guard.

"I thought you were superior to me," Morglum paused to let the words dig in. "I'm not scared." The half-orc had to fight a smile as he turned back around and again led the way out. This time he had struck a nerve and there was no turning back now. Morglum and the two orcs passed through what seemed to be endless tunnels until they finally smelt the fresh air of the surface world and felt a light breeze blowing in. Ahead of them, they saw four vampires crawling about on the walls and ceiling of the cave leading outside. The three of them continued ahead hoping that the vampires would simply let the pass.

"I smell blood," one of the vampires hissed as it dropped down from the ceiling to block the path of the orcs. "One of you is bleeding."

Morglum suddenly remembered the still warm blood that covered the blades of his axes and smacked his forehead an open palm. The other three vampires scurried down the walls and joined their fellow brother of blood in blocking the orcs.

"No one here is bleeding," Morglum argued.

"Yet," one of the orcs joked.

"You just smell the blood that will soon be running down Morglum's face after we beat him to a pulp outside." The other orc joined in the laugh.

"You are not allowed outside says the Master." Another vampire hissed.

"Our Chief doesn't let us outside either and he is our only master," Morglum dared to say.

"Yeah, we don't serve your master we have our own." One of the orcs spat. The vampires hissed as they lunged at the defiant orcs. Each of the vampire guards were once members of their tribe. Orc vampires as they were seemed to be as stubborn as the rest of them. Two of the orc vampires nearly overwhelmed one of the orcs immediately while the other two went after Morglum and the second orc. Morglum instinctively drew his great axe having enough room to swing it there and hoped that it would stop a vampire as he swung it with all of his might. The axe blade came down into the top of the orc vampire's skull and did not stop until it reached its abdomen. In a puff of dust, the orc vampire was gone and Morglum was left in shock. Never before had he heard a vampire vanquished so easily. Both of the orcs drew their great swords and swung wildly as they roared. The orc nearest to Morglum followed his example and destroyed one of the orc vampires in a single swing of his mighty sword. The other orc was being beaten to death by the two orc-vampires, having great difficulty defending against their attacks. The vampires were allowed to feed on anything trying to enter or leave the caves according to their master and after they finished beating these orcs to a pulp, they would lick the blood from the floor as well as their hands. Morglum did not like what he saw and even though he planned to kill these orcs anyway, he was not about to let them die at the hands or fangs of a vampire today. Together, Morglum and one of the orcs cut down the last two orc-vampires saving the frantic and wounded orc guard they were beating to death.

"I thought Chief Gaji said that he fought the Master Vampire and could not kill him," the dominant orc guard barked in absolute shock.

"Your chief is weak in his old age. You are truly mightier than he." Morglum barked in response.

"Challenge," the other orc suggested as he stared at his friend the dominant orc standing beside a superior half-orc.

"I will challenge, after I finish with you outside." The orc laughed. A sharp object penetrated the leather armor enforced with metal studs that covered the dominant orc's back and caused him to flinch in pain.

"You are not worthy of being chief," Aleiz whispered into the orcs ear from the shadows. He stood behind the orc as he pulled his kukri free of the wound. The orc spun around with his falchion with a wild swing and forced the vermin-kissed elf back. The battered orc spotted the vermin-kissed elf briefly as his friend swung on it and moved to assist him against the second foe. Morglum caught him unawares and slammed his great axe blade into the chest cavity of the already wounded orc to send him off to meet the orc god, Bolnarg. The blade had stuck so deep that Morglum had to kick the dead body free of his axe blade. Aleiz rolled in and cut the hip of the orc before coming up to a standing position too close for the orc to swing his large sword at him with great force. Aleiz was inside the swing and stopped it short with his kukri. Morglum cut the orc down without hesitation from behind. He did not want to give the vampires or orcs time to come after them.

"Come on," Morglum barked as he led the way out of the cave. The wind was chilly and the sky was dark. They both felt the sapping energy of the sun and wanted to vomit where they stood. Aleiz eventually did and Morglum had to help the jet black-skinned elf to his feet as they looked around for somewhere they could go. To the south were the Great Plains and then the Great Forest. They stood at the base of a mountain range and knew that on the other side was the Great Frozen Wastes.

"South," Aleiz managed to gag. Morglum nodded his head. There had to be some kind of settlement still standing with life. Morglum believed that his orc tribe was not the only life that remained on the surface world. He flung Aleiz over one shoulder so he could better carry his great axe in one hand using the long haft as a walking stick.

"Aleiz, why were those vampires so easy to kill?" Morglum asked hoping that the vermin-kissed elf knew something that he did not. Aleiz gasped before climbing down from Morglum's shoulder.

"There are many types of vampires my friend. Top of the ladder are the master vampires, which are pure bloods that grew in power somehow, then pure blood vampires and then more commonly spawn servants and lowest on the food chain are fledglings. Those are what you just encountered." Aleiz explained.

"Fledglings?" Morglum gasped as he continued his stride. Aleiz followed still having issues with the sun's rays sickening him.

"Yes fledglings," Aleiz repeated. "They are the weakest of all vampires."

"Why have we not encountered them before?" Morglum asked.

"They are commonly found in large nests which are very rare on the surface. A vampire has many spawn servants and a powerful vampire spawn have servants as well and those are more common here." Aleiz finished explaining what he knew.

"Thanks! I was beginning to think that my great axe had some sort of power or something." Morglum joked as they wandered deep into the grassy plains.

"Do you think they will come after us?" Aleiz asked with hopes that they would not.

"The vampires would not because they need to defend their cattle, but my father would if the Master Vampire allowed him to." Morglum answered with great thought.

"Have you seen the Master Vampire? Is he also an orc?" Aleiz suddenly was the one full of questions.

"I have not seen him, but my father detests him as though he was a surface elf." Morglum responded.

"A surface elf vampire? The whole lot of them needs to be cannon fodder for the vampires." Aleiz choked.

"Your people hate the surface elves as well. They forced us into the darkness long ago." Aleiz explained.

"And they claim that we are the evil ones," Morglum laughed and Aleiz managed a chuckle with him between dry heaving.

"I've got to get you out of the sun. The plains were a bad idea." Morglum noted as he looked around.

"It's the way to the Great Forest," Aleiz spat.

"We could have gone deeper into the mountain range or beyond to the Great Frozen Wastes." Morglum offered.

"That's home to the most powerful undead from what I've heard." Aleiz gasped. "Why would we ever go there?"

"Why indeed?" an unfamiliar voice asked from ahead of them. Morglum and Aleiz looked forward suddenly with their weapons ready. A cat-man with white and black tiger stripes on his fur aimed a longbow their way and a half-elf female stood nearby ready for battle, wielding a scimitar.

"That is our business," Morglum barked ready to leap upon the two strangers at any moment.

"We are on our way to the Great Frozen Wastes to put an end to the darkness that sickens your friend," Taegrid offered still aiming his bow in their direction.

"We do not want to fight you. We only ask if you would join our quest." Sametria claimed.

"We are on our way to seek refuge in the Great Forest," Aleiz gasped. He was first to lower his weapon. Sametria lowered her sword as well, but Taegrid and Morglum remained constantly vigil and did not lower theirs.

"There is no refuge left to take in the forest. It was our home and the wraiths have slain all who once dwelled there. It is a haunted dwelling of rogue wraiths now. You would be going to your deaths if you ventured in there." Sametria warned.

"That's funny," Aleiz chuckled.

"What's that?" Sametria asked.

"Well you say that we would be going to our certain dooms if we enter the Great Forest, but yet you are heading into the Great Frozen Wastes where it is said that Viscus' servants of great power dwell." Aleiz replied.

"It is better to knowingly go to your dooms with a goal to make the world better than to cower and hide and wait for death to find you." Taegrid shared his opinion. It sounded like a challenge to Morglum. To battle the most powerful undead and live to tell the story would be a great honor. Even if he died trying, at least his legacy would be remembered.

"I am Morglum son of a human woman I only knew as mother and orc Chief Gaji Bloody-Knucks. I will go with you if you first aid me in avenging my mother's wrongful death and slaughtering the orcs and vampires inside those caves." Morglum wanted to check their story by first determining how brave they really were as well as how skilled.

"It would please me to kill some orcs," Taegrid growled as he lowered his bow.

"Vampires would help prepare us better to face the wraiths," Sametria added.

"We will help you then Morglum Bloody-Knucks," Taegrid offered and surprised Aleiz as much as it did Morglum.

"My father is powerful and one called the Master Vampire protects my tribe from the wraiths." Morglum warned.

"So this will take some planning," Sametria determined.

"A lot," Aleiz assured the half-elf.

"I am Sametria and this is Taegrid Prowler the last of the cat people." Sametria introduced.

"I am Aleiz Alvraloth," the vermin-kissed elf said with a slight bow.

"Well met. I have never seen a vermin-kissed elf in person. Are you as evil as the elves of the surface world claim?" Sametria asked with sincere curiosity. Aleiz said nothing. He only shrugged in response.

"We need somewhere to take shelter from this wicked sun," Morglum balked.

"There is another series of caves in the plains where we had camped last night. We planned on returning there again tonight if you care to join us." Sametria offered.

"Lead the way," Morglum waved as he finally lowered his great axe. Together, the four of them trekked the five miles back to the caves that a lion once claimed as its den. All that remained of the mighty animal when Taegrid and Sametria found the den was a tainted beast filled with sapping energy from the black sun that it had little protection from and they were forced to kill it. Sadie, the pet wolf of Sametria remained in the den bandaged from the battle with the lion and standing guard when her companion and Taegrid returned with two new allies. The wolf was not alone however. A wounded elf lay motionless and unconscious just inside the cave. Taegrid noted the drag marks from where the elf had apparently collapsed and Sadie apparently dragged him the rest of the way to the shelter of the cave from the sickening rays of the black sun.

"Your pet seems to have found something," Taegrid pointed out the obvious as they entered the cave. Sametria inspected the elf and noted the coldness of the elf's body. The coldness seemed to emanate from his chest where beneath his clothing could be seen faint scratch marks.

"This is the wound of a wraith," Sametria claimed with panic in her tone.

"There must be a wraith about," Taegrid growled as he sniffed the air and looked outside the cave with his keen eyes.

"A wraith?" Morglum barked in protest.

"We would not fare well against such a being," Aleiz added his two cents.

"This elf seemed to survive just fine and he is alone," Sametria argued.

"Yes but he is a practitioner of the arcane arts," Aleiz pointed out noticing the pouch of arcane components hanging from the elf's belt and the decorated robes he wore that marked him as an arcane arts practitioner.

"Arcane arts or not, he has survived the touch of a wraith." Sametria reminded. "That means we stand a chance as well."

"Tend to his wounds the best you can Sametria. I will stand watch with Sadie." Taegrid said before disappearing outside with the wolf following beside him. Sadie had grown fond of the cat-man and tolerated his feline heritage only because he, like Sametria seemed to be empathic towards animals. Sadie simply enjoyed their company, but especially Sametria's. The half-elf druid opened the elf's shirt fully as she chewed some herbs in her mouth to moisten before spreading them over the wound. Morglum watched tentatively as the druid tended the unconscious elf.

"I think we will do fine with her on our side to clean our wounds." Morglum whispered to Aleiz. Aleiz just cringed, as he knew that the half-elf had heard Morglum speak.

"I am good at more than tending wounds Morglum," Sametria assured them as she closed up the elf's shirt over the herbs.

"I bet," Morglum responded before he realized what he had said. Sametria stood up with her scimitar drawn in the blink of an eye. Aleiz leaped back on his heels. Morglum had raised his battle-axe to block, though Sametria had intentionally stopped short.

"I could easily kill you Morglum, but that would be foolish for our enemies are things that are already dead, not each other." Sametria scolded the half-orc who stared blankly at her as though her words meant nothing.

"You could kill me, but I could just as easily kill you to." Morglum dared to say. Sametria paused. She understood that males of any race were prideful and males of the orc race were more arrogant than most. Sametria smiled and then sheathed her sword once again.

"Very well Morglum. Let us hope we never have to put that to the test." Sametria said with no tone of threat or cowardice. It simply sounded like she agreed and that appeared to be enough for Morglum to respect her and lower his battle-axe as well.

They remained in their hidden cave until the elf recovered from his wounds. The elf awoke in a panic at first and even thought of sending a spell or two at his present company.

"Who are you?" The elf asked. Morglum huffed in response.

"Surface elves are far too jumpy," Aleiz protested and the elf glared at his jet black-skinned cousin coldly.

"I shall deal with you soon enough," the elf threatened.

"We are not going to hurt you. I am Sametria a druid of the Great Forest and I am the one who mended your wounds." Sametria claimed as she knelt close to calm the elf. Gilthanus saw that she was a half-elf and suddenly calmed just a bit.

"You keep company with vermin-kissed elves and half-orcs?" the elf asked suspiciously.

"These ones are not our enemies. We are allies with a common goal. We are in search of a way to end the dark reign of Viscus. You are welcome to join us, but you will have to put your racial differences behind you if we are to succeed." Sametria offered as she extended a hand and stood up to her feet. The elf took her hand and allowed her to help him stand.

"I am Gilthanus. I have run away to see the world and acquire great riches." The elf admitted. Aleiz smiled.

"We are not so different then my cousin. For those are my goals as well." Aleiz confessed.

"The vermin-kissed elf is called Aleiz, the cat man is Taegrid Prowler, the wolf that brought you here is my companion Sadie and the half-orc is named Morglum." Sametria introduced everyone and the elf sorcerer simply nodded to each of them as she did.

"Well met then. I shall join your cause then, until I see fit to leave it." Gilthanus offered.

*****

Chief Gaji Bloody-Knucks sat hunched over in his stone throne pondering his thoughts after hearing what his half-breed son had done. He was almost proud of his son for killing so many vampires on his way out with the vermin-kissed elf, but because he had also killed three of his own tribe, Chief Gaji had to decree that Morglum was exiled and if he ever returned, the half-orc would be put to death on sight. That had not been enough for the Master Vampire, however. For killing four of his fledglings, the orc tribe suffered a loss among their numbers. The vampires feasted that day on twice as many of the orcs. Chief Gaji was deeply angered, for one had been a repeat lover and wife of one of his trusted captains. Chief Gaji was still very prideful and though he was middle aged, he was full of life. He had made a deal with the Master Vampire to keep them safe from the wraith forces in exchange for providing the vampires with a few orcs to feed upon from time to time. Chief Gaji had gotten lazy over the last few years and now his armor no longer fit him. He knew that if he did not do something soon, there would be no orcs left to lead. He had been quite the warlord and chief in his day. He felt it was time to renew his younger years and take back their caves from the vampires. Chief Gaji looked over to his armor that rested on the stone floor. He would not have time to fashion a suit that would fit him properly. He had to act now. Chief Gaji then looked to the weapon that had been passed down from chief to chief for the last two hundred years within their tribe. It was called the Pride of the Bloody-Knucks Chief. The magical weapon was a weapon that the first orc who established their tribe had looted from a great dragon all those years ago. It could alter its appearance to suit its wielder by forming into whatever weapon the chief desired. Chief Gaji Bloody-Knucks preferred the great axe and so it appeared as a great axe. It is very sharp blade glistened with magically secreted acid. The orc chief took up his enchanted great axe as he stood from his throne. He saw the vampires that were to watch over them and report any abnormal behavior back to their master. Chief Gaji Bloody-Knucks hopped up on his stone-carved throne as though it were a central stage.

"Orcs of Bloody-Knucks," Chief Gaji beckoned. "Hear your chief's call to arms once again. We have grown lazy and the hunger for war has long been yearned to be tasted again. If you desire your lives and your ways of life then follow me now against the vampires who feast on our brothers and sisters, children and wives." The orcs hearing their brave chief speak were drawn to his speech. They listened to the power of his voice and watched the strength in each muscle on his massive body clench when he spoke each. His orcs gathered as Chief Gaji had hoped. Moreover, as he feared, the vampire guards had vanished to their master.

"Bloody-Knucks-, Bloody-Knucks-!" The orcs began chanting in unison as their chief continued to speak.

"First we will free ourselves of these retched vampires," Chief Gaji roared. The Master Vampire entered the great chamber with an onslaught of vampire minions following him. He was an elf of once great reputation throughout the realms. He was turned and became a pure blood vampire that evolved into a master over the years.

"And what next Gaji?" The Master Vampire asked stealing the hope from his people with his mere presence and disrespecting the chief. "What next after you overthrow those that keep your people safe?" Chief Gaji looked around at his people. They had suddenly silenced from the Master Vampire's dreaded presence.

"I will keep them safe," Chief Gaji declared. "I am their mighty war chief and I will prove it to them once again by defeating you in battle." The orcs challenge was heard and his tribe watched and listened for the Master Vampire's response. Honor from combat was held in the highest regards among orcs and becoming chief was no easy feat. It meant fist fighting every contender for the title and Gaji had done that. The Master Vampire had stolen that glory for many years now, but Gaji wanted it back. He was ready to take it back and the master vampire knew it. He also knew that no matter who won the battle, he would lose control of his cattle. The Master Vampire imagined defeating the proud war chief in front of his own tribe and draining him completely to make a point. The fear would be restored temporarily, but these were tribal orcs. They needed an orc chief and that meant that he would have to wait until one had been declared to restore his control or possibly have another Chief Gaji to deal with. It was too risky for them, the Master Vampire decided.

"Then we will leave your caves to you Chief Gaji Bloody-Knucks. Nevertheless, the next time you see my kind we will not likely come to take you in as cattle. Or perhaps the wraiths may find your tribe unprotected and then who will drive them away?" The Master Vampire attempted one last time to sway the orcs with reason.

"I will destroy everything that invades these caves including you if you don't leave soon." Chief Gaji roared. The master vampire smiled slyly before leaving with his horde of vampire minions in tow. The orcs began chanting once again, "Bloody-Knucks, Bloody-Knucks!" The vampires heard the orc chanting as they left. Their war cry's echoed loudly out of the caves and across the lands like a war drum. The tribe was with the chief again. Now he needed to raise his army.

"Who would be my captain and second in command?" Chief Gaji called out to his people. "One of you will earn this title if you desire it and have no other but me to boss you around. It is like being chief under the chief." Many warriors among his tribe answered his call and stepped forward. The orcs parted and formed a battle circle around the throne of their chief allowing the competitors plenty of room.

"Let the challenge begin then," Chief Gaji commanded and the orcs began wrestling one another. One on one the orcs fought to decide which of them was the strongest and most worthy to stand at their chief's side.

*****

The Master Vampire led his minions away from the orc caves and out into the Great Plains to find a new haven where they could better establish their nest. The Master Vampire saw a lone wraith scouting the area for living beings to drain life force from and instead it spotted an army of vampires.

"You would be wise to join Viscus," the wraith hissed.

"If Viscus had his way then there would be no cattle left to feast upon and we all would come to our end except for Viscus' chosen few. That would just be foolish. However, I am never one to turn down an opportunity when I see it. There within those caves at the base of the mountainside is a tribe of orcs. I am finished with them." The Master Vampire announced.

"You give up cattle so easily for what in return do you ask?" The wraith asked curiously.

"If next your kind crosses me and my minions, turn your forces away and leave us and our cattle alone." The Master Vampire responded.

"I will tell my master of your cooperation Lord-?" the wraith offered the Master Vampire a title of respect but knew not his name.

"Lord will do nicely or Master if you prefer." The Master Vampire stated. With a slight bow, the wraith flew away over the mountains with all haste to return to its master.

"Let's see how the orcs fair when the wraiths arrive," the master vampire laughed as he led his forces out into the plains once again. The Master Vampire leading his minions through the wild Great Plains filled with tainted beasts, but they fed upon them anyway. The taste of a tainted meal was to a vampire like drinking muddy water. It kept them alive and strong, but the taste was foul.

The small army traveled for two weeks until they found a ruined keep. The Master Vampire knew very well that it would not be empty. Something or someone would be using it as shelter. He hoped for someone dwelling there, for that meant cattle and good blood to drink every night. Chief Gaji was a fool for asking them to leave. If not for his belief that cattle needed to exist for a food source, the wraiths would have had their way with the orcs years ago. Now plumes of smoke rose from vents in the mountains and that meant that the orc forges were again in use. The Master Vampire saw the dark smoke plumes far away and smiled.

"War is upon you Chief Gaji Bloody-Knucks. What will you do?" The master vampire asked to himself quietly before turning to lead his minions within the ruined keep. Arrows rained down at them suddenly as they approached.

"Cattle!" one vampire spawn shouted with glee before taking an arrow through the heart and falling to the ground motionless.

"Take the keep," the Master Vampire instructed as he slowly moved in towards it. "Remember to take them alive." The vampire forces charged while the master was more patient with his approach.

Arrows were suddenly trained on him rather than his forces and that meant they would get through. The master with blinding speed, dodged every arrow sent at him, springing into action. He was a true vampire and had powers unattainable by mere spawn. Regular arrows could not fell him as they could some of his minions. The master hissed as he sped for the wall and ran straight up it like a spider, leaping over the battlements and coming down upon a group of archers. The archers were knocked off the catwalk and fell to the courtyard below having the wind blasted from their lungs and the awaiting spawn ready to bind them with rope and disarm them. The master had trained his minions for over a century and his tactics almost always worked perfectly. His minions would distract with their charge and then he drew the attention notably as their master with most or all efforts focused on him, allowing his minions the opportunity to get inside. Once he was inside he helped by stunning their prey while his minions took the cattle prisoners. The ruined keep was overrun and taken in a just a few short hours. Many fledglings had fallen, but the spawn and pure bloods had not.

"Herd them into holding pens," the Master Vampire instructed after inspecting the large number of cattle they had attained. They were all very pleased mainly because orc blood was not quite as tasty as surface dwellers blood such as elves being like a fine wine and humans being a cheaper, but tasty version of the same wine. Pleased with his decision to leave the orcs, the master prepared himself to speak with the human's leader so that he could better control them and allow them to go about their lives. The Master Vampire entered the great chamber they used to hold their bound cattle and looked upon them all. His eyes seemed to draw their attention to him.

"I am, well you know what I am. You can call me master. I offer you your lives and the freedom to live them out as you would with my protection." The Master Vampire offered.

"At what cost to us," one man asked boldly seemingly stronger willed than the rest of the folk. The master vampire studied the man. He was badly bruised and battle scarred. It must have taken a great number of his minions to bring this one down alive.

"I only require blood, as do my minions. If you cooperate, it will leave no one dead. We will simply take our fill for the day and let the selected cattle go back home to recover." The master vampire answered honestly.

"Will it not turn them into vampires?" The man asked.

"No. Only if the victim is fully drained will he or she die and come back as a vampire. We do not want life as you know it to end or else we would be without food. We are in a way on your side against the wraith forces. Together we may eventually become strong enough to bring their reign of destruction to an end." The Master Vampire responded charismatically obviously gaining the people's attention and cooperation.

"We will cooperate as long as there are no casualties. Everyone will be accounted for and we will do a morning and nightly roll call." The man demanded. The master vampire knew he had no choice on the demands and nodded in agreement.

"As you wish," the Master Vampire said with a voice that seemed to calm the rest of the folk bit not the lone man speaking up. The man agreed anyway. He did not trust any undead, but his people could not effectively defend themselves. He had been their savior for the last few years and now they would have the protection of a Master Vampire and his minions. It was their best chance at survival after seeing the wraith scout a few weeks back pass through. After the agreement was made, the Master Vampire signaled for his minions to release their cattle from their bonds so that they could go about their lives.

"Be sure to select those who will be the givers this night. We are hungry." The Master Vampire instructed as the humans were released from their bindings. The master was pleased with himself. He had lost a tribe of orcs and gained a large group of humans. Yes, it was a smaller number of cattle, but they had gained a greater quality of food. In time, they would breed and create more offspring and their numbers would grow. Perhaps more survivors would come and take refuge with them. Either way his higher quality cattle would grow in numbers.

Chapter Three:

Every orc warrior was determined to make a name for its self. Many challenged one another for the title of Chief Gaji's captain, but those who failed were carried away to recover from their superficial wounds. Of the seventy able bodied orcs that were old enough to fight only one would be given the title of captain. Chief Gaji watched as one particular orc arose from the ranks. He seemed more skilled than the mighty, Chief Gaji. Normally Chief Gaji would have been threatened and wanted to kill the orc that could easily take away his title, but this one was loyal to him and had proven it by never challenging him for title of chief. Chief Gaji leaned forward and realized that it was his oldest son Foogart. He had forgotten about that one during his drunken years with so many different consorts. He was the son from a former mistress orc that was long ago slain in battle. Chief Gaji remembered her well. She was fierce in battle and in bed. Her loss was a great one. It was no wonder this orc before him was so dominate among his tribe. He was the offspring of too great orc barbarians. He had fought for hours of combat and in the end, only Foogart stood. He was bruised from head to feet with one eye swollen completely shut and the other open just a crack. All other orcs laid before him groaning in agony. Foogart did not groan in pain at all. One arm appeared broken and he limped as he moved forward towards the stone throne where Chief Gaji now sat grasping the Pride of the Bloody-Knucks Chief.

"I am Foogart," the orc roared as he approached and pounded his chest not with the useful arm he had, but with the broken arm to show his pride before his chief and father. Chief Gaji took the sign as though he may want to challenge him and leaped forward, slugging the wounded orc as hard as he could in the gut and blasting the wind form his lungs. Foogart fell back and landed on his rump. Chief Gaji stood over the proud orc and huffed. Foogart crawled to one knee and bowed before his chief and father.

"I am Foogart and I claim the right," Foogart began, but Chief Gaji swung a heavy fist into the side of Foogart's head and sent him falling to the stone floor. Again, Chief Gaji stood over his broken son and watched his stubbornness prevail. He again crawled to one knee, bowing to his chief.

"I am Foogart and I claim the title of captain." Foogart shouted before his father could hit him again. Chief Gaji halted his fist in mid swing. He froze with amazement. Foogart was truly loyal to him. Chief

Gaji looked to his tribe who watched the trial their chief was holding vigilantly.

"This is your captain. This is Foogart, my son." Chief Gaji roared proudly and the entire tribe cheered for their captain and chief. Foogart managed a slight smile to his father before he finally collapsed from exhaustion.

Several days had passed and the orcs had already recovered from the majority of their wounds and begun fabricating weapons and armor for battle. Foogart trained soldiers for battle that would be under his command and loyal to him. This was a dangerous issue for Chief Gaji, but as long as they remained loyal to Foogart and Foogart remained loyal to him, it only strengthened their army. Foogart was no war chief and he did not follow his father's example to become a warlord. He had the charisma and leadership skills to command troops. If it were anyone other than his son, Chief Gaji would feel very threatened for fear of his tribe splitting off. Foogart had taken a beating from nearly a hundred orcs and then from his own father before the entire tribe. He had proven himself loyal to his father and to the tribe. Many orcs heard their call to arms and journeyed from across the mountains or from deep within the subterranean realm to join their tribe that had over the course of a few weeks evolved into a clan. A young dragon with green scales arrived at the orc caves. It had heard of the great Foogart and Chief Gaji by reputation and hoped to use the orcs to obtain great wealth that all dragon-kind desired. The dragon went by the name of Faerxerous had joined with Foogart for a price. Foogart's forces were far greater than his father had ever attained. He was mightier than the chief of his tribe was, but Foogart was only that way so he could better impress his father. The forges echoed with the pounding of metal ringing out as Foogart approached his father who trained with his enchanted great axe called the Pride of the Bloody-Knucks Chief. Every orc hoped to wield the weapon of the chief not just, because it was the symbol of their leader, but because of its destructive power and ability to adapt to its wielder by transforming magically into the weapon the wielder desired. Foogart watched his father's movements as he approached. Even with the slight belly over hanging his trousers, the orc moved with great skill and speed as well as force. The chief struck the straw dummies fashioned for him to train with repeatedly until only wooden posts remained. They had seen humans train this way and had adapted it into their own training techniques over the years.

"Chief Gaji," Foogart called out as he bowed before his father. Chief Gaji turned to see Foogart kneeling and approached his son.

"Stand up Foogart," Chief Gaji instructed.

"I am wondering what you plan on doing about Morglum and the master vampire." Foogart asked drawing an angry glare from his father.

"Are you trying to tell me what to do?" Chief Gaji barked. Foogart shook his head frantically. His father was far too suspicious of him.

"No, I only ask because we have amassed a great army and thought if you will it that we should send scouts out to locate both of our enemies." Foogart explained. Chief Gaji was impressed at how intelligent his son was for an orc. He was even smarter than Gaji as well as stronger in battle and a better leader. He was smart enough to realize his son's intelligence; Chief Gaji had an idea.

"What would you suggest?" Chief Gaji asked the advice of his son. Foogart was taken by surprise and thought it a loaded question.

"I would only suggest if asked to Chief Gaji," Foogart barked loyally.

"Then suggest," Chief Gaji ordered. Again, Foogart was surprised and looked at Chief Gaji intensely trying to figure out his intentions.

"I would send out two small scout groups, one to track Morglum and the vermin-kissed elf, and the other to track down the Master Vampire and see what he is up to." Foogart replied. Chief Gaji thought that it sounded like a good plan.

"Then do it and report back to me anything that you learn," Chief Gaji instructed.

"Yes my chief," Foogart barked with a bow and took his leave to put together his scout patrols. He left his father alone to ponder whatever thoughts he had on his mind. Chief Gaji indeed had a lot on his mind. He knew his son was loyal, but his people would see how much leadership his son had and begin a feud if he did not do something. He needed a plan to get rid of the only orc mightier than him and he hoped that something would come from whatever the scout patrols discovered.

Foogart assembled two groups of six orcs and stood them before him armed and ready to be sent out on their missions of war. The orcs longed for battle, but Foogart seemed to go about things differently. He was tactical rather than sending orcs to certain death in battle, he was sending them to simply track and observe before returning to him and reporting what they had learned. The orcs were shocked at first but they were excited to be out of the caves in the open where monsters could be battled. The trackers of each group found both trails of their marks and split up. One headed into the open plains while the other followed a trail to the mountains.

*****

The six companions took to the road leaving behind the Great Plains and avoiding the cave home to the orc tribe. After two weeks of navigating the mountains, they heard loud drums echoing throughout the mountains. Morglum knew what it meant and fear swept over him. Would his father come after him? He was not certain.

"What is it Morglum?" Aleiz asked curiously knowing well the sounds of war drums.

"My tribe has taken claim of their caves again. The vampires have either gone or been defeated." Morglum explained.

"So who is he at war with?" Aleiz asked.

"Me," Morglum gasped fearfully. The six companions had to keep to mountain trails and to navigate the mountains. They hoped that none of the denizens of the mountains would bother them as they journeyed through the long trek of mountains. Sametria and Taegrid led their new companions through the mountain pass as best as they could for never having traveled through it before. The air was thin and cold. It screamed as it blew, constantly reminding them of the cold wastes that lay ahead. Snow covered the landscape at higher elevations as well as their horizon and the rest of the mountains ahead of them.

"This is where it gets very cold," Sametria warned her companions.

"That's alright. I'll use Sadie's fur to keep me warm." Morglum joked but got a dangerous growl from Sadie and a wicked glare from Sametria in response. Taegrid looked over the edge and saw a hidden path that they did not know existed. His eyes widened as he saw an army of undead marching through the winding path below. It was narrow and allowed perhaps two at a time passage, but it provided protection from any who would attempt an ambush from above as the mountain walls constantly shifted and at some points completely covered the winding path.

"Look," Taegrid whispered to his companions as he pointed down below. They all looked and felt the hair on the back of their necks stand on end.

"They probably march for the orcs," Morglum growled. Taegrid looked to Sametria.

"What if there are other settlements we were unaware of?" Taegrid asked with a panicked tone. Sametria thought for a moment as she looked around and examined their surroundings. Her head stopped as her field of view became obstructed and standing upon the path behind them were a handful of skeletons and a hovering wraith.

"They are not your concern. I am." The wraith hissed catching the attention from the rest of the group. Gilthanus saw the wraith and it saw him.

"You-, I will finish you off this time!" The wraith hissed with a venomous tone.

"I don't think so," the elf sorcerer argued as his companions drew weapons. This was to be their first battle as a group and they all hoped for the best. The path they traveled was just a little wider than the one below, allowing for side-by-side marching with just a little breathing room. They had a wall to one side of them and a cliff on the other side that spelled certain doom. The skeletons marched towards the companions with their curved scimitars drawn, passing through their commander the wraith as though he was not even blocking their path. The wraith laughed wickedly. Taegrid loosed an arrow at the skeletons, but his first shot passed harmlessly between the ribs as no mass of flesh clung to the bones to be struck. Aleiz tried to hit one of the skeletons with his crossbow before backing away. He and Gilthanus were holding up the rear with Sadie. Their rear was the direction the undead forces approached from. Gilthanus kept his keen eyes trained on the wraith and readied a spell to send at it when he had the chance. Sametria and Morglum pushed passed their companions to meet the skeletons in combat.

"Guard them Sadie," Sametria instructed her wolf as she passed by and Sadie listened. She growled threateningly at the undead forces, but she stayed to protect the others. Morglum slammed his great-axe down and shattered one of the skeletons into bone chips. Sametria stabbed her blade but it scraped between ribs as Taegrid's arrow and Aleiz's bolt had. Another skeleton moved up to replace the one that had fallen and swung on the half-orc, but the blade missed wide. Sametria was also swung upon and ducked low with her scimitar overhead to deflect a second blow if needed. The wraith took to the sky cackling as it circled the companions in wait. Gilthanus waited no more and sent a magical spell at the wraith. The spell took hold of the incorporeal body its energy exploded on impact and angered the wraith. The spell stung the wraith but nothing more, similar to an explosive bee sting. One hurt but many could be fatal.

Taegrid knew it would be a waste of arrows to fire anymore and instead began leading those who would follow along the path.

"Come let those in the rear provide us cover and if they fall the next in line will take arms." Taegrid instructed as he began moving along the narrow path. Aleiz did not argue and followed. They knew that given the circumstances there was little that they could do. Sametria continued to parry the attacks of the skeleton she faced not wanting to give up any ground. She scratched the skeleton from time to time but it would take some time to destroy one at that rate. For now, she would just hold the line while Morglum cut them down one by one. His mighty swings from the great axe he wielded shattered them as though it were a war hammer wielded by a man. Morglum's muscles were toned with definition and bulged as he swung his great axe. He was truly a mighty half-orc. Gilthanus refused to leave the one who tended his wounds and nursed him back to health. He thought he was their only chance at destroying the wraith and that is what he was going to do. The wraith wanted to attack them from behind, but Gilthanus sent a second spell streaking at the wraith and it exploded on impact as well, knocking it off course.

"You cannot destroy me. Your spells could fail you at any time." The wraith warned, but Gilthanus would not leave. He was not afraid of this creature no matter how dangerous it was.

"I defeated you before," Gilthanus reminded the wraith hoping to anger it more and cause it to make a mistake.

"I retreated yes, but you did not win the day. You survived because I was merciful. This time I will not be." The wraith lunged in at the elf suddenly. Gilthanus dropped to the ground flat on his belly and the wraith passed over him dangerously close almost scratching his back as it passed by and disappeared within the mountainside. Gilthanus spun around on his belly and watched the mountainside as he started to stand to his feet. Sadie barked at the rock wall and Gilthanus knew it was coming back. He dropped again as the wraith passed over and sent his spell at it. This time the spell did not take hold, but the wraith did and scratched Gilthanus along his arm. The touch was cold and sickened him like the rays of the sun magnified, but the sorcerer fought through it and stood to his feet sending another spell at the wraith as it turned around to swoop in again. Sametria and Morglum could take the skeletons. It was up to him to take the wraith. The wraith was a powerful undead that could withstand a great deal. Gilthanus ached from the wound that drained him of some of his life force, but as the wraith swooped in again he released a beam of life giving energy at the critical moment. When the wraith impacted with his body and would have normally passed through his body to leave him drained, the spell struck and vaporized the wraith. Because it impacted with the life giving energy summoned by Gilthanus, it was as though the wraith had become solid matter for an instant and the force knocked Gilthanus back against the rock wall hard. He slid to the ground motionless and gasping for air. Sadie whimpered as she approached the elf and sniffed him. She howled to warn Sametria that one of theirs had fallen.

"Gilthanus has fallen. I must tend to him right away." Sametria warned the half-orc.

"None of these bone heads will get by me," Morglum vowed. He took a central station to block the approach from either side of the path and Sametria ran over to inspect the unconscious elf. She sheathed her sword as she knelt beside him and placed a gentle hand against his head as she chanted a spell. Healing energy filled him and closed some of his wounds. He was cold to the touch but not as bad off as he had been when they last found him. His eyes began to open.

"Thank you again," Gilthanus said sincerely as he came to and saw the half-elf tending him.

"You earned it my friend," Sametria stated as she helped Gilthanus to his feet.

"Where is the wraith?" Gilthanus asked suddenly frantic and looking all around. Sametria smiled and smacked him on his shoulder as Morglum hacked down the last skeleton on the path.

"You sent it to Oblivion," Sametria commended the sorcerer who was actually amazed with himself.

"It worked," Gilthanus gasped in shock as Morglum tromped over to them.

"We should catch up with the others and get out of the open before more of them find their way up here." The half-orc suggested.

"Or before more wraiths come," Sametria added.

"Agreed," Morglum said. "This elf seems to be the only one useful against the blasted things."

"Come on Sadie," Sametria called as she led them up the trail to catch up to their other companions. Taegrid had led them to the end of their trail and had his bow trained upon them as they rounded the bend. He saw that it was the rest of their group.

"Where is the wraith?" Taegrid asked as he lowered his bow.

"The elf vaporized it," Morglum answered as he smacked Gilthanus on his back proudly and nearly knocked him over.

"That takes care of one problem. Look." Taegrid noted as he pointed out that the long trail had ended. Gilthanus looked and pointed at something his keen elf eyes saw. Aleiz now saw it as well. Taegrid had blocked his view before. Across the gap on another mountainside was an ancient rope bridge dangling in the wind against the mountain wall. Gilthanus pointed out where it had once been attached at the paths end and Sametria moved to inspect with Taegrid.

"The ropes were cut," Sametria and Taegrid said in unison.

"How to get across?" Morglum asked as though he could come up with the answer.

"Do you have any spells to aid us?" Aleiz asked the surface elf sorcerer.

"I regrettably do not my cousin," Gilthanus showed Aleiz more respect than any vermin-kissed elf had been shown from the surface elves in many centuries on Athyx just by answering his question without a rude remark, but to refer to him as his cousin was what caught him more off guard. Aleiz nodded his thanks silently and Gilthanus understood his quiet reaction.

"We have come to the mountains with no rope," Gilthanus stated more than asked.

"If we go all the way back we will have to face that army of undead and the orcs." Morglum reminded.

"We will go forward," Gilthanus said suddenly as he pushed past the two rangers to where the rope bridge had once been and began feeling along the rock face. "There was a symbol here long ago." Gilthanus wiped away some dust to reveal the rest of the rune that hid a secret door in the mountainside.

"How do we open it?" Aleiz asked as he began inspecting and found no apparent way to open it. Morglum slammed his heavy axe head against the stone face and sparks flew. A large chunk of stone fell at his feet leaving a chip in his axe blade.

"I'll open it," Morglum claimed with determination. He brought his great axe up for another swing and slammed the axe blade against the rock face in the same spot. This time a large piece of his axe blade broke off, but the hidden doorway was revealed and a dark tunnel could be seen on the other side through the small opening he had created. Morglum looked very upset that his favorite axe was broken, but he swung it again to widen the opening. He beat the rock until his great axe was nothing but a pole with remnants of an axe head on it and tossed it to the ground.

"This is going to have to do," Morglum grumbled. The opening was wide enough to crawl through. They knew it would take some squeezing effort for Morglum to get through, but the rest of them would fit with no difficulty.

"Sorry about your axe," Sametria apologized knowing that he had made a sacrifice for them.

"I'll make a better one," Morglum said waving a hand as though to brush the thought away. Aleiz was first to enter the hole leading into darkness. Gilthanus followed and then Taegrid. Sametria helped Sadie through to Taegrid and then Morglum. Sametria took one last deep breath of fresh air before climbing through.

"We need light," Sametria reminded her companions. A quiet chanting of a spell and Gilthanus had a long sword in hand radiating light as though it were a torch.

"I will have to cast another in a short while. My magic is still developing in strength." Gilthanus warned.

"It will work long enough for us to find some supplies," Gilthanus said pointing into a cavern apparently used as a storeroom.

"Torches and food," Sametria noted as they approached the crates.

"Rotten food," Morglum said after sniffing the air.

"Who did this belong to?" Taegrid asked pointing out writing.

"It's dwarven," Morglum answered as he recognized the writing. He could not read it, but he spoke it and recognized it.

"Gather whatever we can use. Aleiz scout ahead, but not too far ahead." Sametria instructed.

"These caverns have been abandoned for some time." Taegrid warned as he noted the dust and webs about them.

"What could cause dwarves to leave their homes in the mountains?" Gilthanus asked as they gathered supplies. Aleiz was already on the move through the nearby tunnels. He checked for any pitfalls or hidden stone traps that still might function along his way. Due to the trained eyes of Aleiz, they avoided a pit trap that still functioned and marked it with a dwarven helm nearby. A thought came to him. Why was there a dwarven helm in the middle of a hallway with no sign of any dwarf or dwarf remains? Aleiz looked up and noted several dwarf sized cocoons hanging from a web covered ceiling and walls.

"Damn," Aleiz cursed knowing that he would only further anger his people and goddess by killing giant spiders they encountered. "It's a good thing Na-Dene is imprisoned or dead I guess." Aleiz balked. He returned to his companions at the storage room. A torch now lit the chamber where his ally's gathered supplies.

"We have rope now," Gilthanus joked when he saw Aleiz had returned. However, all of them went silent from the expression on the vermin-kissed elf's face.

45

"What did you find?" Sametria asked drawing a scimitar in hand.

"Dead dwarves," Aleiz answered regrettably.

"Killed by what, could you tell?" Taegrid asked. Aleiz looked the cat man dead in the eyes.

"Spiders," Aleiz paused to draw out the dramatics of the issue, "Spiders the size of you and me or larger."

"Oh is that all?" Morglum asked drawing his battle-axe and checking its sharpness with his thumb.

"He is afraid," Gilthanus noted knowing the vermin-kissed elf history. "His people worship the vermin-kissed goddess Na-Dene and she adores vermin such as rats, centipedes, spiders and pretty much anything in the category of vermin. It is blasphemy to kill them."

"That is correct," Aleiz confirmed.

"Do you intend to return to your people?" Sametria asked catching a strange look from the vermin-kissed elf.

"No," Aleiz dared to say.

"Then killing the spiders with us, if we have to, shouldn't be a problem for you." Sametria pointed out. She knew there had to be more to the story.

"My people probably believe me to be dead. If I am discovered they will brand me as a deserter and they will hunt me down." Aleiz suddenly admitted fearfully.

"Then we will protect you," Morglum vowed to his friend.

"But who will protect you?" Aleiz asked catching their attention even more.

"The vermin-kissed elves are dangerous Aleiz, but they are not worse than what we have just faced outside." Gilthanus reminded the vermin-kissed elf.

"Some of them have turned to the worship of Viscus. Those that have, decided to leave the city. They are allies to those we have just faced and anything that would attract their attention is just a very bad idea. A civil war has begun between the vermin-kissed elves faithful to Na-Dene and the vermin-kissed horrors who believe they are more faithful and that we should have done something to help our goddess." Aleiz explained.

"We are companions now. We watch each other's backsides, even if we fall at the end of a blade during the process." Sametria claimed and the bond between the six companions grew that day within the darkness of the dwarven graveyard.

"We have few options before us. What do we want to do?" Taegrid asked his allies.

"I think riches are here to be found," Gilthanus pointed out and Aleiz was suddenly interested.

"I think our best chance of survival would be to slaughter spiders and see what the dwarves left behind for us." Aleiz said suddenly changing his outlook on the matter.

"Let us be cautious then. Taegrid, Sadie and I will lead with Aleiz scouting for traps just ahead of us." Sametria suggested and no one argued.

"I'll watch the flank in case anything tries to attack our backs." Morglum offered. "But know that I will bowl anyone over that gets in my way if I am needed up front." Gilthanus shrugged.

"I guess I'll stay in the middle and go where I am needed." Gilthanus offered.

"You are our only arcane spell caster Gilthanus. We have to protect you as well." Taegrid explained. The six companions began their long and perilous journey through the spider infested tunnels with hopes of finding great treasures and living to fight another day.

Chapter Four:

The orc trackers had followed the trail of Morglum and discovered that he had joined with others besides the vermin-kissed elf he helped escape. During their scouting expedition, they had also seen the approaching undead army heading towards their home.

"What should we do?" one of the orc trackers asked the group.

"We are to track Morglum and report back to Foogart," one of them repeated their orders.

"What if Foogart is not alive when we come home to report?" another orc asked with a good point. The orcs wanted to fight and there was a war coming to them.

"I say we tell him Morglum died in the mountains and warn him about the undead army." The first orc suggested. They all agreed. The orcs were bred for war. If Morglum wanted to leave them behind, then they felt that they should let him. They did not care for a half-breed anyway. The orcs sped their way back down the mountain path hoping to stay in front of the undead army that was no longer in their view. The wind blew their long thick black hair as they ran. They ran so fast that they were kicking rocks that were in their way. The orc scouts were no longer trying to be careful or remain hidden. They were in a hurry to get back to their home and warn their chief of the approaching danger and their hastiness had gotten them discovered. Several wraiths rose up from below and screeched at them when they were spotted.

"Wraiths!" one orc warned as he looked up to the gray sky. The other five orcs never looked back, even when they heard their comrade fall to the wraiths that now streaked after the next orc in line. The black shadow-like ghosts passed through the orc as though he were insubstantial and with each pass, the orc was drained a bit more of his life force until it fell to the ground, cold and lifeless. Four orcs remained and they ran as fast as horses, nearly falling over the edge of the pass trail at each turn. The wraiths continued to stalk their prey and assaulted a third and then a fourth orc. They ripped through the orcs bodies, devouring their souls with each pass. It did not take long for a group of wraiths to kill even the mightiest of mortals. They swooped in and killed the fifth orc only inches behind the final member of the scouting party. The sixth and final orc saw the end of his path ahead. He heard the wraiths screech from behind him as they killed his last fellow orc. His chest pounded. This was not how orcs or anyone else in the world wanted to die. The orc looked over his shoulder and saw the wraiths were upon him and suddenly decided to leap over the edge.

"Bolnarg!" the orc cried out as he fell to his death, crashing hard upon the rocks hundreds of feet below and breaking every bone n its body on impact. The wraiths were pleased with the outcome and let out eerie screeches before they returned to their approaching army of undead.

*****

Aleiz had led his companions into a chamber just beyond the trapped hallway where he had found several dead and cocooned dwarf corpses. Inside the chamber, there was a mass of webs that they had to burn their way through. Ahead of them was what they thought they were looking for. It was the dwarven armory, but they would not get to examine the dwarven goods so easily. Several man-sized, spiders crawled from out of the shadows upon the ceiling and the walls. They moved right at the intruders.

"This is it I guess," Aleiz grumbled as he took aim with his crossbow. Arrows, bolts and spells struck the spiders as they approached. The spiders attacked, forcing the intruders into melee. Taegrid counted the spiders as he dropped his bow and drew out his sickle. The cat man swung the curved farming tool at the spider's hairy body as it came in at him with large fangs dripping venom. Morglum clove one in half and quickly engaged a second while his friends still fought their first. The spiders were savage and mindless having no fear for their own safety. Morglum had cut down three spiders before Taegrid cut down his first. One over powered Gilthanus and sunk its massive fangs into his shoulders pumping its strength robbing venom into his body. Gilthanus screamed in pain as he tried to pull the fangs free of his body. Morglum roared as he charged in and kicked the giant spider off his friend and slammed his axe home to finish it.

"Sametria, Gilthanus needs you." Morglum shouted as Sadie killed a spider.

"I'm slightly busy," Sametria groaned, still fighting her first spider. Morglum roared as he charged in and relieved Sametria of her foe.

"Now you're not," Morglum barked. Sametria sighed as she turned to tend Gilthanus. Taegrid dropped a second spider as Aleiz killed his first. Morglum finished whatever other spiders roamed within the chamber.

"That's two for me and one for each of you," Taegrid said proudly to Aleiz and the wolf.

"I got six," Morglum said matter-of-factly as he strolled by to see how Gilthanus was doing. The poison burned Gilthanus' veins. Sweat beaded on his brow as Sametria sucked as much of the poison out of the wounds as she could and spat it on the floor next to them. When she had finished, she packed the wounds with herbs that would absorb more of the toxin and ease some of the elf's pain allowing him to rest easier.

"Rest now my friend," Sametria said with a soothing voice as she wiped the elf blood from her lips.

"How is he?" Morglum asked as though he genuinely cared.

"He will live," Sametria answered.

"You have a gift for healing," Morglum complimented the half-elf.

"I am a Nature's Allie, it is what we do." Sametria responded matter-of-factly.

"Mighty Morglum, that's what I'm going to call you from now on." Aleiz joked.

"It has a nice ring to it," Morglum returned the laugh.

"We will have to spend the night here," Sametria warned everyone pointing out the unconscious elf.

"He is quite frail now isn't he," Taegrid scoffed.

"He is one of us and we will treat him that way," Sametria scolded the cat-man.

"I know he did after all destroy a wraith single handedly." Taegrid reminded himself and the others. "I'll check the perimeter."

"I'll go with you," Aleiz offered as he followed the cat man who now carried a torch in one hand. Dwarf sized armor littered the chamber as well as empty weapon racks. Eventually Aleiz and Taegrid happened upon several crates of ammunition. They found crossbow bolts, arrows and throwing axes as well as a weapon rack with cobweb-covered weapons still hanging on it.

"What do we have here?" Taegrid asked rhetorically as he picked up a massive longbow from the rack and wiped the webs and dust from its length. Sparks crackled from its string when he grasped it as though it housed some kind of magical properties. It was a finely crafted weapon. In fact, it was so fine that it required a greater strength than Taegrid's to draw back the string.

"Too bad you do not have the strength to wield that bow," Aleiz taunted. Taegrid glared at the vermin-kissed elf.
"I will strengthen my muscles and in time I will be able to draw back the string. In the meantime, I bet Morglum could make use of it." Taegrid thought as he slung it over his back along with a quiver of arrows.

Morglum cleaned the spider matter from his battle-axe as he stood over Gilthanus and Sametria with Sadie pacing the floor nearby.

Sametria prayed to her nature god believed to have been slain by Viscus. Tevlos was her deity no matter if he had perished or not. It was natural for one to die for the rebirth to take place. Perhaps Tevlos would be reborn and Athyx would again become beautiful. Sametria day dreamed as she prayed over Gilthanus. She felt her bond with nature and her wolf growing every day. She believed Tevlos blessed her even in his absence as it were. Unlike holy clergies such as priestess, the druids drew their power from the nature that surrounded them through the essence of Tevlos. Even with his absence, druids still wielded power while his priests could not. Unfortunately, because that was the case, Sametria also sensed that nature was mutating so rapidly that it would not be natural for much longer. She knew that her time was limited on this world, but now it was even more limited because without the forces of nature, life could not exist. She was even more determined to find a way to restore her world now than ever before. She felt nature crying out for her help.

Sametria's attention was brought back to the here and now when she heard what sounded like scampering feet trying to be quiet out in the dark tunnels. Aleiz and Taegrid returned to their friends sides. Sadie was staring into the darkness baring teeth and growling quietly.

"Did you hear it to?" Morglum asked the others. They all nodded as their weapons were drawn at the ready.

"More spiders..." Morglum contemplated.

"I don't think so," Aleiz responded trying to see what the creatures were that they heard. Now they heard whispers out in the tunnels. Gilthanus opened his eyes and grabbed Sametria's wrist.

"They speak dragonese," Gilthanus warned.

"Dragons?" Sametria asked the sorcerer before he passed back into unconsciousness. "What else speaks dragonese?"

"I think we're about to find that out," Taegrid answered as he through his torch by the doorway and notched an arrow. A small red-skinned creature resembling a lizard-like humanoid poked its head into the room to see the intruders and spat unfamiliar words at them.

"Gilthanus what is it saying?" Sametria asked, but the sorcerer was out cold. More of the creatures came into view brandishing spears forged for their size.

"They are kind of cute," Sametria claimed.

"They stink," Morglum barked. One of the creatures entered the room fully and hopped up and down in a threatening manner shouting something at them in its language. The conscious companions could not help but laugh at the sight.

"I don't think it likes what you said Morglum," Taegrid chuckled.

"They're kobolds," Aleiz said as he recognized the creatures. "My people enslave their kind as well as others." A large group of the kobolds scurried into the chamber behind the first and in unison; they hurled their spears at the intruders. Morglum sheltered Sametria and Gilthanus with his own body allowing any spear that would hit his two friends bounce harmlessly off his armor. Aleiz and Taegrid rolled to opposite sides before coming back up to their feet. Taegrid loosed two arrows as Aleiz charged in with his kukri.

"Are you alright?" Morglum asked Sametria. Sametria inspected the heroic half-orc for any wounds.

"You're fine, now go cut them down." Sametria barked as she leaped to her feet with her scimitar now in hand. Two kobolds were wounded right away one from Taegrid's arrows and Aleiz wounded another. One of the kobolds began hooting something outside the doorway before moving out of the way. Several spiders of the same size they had just faced earlier entered the room with kobold riders directing them and armed with spears.

"Sadie, stay and defend Gilthanus." Sametria ordered her wolf as she charged in beside Morglum. The little creatures lunged forward with their spears to try to drive back the intruders. Taegrid dropped the first kobold with two more arrows and quickly took aim at the next in line.

"Did I say these things were cute?" Sametria asked her friends with distaste as she cut a wound along the chest of a kobold. "I meant I really don't like them at all." Morglum laughed as he split one of the small creatures in two, right down the center with his battle-axe. The companions could not help but laugh as they were forced to slaughter the kobolds. The laughter stopped when the spider riders that had taken the time to ride up onto the ceiling coached their mounts to fire webs at the intruders. Sametria was pinned to the floor unable to defend herself and the kobolds came in with their spears. Morglum was pinned to the floor nearby and he roared in protest. Sadie was trapped in a web with the unconscious Gilthanus. The wolf barked repeatedly as she tried to chew herself free. Aleiz and Taegrid rolled out of the way before the webbing could entangle them.

"Hang on!" Taegrid shouted as he sent two more arrows into the approaching crowd of kobolds. Aleiz killed one of the smelly kobolds and turned to engage the next. Sametria chanted a druid spell and she felt her muscles begin to strengthen beyond their normal capacity. Morglum erupted from the webbing ripping it from his body and roaring in anger. The kobolds stopped their charge briefly. A second, and then a third web engulfed the half-orc holding him fast. Once the half-orc was again held firmly in the webbing, the kobolds came in and began stabbing at him through the webbing. He felt several spears almost piercing his armor and growled in frustration. Luckily, for Morglum and Sametria, they were not defenseless. The webbing aloud for some movement however minute, allowing them to defend themselves to a degree. Sametria followed in Morglum's example and ripped her way out of the webbing, surprising the kobolds that came in to stab her with their spears. Before another web could net her, she engaged the kobolds and kept them close so the spider rider could not target her again. Taegrid killed a second kobold with two arrows sticking out of its small head. Morglum broke free of the webbing again and followed Sametria's example and stayed close to the kobolds to avoid being webbed again.

"These things are smarter than they look," Morglum spat.

"That's because if they are ever captured and enslaved by more powerful races, they are used and cannon fodder." Aleiz explained as he turned a kobold spear away from him harmlessly. The kobold infantry tried to scatter away from Aleiz, Sametria and Morglum to allow their spider riders to rain down webbing upon them. Morglum and Sametria were caught again in the thick webs.

"Did I mention that I really hate kobolds and spiders?" Sametria growled. She could hear Sadie still barking and trying to free herself. She saw the kobolds pivot and turn back at her. Taegrid fired his bow at any kobold that tried to get near his entangled friends as he dodged webs that were spun at him. Sametria and Morglum broke free of the webbing again only to be webbed a third time just as they ripped free.

"Son of a goblin!-" Morglum cursed as the kobolds stabbed at them with their spears again. Taegrid's arrows kept the kobolds from getting close enough to really hurt Morglum or Sametria with their little spears. Morglum and Sametria were becoming exhausted from breaking free of the webs repeatedly, but they had to keep it up or the kobolds might soon find an opening in Taegrid's arrow barrage and wound them with a spear. Taegrid killed a third kobold with a flurry of arrows as it tried to run in at him. Sametria and Morglum broke free of the webs and leaped at the kobolds who had readied their spears. The choice before them was not very promising. They could either accept the end of a kobold spear with a chance of killing one or be entangled again and risk being killed. Both happened to react the same way and embraced the fates of the spears. Sametria was tired and her muscles were sore, but she managed to score a cut on a kobold as she came in.

Aleiz killed a second and moved in to help Sametria. The kobolds were growing frantic. Sametria killed her first kobold and Morglum cut down his second. The spider riders could do nothing until they had a clear shot other than keep trying to entangle the cat man archer who managed to evade their snares every time. Taegrid killed another before turning his attention to the kobold riders and firing on them. The kobolds cackled something before turning and scampering back out of the dwarven armory. The spider riders followed catching a few arrows in their rears as they left.

"That was fun," Aleiz stated with sarcasm. Sametria ran over and cut Sadie free of the webs before removing the rest of the webbing from an unconscious Gilthanus.

"Barricade the doors and make sure there are no other entrances they can sneak up on us from." Sametria instructed her friends. Morglum began trying to reattach the dangling doors enough for them to be closed and barred. Aleiz checked the large chamber for secret doors that the kobolds might try to attack from. Sametria made sure that Gilthanus was cared for, even with her fatigue. She still watched over him waking to check him every few hours. Aleiz had found a single secret entry to the armory, but it looked like it had not been used in years. Morglum watched each of his friends do the things that they were best at and studied how they did each task that was set before them. Fighting came easy for Morglum because he was a barbarian. He also knew when to get angry and reckless and when not to. He was intelligent enough to know things that the average orc would easily overlook. He just could not read or write. That did not make him stupid, just illiterate. They needed rest and it was possible that the kobolds would return at any time with a larger force to try to finish them off. They hoped that the smelly little creatures would have learned their lesson and leave them alone.

Rest did them all well. No monster of any kind attempted to intrude upon them as they slept. Gilthanus was awake, but still very weak, too weak in fact to carry his own pack. He was angry that giant vermin could take him so easily. Morglum carried his pack for him as well as his own.

"Thank you Morglum," Gilthanus said wholeheartedly as they prepared to leave the dwarven armory. A loud knock came from the barred door and caught their attentions. Weapons were drawn. Taegrid and Morglum moved toward the door ready with battle-axe and bow.

"Who is it?" Morglum asked. A strange cackle was heard from the other side of the door. They knew right away that it was the kobolds. "Go away you smelly lizards or I will slaughter the whole lot of you."

"Wait," Gilthanus called out to them as he approached the door. He began speaking in their language to them.

"What did you say?' Taegrid asked when silence fell over the kobolds.

"Hello I believe," Gilthanus answered.

"Sounded more like what's your name and last night was great to me." Morglum joked. The kobolds again began speaking to them through the door.

"What are they saying?" Taegrid asked. Gilthanus listened carefully and translated every word they spoke.

"We are sorry for attacking you. Please show us mercy. We help you if you help us." Gilthanus translated in the common tongue.

"Do you think it's a trap?" Sametria asked Gilthanus who shrugged in response.

"Assume that it is. What is it they want our help to do?" Taegrid offered his two cents of wisdom.

"What do you need our help with?" Gilthanus asked the kobolds in their draconic language. The kobolds responded right away and sounded quite excited that the intruders were considering adding them at all. Whatever color Gilthanus had in his complexion faded in an instant as though the blood in his body had suddenly been drained. Gilthanus first looked to Aleiz and shook his head in denial.

"What is it?" Aleiz gasped fearfully.

"A vermin-kissed horror stalks them at night. They thought us its minions because they saw Aleiz. They want us to kill it for them and they will show us the way through the mountain and give us whatever we want from the dwarven hoard they have in their lair." Gilthanus translated reluctantly.

"Is it just one?" Aleiz asked curiously knowing his culture better than anyone present. Gilthanus asked the kobolds in their language and they answered right away. Gilthanus turned his face to the floor with a sigh before turning to face his friends.

"There are three of them," Gilthanus informed his companions.

"Three vermin-kissed horrors'-?" Aleiz gulped. "We might as well go and face the undead army and get it over with."

"Why do you fear your people so much?" Taegrid dared to ask. Aleiz met the cat man's gaze.

"The worst thing that might happen to you in your life is death or complete destruction from life-sapping energy devouring your soul. My people would just assume keep you alive in eternal torment. A fate far worse than anything you might ever imagine." Aleiz responded with fear in his tone.

"If we kill these vermin-kissed horrors, will you believe that we are worse than your people?" Morglum scoffed at his friend. Aleiz looked at the Mighty Morglum.

"You would have to be more frightening than the vermin-kissed elves. You will have to embrace chaos to defeat chaos." Aleiz answered.

"I'm Morglum the Mighty and I am quite chaotic." Morglum said with a wink. "Tell the filthy things we will do it." Gilthanus looked to everyone else first and saw as they all approved with nods. The elf sorcerer informed the kobolds that they would accept their terms for what they offered. Gilthanus added that they would have to be given the treasure first and waited for a response. The kobolds were silent for a moment and whispered amongst themselves before finally agreeing.

"What was that all about?" Sametria asked as they all gathered around the door.

"I told them we agreed, but we would have to be given the treasure first. They agreed." Gilthanus explained with a smile.

"An elf after my own heart," Aleiz laughed. Morglum removed the door bar and swung it open. The door opened part way before ripping away from the hinge and falling to the floor, nearly crushing several kobolds. The kobolds scattered and parted as their leader pointed down a dark tunnel.

"The treasure is that way?" Gilthanus asked in the dragonese language. The kobold chief hopped up and down before leading the way down the dark tunnel. Knobs and spider riders surrounded them on all sides of the wide tunnel, parting as they passed with the kobold leader. There were so many kobolds that Sametria gasped in disgust.

"These things must breed like rabbits!" Sametria spat as the kobold chief stopped in front of a set of dwarven decorated double doors.

"The treasure is on the other side?" Gilthanus asked in dragonese. The kobold nodded and took a key from beneath his shirt that hung on a gold chain and handed it to the sorcerer.

"Take what you want, but please kill vermin-kissed horrors." The kobold chief managed to say in the common language of the surface folk.

"We will as long as you do not lie to us about the treasure." Gilthanus promised. Gilthanus took the key and handed it to Aleiz who promptly inspected the door to see if there were some hidden traps. Aleiz made certain that it was safe before he inserted the key and turned the locking mechanism. Morglum yanked the heavy doors open when Aleiz moved. Beyond was a chamber full of great riches the likes a dragon might have in its hoard. Aleiz and Gilthanus stared at the riches for a long moment before looking at one another. The kobolds watched the intruders intently as they entered the treasury they had rightfully stolen from the dwarves. Hills of gold, silver and platinum filled the treasury, but that was not what the companions thought interesting. There were bricks and rods of various valuable materials that the dwarves forged weapons out of. Again, that was not what interested the companions. A scimitar designed so that the pommel and hilt resembled an oak tree with the tree roots gripping the blade at the guard seemed to call out to Sametria. The half-elf picked up the blade and examined it carefully. It was the finest artisanship she had ever seen with a sword of its kind.

"That is a nice looking sword," Taegrid offered as he stopped to see what Sametria had found to her liking.

"How much of this do you think they will let us have?" Aleiz asked with excitement.

"We should not be greedy Aleiz. They still outnumber us about a thousand to one." Taegrid warned the vermin-kissed elf.

"I might have to come back here some day," Aleiz shared as he knelt low to take a closer look at a black cloak that seemed to writhe.

"What is this?" Aleiz gasped as he picked up the strange black cloak.

"I would be careful Aleiz. Not everything is beneficial." Gilthanus warned. Aleiz looked up to the sorcerer with a great smile as he dared to put the cloak over his shoulders and clasp it in place. Nothing happened to him. Both of them sighed with relief.

"One day your arrogance may get you killed." Gilthanus warned. Aleiz smiled as he watched his cloak writhe upon his shoulders as though it were crafted from shadows or a wraith.

"You take and you leave," the kobold leader spat in the language of the surface dwellers. Gilthanus nodded in understanding.

"Aleiz and Sametria you have to leave the treasury now that you have chosen your payment." Gilthanus explained. Sametria understood and took her leave, grabbing the vermin-kissed elf on her way and pulling him along before he could pocket anything else. Taegrid looked for something that he hoped would alter his strength magically so that he could wield the mighty longbow he found earlier. A set of bracers caught his eye and tried them on. He did not feel stronger but tried to lift a large chest anyway and nearly pulled a muscle in his back. Taegrid left the chest where it was and slammed his arm down on it to rest in defeat but his arms did not touch when they stopped. They were a good half inch away from the chest and could not be forced down any further. It was as if an invisible layer of armor seemed to surround his body.

"I guess that will do," Taegrid whispered with a little disappointment before leaving the treasury. Gilthanus picked up a ring at random and left the treasury with it in hand. Morglum still looked around for something he might find useful.

"All of this is dwarven crap," Morglum barked until he found something so unique and blasphemous that he had to have it. A great axe fashioned from mithral rested against the wall in the back of the chamber. The carvings were so artistic and creative that Morglum had to take a closer look. The long handle and the axe head was one solid piece. The front head was an axe blade carved to resemble the face of a roaring orc and the back end was a war hammer rather than another blade resembling the face of a screaming dwarf. Morglum knew that it meant dwarves hated orcs most, but he preferred to think these artisans had made the great axe for him personally.

"This is mine," Morglum roared as he held the mighty, great axe over his head and laid claim to it.

"You get treasure. Now kill vermin-kissed horrors." The kobold leader barked in the dragonese language. Gilthanus nodded.

"He says it's time for us to keep our end of the bargain." Gilthanus informed his companions.

"Tell him to point us towards the damned monsters so I can cut'em down," Morglum demanded as he joined his friends. Gilthanus looked at the half-orc curiously.

"Are you alright?" Gilthanus asked him.

"I was just trying out my dwarven accent," Morglum chuckled as he showed off his fine mithral great axe. Morglum could not get over how light the great axe was. It was exactly the same weight as his battle-axe forged from steel. The kobold pointed down a large tunnel that ended in another set of double doors barred on this side.

"They must be in there," Gilthanus stated the obvious. Morglum removed the bar from the doors and leaned it against the wall to his right.

"Are we ready?" Morglum asked as he grabbed a rung on one of the doors. He looked to everyone before he dared to open one of the double doors. Taegrid had two arrows notched in his bow and nodded. Gilthanus put his ring on and waited for a moment as he prepared a fresh torch for something to happen, but nothing ever did. Now was not the time to try to figure out what his ring might do if anything.

"I am ready," Gilthanus claimed as he raised his torch out at eye level. Sametria had her old scimitar sheathed and her new one in had swinging it intently. Each swing produced a whisper of a single name, "Tevlos." Somehow, her deity was calling out to her around every bend. She only wished she knew what exactly he wanted her to do. Taegrid stepped closer as everyone heard the whispered name and looked at the sword as intently as Sametria.

"I am surely ready," Sametria finally answered as she stopped swinging the scimitar. It was crafted of adamantine, the hardest of all known elements on Athyx. Aleiz simply nodded at Morglum when his eyes fell upon the vermin-kissed. Morglum held Mar Doldon the dwarven crafted mithral great axe in one hand as he yanked the heavy door open. Gilthanus stepped forward with the torch he held to light their way beyond the doors. A large tunnel led into darkness covered with webs. Gilthanus and Morglum entered first with Taegrid and Sametria moving in second and then taking the lead. Aleiz and Sadie followed in the rear. The kobolds slammed and barred the doors behind them barking and laughing mockery in their language. Morglum looked to Gilthanus.

"What are they saying now?" Morglum asked. He saw the facial expressions change as though Gilthanus already answered his question.

"They are laughing that our greed has blinded us so easily. They are saying they tricked us to our dooms." Gilthanus managed to translate what little he could accurately hear. Morglum slammed his body into the heavy door and found out very fast why it has kept the vermin-kissed horrors out for so long. His shoulder did not even budge the door now that it was barred again.

"One day we might come back. If ever you see us again, I will slaughter the whole lot of you." Morglum roared. Morglum's outburst was very loud and they all heard something.

"Shush," Sametria warned, as the sounds got louder and louder.

"I'm so angry," Taegrid growled.

"We were set up," Sametria claimed. "But we made a deal and they kept their end of it. Now we will keep our end. But so help me from this day forward, no kobold I meet will be safe." The tunnel was large enough for a hill giant to walk through with a second hill giant at its side. Whatever was coming cold be very big or there could be a great number. Either way, the companions faced an issue. They had only one way to go and that was forward and possibly to their deaths. Sadie growled, as she smelt whatever was coming.

"Stay girl," Sametria commanded knowing the wolf wanted to charge out and attack to defend her friend. Five massive spiders came into view of the dim light cast by the torch. They were as wide as hill giants were. Two scurried along the floor, with two more along the ceiling and one on the wall to their left. Aleiz ducked into the shadows after seeing the size of the incoming spiders. Taegrid fired his bow and Gilthanus let loose with his spells while Morglum and Sametria charged straight in at them. Sadie followed her companion growling all the way. Taegrid and Gilthanus focused on the two spiders crawling on the ceiling towards them. Morglum and Sametria charged in at the same giant spider with fangs bigger than their weapons. Sametria cut of the fangs as they came down to sink into her frail body and Morglum hacked Mar Doldon deep into its head, killing it instantly. Aleiz leaped out of the shadows at the spider that stood next to the one Morglum and Sametria had just killed and sunk his kukri deep into its bulbous body. Sadie latched her teeth onto one of the spear-like legs of the spider Aleiz was dangling from. It seemed to fall over to one side twitching its legs in panic. The spiders on the ceiling spun webs down at Taegrid and Gilthanus, entangling them fast to the floor.

"These ones are a lot more accurate," Taegrid moaned as he tried to break free of the webbing.

"No they just cover more area with their spinners," Gilthanus corrected as he tried to cast a spell while entangled that might help them. The spider came down from the wall and tried to sink its fangs into Sametria. They were like spears dripping with venom as they came down at the half-elf. Sametria rolled out of the way, as the fangs struck the floor where she had been standing.

The webbing was too strong for Taegrid to break free. He growled in protest. Gilthanus concentrated as he tried to aim his spell to hit the webbing. A fan of flames emerged from his hands and seared the webs from his body. Gilthanus sat up and carefully aimed his spell towards Taegrid. The webs melted away from the cat man, singing his fur just a little.

"Are you alright?" Gilthanus asked his friend when he saw smoke rising from Taegrid's fur. Taegrid nodded.

"Thanks," Taegrid said as he rose up and fired more arrows at one of the spiders. Morglum and Sametria struggled to avoid the giant spider legs that constantly came down at them like spears as it moved to look for its prey and sink its fangs into. Aleiz ripped his kukri free and dropped to the floor near Sadie who still ripped away at the spider leg until it finally came loose at one of the joints.

"Whoa!" Aleiz laughed in shock at the wolf. The two spiders came in and dropped down from the ceiling at Gilthanus and Taegrid. Taegrid leaped to the side to keep from being speared by the massive fangs. Gilthanus did the same, but a leg caught his clothing and ripped away a large piece of material exposing his leg.

"Too close, too close." Gilthanus whined as he backed away like a crab on his rear. Taegrid came up from a rolling position and fired his bow at the spider that nearly pounced on him. Gilthanus cast a spell and his hands erupted with fire. The wide fan of flames singed hairs off both spiders. Sametria smacked the fangs aside with her scimitar creating an opening for Morglum to bring Mar Doldon down into its head and killing the giant spider. Sadie ran up to Sametria holding the spider leg in her mouth to show off to her friend proudly as Aleiz made certain the spider was dead by spilling its guts and slitting its abdomen open with his kukri.

"Won't that anger Na-Dene?" Morglum asked with a slight chuckle to his vermin-kissed elf friend.

"We're not finished yet," Sametria pointed to the two remaining spiders that had gone after Taegrid and Gilthanus. Morglum whirled Mar Doldon before storming in at the spider that was trying to eat Gilthanus. He knew Taegrid could take care of himself, but that elf always got himself hurt thinking he could fight like the rest of them. The spiders leaped at their prey hoping to come down and sink their fangs within their flesh. Taegrid rolled out of the way, but one of the spider's legs scratched Gilthanus as it tried to pin its prey. Taegrid put two more arrows in the giant spider as he come to his feet, but the spider still survived.

"Damn," Taegrid cursed as he backpedaled away from the spider. Gilthanus dropped the torch and drew his long sword to defend himself against the spider in melee while he stood to his feet. Morglum came in roaring as he brought Mar Doldon down upon the large spider. The mighty, great axe sunk deep into the spider's body spilling out thick mucus. Aleiz charged in behind Morglum and slid beneath the spider, stabbing his kukri into the spiders under belly as he slid up towards its head and slit it wide open, killing the vermin where it stood and covering himself with the thick spider mucus. Taegrid put a single arrow between the spider's fangs, ending its life.

"That wasn't too bad," Taegrid said as he rounded his foe and came into view of his companions. He saw Gilthanus clutching his wounded leg and Aleiz crawl out from beneath the dead spider covered in thick white goop. Sametria came walking up with Sadie at her side, still carrying the spider leg in her mouth and then dropping it at Taegrid's feet as if to show him. Sadie sat down with her tongue out and panting for air with glee.

"She is pretty proud of herself," Sametria laughed as she patted the wolf on her head.

"You have trained her well," Taegrid commended the half-elf as he also patted the wolf.

"Are you alright Gilthanus?" Sametria asked from across the way.

"It's just a flesh wound," Gilthanus responded. Sametria approached her wounded friend. Taegrid and Sadie followed. Sametria wiped her sword clean before sheathing it and kneeling to check the wound.

"Was it a fang?" Sametria asked as she looked at the wound. The poison from the spiders still weakened Gilthanus from the other day, but he was recovering and these spiders never sunk a fang in.

"It was a leg. The venom from the other day still weakens me, but I am regaining my strength. These spiders did not get the best of me as the others did. I learn quickly how to battle my foes." Gilthanus replied.

"When are you going to learn that you are a sorcerer and not skilled enough to wield that sword you carry?" Morglum asked more to protect his friend than to belittle him.

"I am getting better with it," Gilthanus replied knowing what the half-orc meant by his question. Sametria chanted a spell that revitalized her friend and caused the wound to scab over. She stood up and looked the elf in his eyes.

"You are doing very well Gilthanus. Just try to keep up what you are doing and keep yourself out of danger." Sametria said evenly.

"If you mean for me to run when I am under pressure, I would have if not for the barred doors." Gilthanus laughed. Sametria smiled and patted the elf on his shoulder. Aleiz brushed the thick goop from his clothes as much as he could without having to bathe.

"These were not vermin-kissed horrors," Aleiz noted to his friends.

"We are aware of that Aleiz. In fact I think the vermin-kissed horrors herded these spiders in here just to study how we fight so they might better defeat us in battle." Sametria pointed out.

"So you do understand the ways of the vermin-kissed elves," Aleiz said in response to Sametria's knowledge as every one of them heard a whispering coming from the shadows. Gilthanus recognized the whispers for what they were.

"Spell casters," Gilthanus warned his friends as three flashes of light streaked from different vantage points right at them. Three magically summoned bolts of lightning struck Morglum and blasted him against the double doors. He slid to the floor with sparks slowly dissipating from his body as it convulsed for a moment.

"Morglum," Sametria cried.

"Tend to him Sam," Taegrid growled as he led the charge at the three vermin-kissed horrors they had yet to see. Aleiz looked to his motionless half-orc friend before taking to the shadows as his mutated brethren did. Taegrid had two arrows notched and ready for the moment one of the vermin-kissed horrors came into view. Gilthanus was ready with a spell. Aleiz spotted the three vermin-kissed horrors spaced out strategically. Two were on the ceiling and one on the floor. He knew that they spotted him as well. Aleiz thought fast and doused one of the vermin-kissed horrors with a pint of oil he had found in the dwarven storeroom. It was caught off guard and gave Aleiz the opportunity to light it ablaze and reveal it to his friends. The vermin-kissed horror panicked. The sight of the vermin-kissed horror was nightmarish to the heroes. This one resembled one of the large spiders they had just slain, but rather than having a spider head, it had the upper half of a vermin-kissed elf protruding from the spider body. Much like a centaur in the fact that it was half monster and half humanoid, the vermin-kissed horror was frightening to the eyes of the inexperienced hero. Gilthanus and Taegrid saw the illuminated vermin-kissed horror appear and without hesitation unleashed their assault. Two arrows and two magical projectiles struck the vermin-kissed horror and knocked it from the wall. It slammed to the floor with tremendous force blasting the air from its lungs. The two arrows struck its heart, but the creature was strong and fought against the dying process. Sametria knelt beside Morglum and laid him on his back flat. She listened to his chest and heard nothing.

"Breathe Morglum," Sametria commanded as she beat a fist down on his chest. Two more lightning bolts struck near Taegrid. It was not enough that he dove out of the way. The electricity in the bolts was so intense that he felt their power indirectly as he dove out of the way. His fur was singed and his muscles twitched slightly. The vermin-kissed horrors had moved after their fellow vermin-kissed horror was blasted from the wall and it was to the advantage of Aleiz.

Aleiz had one more pint of oil and because the vermin-kissed horrors stood close enough the pint erupted over both of them. He lit the oil and rolled clear before the cursed vermin-kissed elves could get to him. These two had the lower bodies of giant rats. It was common that when cursed, the vermin bond was the chosen vermin curse as well. Taegrid rolled to his feet still smoldering and sent two arrows at one of the vermin-kissed horrors that Aleiz had outlined with burning flames. It was struck in the chest and fell to the floor near its comrade. Gilthanus sent two of his magical projectiles streaking at the first vermin-kissed horror they had wounded as it stood to its feet. The two wounded vermin-kissed horrors drew out their short bows and fired them at the vermin-kissed elf that had lit them up with painful flames. Aleiz ducked low allowing the arrows to pass harmlessly over him and avoiding a magically summoned bolt of lightning sent down from the vermin-kissed horror that remained on the ceiling. Aleiz felt the shock wave indirectly from the powerful bolt, but he was all right. Taegrid saw that the vermin-kissed horrors had targeted Aleiz and took a dead aim at one of the wounded vermin-kissed horrors. Taegrid's two arrows flew with deadly accuracy and struck home, one in each eye socket and piercing the brain killing it instantly. Gilthanus cast another spell sending two magical projectiles impacting the wounded vermin-kissed horror that remained. Aleiz leaped out with his kukri and stabbed it into the vermin-kissed horrors already wounded chest, finding its heart and ending its cursed life. Aleiz ducked beneath the dead body out of sight of the last remaining vermin-kissed horror. The vermin-kissed horror chanted a spell and disappeared from sight, but an outline of smoke remained.

"Damn you," the vermin-kissed horror cursed Aleiz as two arrows passed by the vermin-kissed horror, dangerously close. An orb of acid splashed against the wall just inches away from the monstrous vermin-kissed horror. It drew out twin daggers and hoping to find the vermin-kissed elf that had highlighted it for the others to see and kill him. Aleiz panicked when the dead vermin-kissed horror body was tossed aside, revealing his hiding place. The invisible, smoke outlined vermin-kissed horror again became visible to the eye as it tossed the dead vermin-kissed horror aside. Arrows whipped passed the vermin-kissed horror, as did a misfired orb of acid sent by the elf sorcerer. Sametria charged in with her new scimitar and tried to catch the vermin-kissed horror from behind, but it hopped out of the way and laughed insidiously. Aleiz tried to come around behind the vermin-kissed horror that now faced in the direction of Sametria and his friends, but it must have sensed him coming. The vermin-kissed horror leaped out of the way as Aleiz came in swinging his kukri at its hindquarter. The vermin-kissed horror spun around and stabbed both of its daggers straight in at the chest of Aleiz. His body was suddenly enveloped by his shadow cloak and he disappeared with puff of darkness before reappearing a short distance away from the vermin-kissed horror. As shocked and amazed as the vermin-kissed horror was, Aleiz leaped back in at the vermin-kissed horror in full force. Arrow after arrow missed the vermin-kissed horror coming dangerously close to Sametria and Aleiz as well as the vermin-kissed horror. Gilthanus turned around to see the body of Morglum out of his armor and lying there motionless. The elf forgot the dangers of the vermin-kissed horror and ran over to his friend's side.

Sadie nipped at the vermin-kissed horror beside Sametria and latched onto one of its four rat-like legs. Sadie ripped the leg away from the joint causing the vermin-kissed horror to shriek an otherworldly scream. Sametria stabbed her new scimitar deep into the rat-like body, spilling out its tainted blood. Aleiz climbed up its backside and took the vermin-kissed elf head clean from its shoulders with his curved kukri blade. The third and to their knowledge, the last vermin-kissed horror in the tunnels fell dead.

"Is Morglum alright?" Aleiz asked the half-elf as she pulled her scimitar free of the vermin-kissed horror's body. She looked up to meet the vermin-kissed elf's gaze. His emotions showed through. He truly cared for the half-orc. Sadie pranced away with the spider leg, dragging it back to Morglum's motionless body and laying it at his feet before lying down as well and whimpering as she stared at him. Gilthanus sat beside the half-orc and looked to his friends. Aleiz saw the elf staring at him and he smiled with tears in his eyes.

"He will live to cut more monsters down. He just needs time to heal." Sametria finally answered. "I will scout ahead with Aleiz and make sure we are in the clear for the moment. In the meantime, stay put with Morglum. You stay Sadie." Aleiz and Sametria took to the tunnel after Sametria cast a light spell upon her new scimitar. She liked the scimitar a great deal. Every swing it spoke the name of her god and reminded her that he still had power, even in his absence. The two of them followed the great tunnel for at least a mile watching the shadows and webs for anything living or moving within them. Nothing was seen and nothing dropped down upon them. The tunnel finally came to an end where it opened up to a great chasm and a stone bridge about ten feet wide spanned a great distance to the other side where another tunnel opened into darkness. Webs were spun below and above the bridge. Some even were attached to the bridge.

"What do you think Aleiz?" Sametria asked the vermin-kissed elf. Aleiz inspected tem carefully. Webs were very similar and it was difficult for him to tell if they were spider webs or vermin-kissed horror webs. He shook his head in defeat.

"They could be either. I'm sorry I can't tell." Aleiz offered an apology.

"It's alright my friend. When we come to this road, we must just be ready for anything." Sametria waved for the vermin-kissed elf to follow her cautiously and the two of them turned back the way they came to return to their friends.

*****

The wraith known as Calvin the Mad commanded the first regiment of skeletons be sent into the orc caves. They would be taken by surprise and easily overrun if not by the skeletons, then by the wraiths that followed with the second, third and fourth regiments of skeletons. The orcs had sounded their alarms and the siege had begun. The lead wraith Calvin the Mad remained outside for the time being and waited.

"Should we send the second regiments yet?" one of the other wraiths asked their leader. Calvin the Mad hissed as he looked at the wraith who dared question his ability in front of his minions.

"I could send you to Oblivion right now for your foolishness," Calvin the Mad threatened and the wraith cowered.

"I beg forgiveness my lord. I only meant to help." The wraith pleaded in fright. Calvin the Mad was a savage wraith as his master and they were among the most feared of all wraiths in the world because of the power they commanded. Calvin the Mad glared at the wraith and seemed to ready a backhand to strike the cowering wraith.

"My Lord," another wraith called out interrupting the confrontation. "Dax has not returned." That was correct, Calvin the Mad remembered. He suddenly remembered sending the small group of skeletons led by Dax after the small group they had seen above them in the pass. Dax should have returned by now. Something must have happened to him. A thought came over Calvin the Mad as he continued to glare at the disrespectful wraith.

"You will prove your loyalty to me and find out what is keeping Dax from returning." Calvin the Mad ordered.

"Yes my lord with all haste," the wraith replied and flew off out of sight passing through the mountains to cover ground faster.

"Send the second wave," Calvin the Mad ordered quietly and the five wraiths that were a part of that group sent in the next wave of skeletons with themselves strategically placed within groupings of the mindless soldiers. Calvin the Mad waited for several moments before he sent in third and then the fourth and final wave that he was a part of.

There were massive piles of skeletons throughout the cave tunnels as they moved through. Every now and again, there was a dead orc or two. It was not until they came to the main cavern that more orcs lay dead. Some were clawed or cut to death by the skeletons, but as they had planned, most were slain by the wraiths. Orcs braved against the skeletons with their chief and captain leading them in battle. Both of which were fighting against wraiths and skeletons alike. They were nearly beaten when Calvin the Mad reached the great cavern with his final regiment. He was insidious and devastating with his planning. He knew that the orcs would not be smart enough to stand against them in battle. The scout that had been told of the orcs by a master vampire was to be commended Calvin the Mad thought. He then saw that very wraith cut down by the mighty orc Captain Foogart and Chief Gaji sent another to Oblivion. Calvin the Mad was suddenly curious to what was going on.

"The last of them are here," an orc shouted from behind Calvin the Mad's regiment. The orcs had placed scouts strategically outside and throughout the caves to lay in wait and notify their leaders if they were attacked when the last of them had entered.

"Now!" shouted Foogart and boulders rolled exposing hidden caves where their main forces were hidden and now swarmed at the undead forces. Calvin the Mad hissed. His victory had just been stolen from him and he was very angry. He had underestimated the orcs. Never had he known orcs to be tactical about war. They were more likely to attack in full force at the very beginning, but never had he seen a surprise attack like this. He heard the scream of a wraith as it was sent to Oblivion and the cowardly wraith retreated and left his minions to their dooms. He flew through solid rock walls of the mountain to escape his utter destruction. His master would not be happy with him. Perhaps Oblivion awaited him after all. Calvin the Mad knew he could not return to his master after his failure. He was on his own now at least until he redeemed himself.

Chapter Five:

A barbarian of the Frozen Wastes followed an army of undead that his tribe had run away from. The human tribe wanted to battle, but when they saw the wraiths among the skeletons, they knew better. There was no one among them that had ever defeated a wraith. They had clubs and spears to defend themselves against anything made of flesh. If it was ghostly, then they retreated. It was how they survived for so long after the cataclysm within the Frozen Wastes. This barbarian wanted to change those cowardly ways. He also hated the frozen tundra and wanted to venture out to the sea in a ship to sail the uncharted waters he had only heard tales of. The young barbarian was a savage among his people. His muscles bulged and his beard and hair were long and red braided together as one. He climbed mountains not knowing how to navigate them properly and found the lower pass to the south. He was no tracker, but it was obvious that the skeletons had gone this way. They still had tracks in the snow where the wind could not cover them up very fast with fresh fallen snow. The barbarian wore a suit of chainmail that his uncle had forged for him and carried a short spear as the hunters of his tribe did. He was not a skilled hunter or tracker, but he managed when he went out with the hunting parties. He was Thortwerg, proud and true to his people for his whole life. He felt it was time to think of his self for a change. He wore a thick coat under his armor and gloves to keep him warm. A thick cap covered his head and ears, protecting them from the stinging winds and snow. His thick boots and clothing were made from winter wolf fur. It protected from the cold quite well. Now that he was in the lower pass, the wind did not sting as bad. Thortwerg followed the undead army trail, but he did not run or try to catch them. He stalked them as a hunter stalked his prey. Like the hungry yeti stalked him from the north and now followed him into the pass. Its fur made it blend into the snow background so well, that it may as well have been invisible. Thortwerg stopped dead in his tracks when he thought that he heard something behind him. He turned around slowly and scanned the pass to the north from where he had just come from. There was nothing but white snow and mountainside to b e seen. He heard it again almost right in front of him, but he still did not see anything.

"Yeti," Thortwerg growled as he raised his spear to defend himself from harm. He knew of the yeti. They were savage monsters of the north that could not be seen until they were right upon you without a well-trained eye. A heavy arm smacked him from the side, wrapped him against a muscular chest, and squeezed. Thortwerg rammed his spearhead into the furry chest of the yeti as it squeezed him. He felt his back crack and the air leave his lungs as darkness took him. The yeti had taken him by surprise and Thortwerg realized he would die before he could ever make his dreams come true and see the great oceans of the world.

*****

Calvin the Mad, the wraith had rejoined his only remaining wraith minion and together they roamed the dark tunnels of the mountain that his minion had found during its search for the missing wraith scout named Dax. They assumed the worse after seeing the piles of skeleton bones back along the upper trail of the mountain pass. They had seen a large group of kobolds with giant spider nests that they seemed to be raising as mounts as they passed through within the shadows. The wraiths were invisible to the untrained eye within the shadows or darkness. Calvin the Mad made a mental note of the kobolds dwelling within the mountain so that when he amassed another army of his own, he could return and slaughter the whole lot of them. He felt a sudden wave of freedom come over him and he knew that his master had witnessed or at least discovered his failure. He had been released from his master's control and though to most, freedom sounds very good, but to a wraith, it meant that either his master had been slain or his master was going to have him slain.

"I haven't much time," Calvin the Mad, hissed to his only minion. "My master has freed me and I know he means to destroy me for my failure. This is our time now to prove to Viscus that we are worthy before my former master comes for us both." The minion nodded in agreement to its master. An idea donned on him. The kobolds were his for the taking. They would be his new minions.

"Drain them all," Calvin the Mad ordered to his minion and the two wraiths swooped in at the kobolds, draining most of them while they slept. They would rise as wraiths under their control and they would be set loose upon the orcs.

*****

Chief Gaji and his son the captain of the orcs, Foogart stood dominant over the undead army. They were hurt and weakened from their battle with the wraiths, but nothing they could not recover from in time. Foogart had been wise in his suggestions of placing hidden scouts and hiding their main forces. Chief Gaji was very proud of his son. He remembered the other suggestions his son had made and now was going to make them his own.

"My orcs," Chief Gaji barked gathering their attention to him. "We have been wronged by our former enslaver the master vampire elf. We are waiting for our scouts to return that I sent to track him down and discover his new lair. The second group we had sent never returned, but other scouts we have placed on the mountain saw their loss outside and we knew of the approaching army because of my leadership, because I was so smarts. We will have our revenge on the master vampire soon enough." The chief ended his speech and though Foogart did not care that he stole all credit, Foogart's closest lieutenants did. They had suddenly lost all respect for their chief and shouts began with them.

"Chief Foogart," the orc lieutenants shouted over and over until others joined the shouting and soon many orcs shouted it, too many for Chief Gaji to make an example out of. Chief Gaji could do nothing but challenge Foogart in battle, but he knew Foogart would surely defeat him. An idea came to his feeble mind. He grabbed Foogart and pulled him close.

"You are loyal to me to death?" Chief Gaji whispered to his son in question. Foogart looked his father in the eyes curiously. He did not want to rob his father of his honor. He just wanted his father's approval.

"What is your plan?" Foogart whispered back.

"You lead our tribe, but I still command you." Chief Gaji responded in secret and Foogart understood. He nodded in agreement. Chief Gaji sighed in defeat.

"I am old, but not weak. I am your chief until I am bested or I say otherwise." Chief Gaji roared and then paused for a moment. "This is my son, my Captain and your new chief. I renounce my title as chief and bestow it to him for it was he that truly made the difference using tactics that we have never before used as orcs. He has earned the title of chief. All hail Chief Foogart." Gaji roared the final praise and the entire colony of orcs soon chanted it repeatedly as Gaji passed him the Pride of the Bloody-Knucks Chief. He was reluctant, but did not want his son to lose respect for him or else he might have to fight him and truly lose his title. Foogart took the symbol of his tribe that marked him as the new chief and held it up high. The orcs cheered in response. Gaji lowered his head in shame and moved to leave his son's side but Foogart grabbed his father by the shoulder and held him still.

"Father, you deserve this more than I, so earn back your respect from the tribe. Go after Morglum and return with his head on a pig pole." Foogart suggested. Gaji listened to his son because he proved to be by far smarter than any orc of their tribe. He hoped Foogart was right and he could reclaim his title as chief. If not he would have to try to take it by defeating his son and that would be no easy task.

"I will do this," Gaji claimed.

"Gaji has vowed to serve me and regain your respect by hunting down my half brother the half breed and returning with his head." Chief Foogart announced to the tribe and they cheered.

"Kill the half-breed traitor," one orc shouted as he remembered the orcs that Morglum had killed along with the vampires. Foogart knew that if not for his half brother's actions, the vampires might still enslave their tribe, but he was far too intelligent to remind his tribe of this. That fact was what gave him and his father control of their tribe. They were free of their vampire enslaver and free to war against whomever they chose.

"I Gaji will take my army,' Gaji began to say and quickly altered his phrasing. "Chief Foogart's army granted to me to command and hunt down the vermin-kissed elf and Morglum. I will earn back my glorious honor and bring you his head." Gaji roared with great anger.

Gaji marched that night with his army out of the orc caves and minus his captain. The orc was angry but in the same instance, he was proud at how his son had usurped him and stolen his title as chief of their tribe. He would return and reclaim what was rightfully his and he would put down his son for his treacherous plotting against him. He thought the way his son had stolen his title was cowardly and not like an orc at all. Orcs battled one another to see who was stronger and better in combat to prove their worth. His son had only done that for the title of captain. He had not truly earned the title of chief as far as Gaji was concerned. He remembered what he had learned from watching his son and sent scouts ahead to pick up Morglum's trail as they marched towards the north pass of the mountains. The north was home to some of the most revered undead of the entire world. The most deadly of Viscus' servants dwelled within the frozen wastes and only a select group of the living took refuge among their enemies to hide in plain sight. Most were assassin guilds that did well at hiding themselves from magical scrying. It was rumored that the wraiths planned a great assault on all those that lived within the subterranean realms of Athyx once they believed they had extinguished all life on the surface world.

Foogart's dragon had watched Gaji leave with his army into the mountain pass of the north. It was loyal to Foogart and obeyed him respectfully like a loyal knight to a king. Faerxerous was a green dragon and young for its kind. It was as long as a man was tall, not factoring in the length of its tail. It circled high enough over Gaji that he would likely not notice it, but low enough to still see the orc army. He was Foogart's eyes from the sky. Though Foogart did not send him to spy on his father, Faerxerous felt it was a good idea to at least make sure he headed in the right direction. The green-scaled dragon saw the orc scout party running far ahead of the army to pick up Morglum's trail. So far, it seemed they could not find any sign. He had to of gone that way because it was the only trail to the north for many days. The pass had a high trail and a low trail. The low trail showed signs of the skeleton army marching from the north, and that meant that Morglum had to have taken the high trail or else he would have been slain. His trail would have gone cold for the trackers, due to the hard rocky surface and length of time he had been gone. The orc scouts would not return to the army until they had picked up the trail though. They pushed themselves like a warhorse and kept running the trail until they found something. The orc scouts were swift afoot and ran into a sight of shattered skeletons along the trail.

"Morglum was here," one orc scout barked with fire in his eyes.

"He has picked up a few more allies," a second orc noticed as he saw signs of multiple battles in the small area.

"No matter, Gaji comes in full force." The first orc scout retorted. They continued ahead until the trail ended and they saw a broken great axe haft bearing the Bloody-Knucks symbol near a small hole in the mountainside that looked as though the great axe had been used to make the hole that exposed a hidden tunnel beyond. The orcs would have a hard time squeezing through in their armor. The scouts knew they would need mauls or war hammers to widen the entrance so that they could follow. The scouts turned back to return to Gaji. The green-scaled dragon saw the scouts turning back after discovering the hole and returned to Foogart to report Gaji's progress.

Gaji stood by and watched as two of his strongest orcs took turns slamming mauls against the mountainside, widening the entrance for the orc army to pass through. Gaji knew he would catch up to Morglum soon enough and when he did, no head start or number of allies would protect him from his army and wrath.

"Quickly orcs, Morglum's head awaits my axe." Gaji barked. The two orcs worked as fast as they could to widen the entrance, but it still took them several hours of bashing until the doorway was finished enough for them to pass through without ducking or turning sideways.

"We will set up camp inside," Gaji announced as the army began to enter the dark tunnels. There was an eerie and cold draft about the tunnels as the orcs entered. It was as if whatever orc clan had once dwelled here still haunted the place. The orcs were unsettled about their situation, but they coped and had quickly found a large enough chamber for his army to set up camp. There were thousands of dead kobolds littered through the chamber and they were cold to the touch.

"Morglum surely slaughtered the whole lot of them," one orc barked. Gaji knelt down low to examine the dead kobolds. There was just too many and not a single wound covered their bodies that would have killed them. Poisoned perhaps, Gaji thought to himself, as he looked about the area very unsettled about the sight. He suddenly realized the truth.

"Wraiths!" Gaji shouted in warning to his army. The orcs looked around in panic and saw nothing.

"We do not have wraith killer weapons Gaji," one of his lieutenants whispered to the former orc chief. Gaji grimaced. He missed the Pride of the Bloody-Knucks Chief right about now.

"Back them all out of here, now." Gaji whispered. Wraiths suddenly began to rise up from the many corpses that surrounded the orcs and shouts of protest erupted along with curses and war cries' as the orcs were ambushed by the kobold wraiths led by Calvin the Mad. Gaji pushed through his own army in an attempt to escape. Calvin the Mad spotted the former orc chief and swooped in at him like an arrow that had been fired from a savage longbow and passed right through the massive orc, stealing some of his life force. Gaji growled in protest.

"You foul thing," Gaji roared as he looked all around him for some way to escape, but all that he saw was his army being robbed of their life force.

"It is time to join Viscus," Calvin the Mad hissed as he swooped in at Gaji again.

"Bolnarg!" Gaji cried out in proudly as the wraith sole the last of his life force and left his drained and empty carcass to rot among the kobolds.

"It looks as though we have redeemed ourselves a bit," Calvin the Mad hissed as his trusted wraith minion came to join his master.

"Two armies for the price of one," the minion laughed and Calvin the Mad joined the laughter with his own insidious hiss of a laugh. The wraiths had ended thousands of lives that night and in an instant, it seemed they were the most dominant race in the world. Not even the vampires would stop a force such as the one under the control of Calvin the Mad. Viscus would be pleased with them and place them in high ranks among their fellow wraiths. Perhaps they would be in charge of the powerful Soul Hunter Wraiths. They did not know. They only knew that they had regained their pride to say the least. Wraiths did not tire, did not need to eat, drink or sleep. They were the perfect death squad and they would continue their slaughter by attacking the orc caves next and with their own orcs now raised as wraiths it would make the slaughter even more pleasing to Calvin the Mad.

*****

Sametria tended to her friends wounds, mending them, as she needed through the night. She cast a healing spell the next morning upon Morglum to close some more of his wounds and make him able enough to walk without aid. Morglum and Taegrid still suffered ill effects from their wounds and would heal in time if given the chance, but for now, they needed to push on before the kobolds decided to come after them while they were hurt.

"We found what might be a nest ahead, so be quiet as you can when we get to the bridge and as we cross." Sametria instructed her friends. Aleiz scouted ahead while Sametria and Taegrid led the group. Morglum stood by Sadie in the rear with Gilthanus between them as usual. Aleiz had not returned to them having gone ahead of them across the bridge as Sametria had asked him to when they left camp. The vermin-kissed elf was quiet with his movements and able to move through areas unnoticed if he had to. He was not sure about the great chasm he had just crossed, but the tunnel ahead of him seemed a little peculiar. It was not web covered at all and the walls were all natural, with no sign of any dwarven smiths ever touching them. He pressed ahead quietly for at least a half mile before one tunnel arched upward and a second branched and sloped downward. A howling wind could be heard coming from the tunnel leading up and the cold breeze told him that they were higher in elevation than they thought. The tunnel leading down possibly led into the underworld where subterranean beings such as his people dwelled. He thought of leaving his friends and returning home at that very moment. He could not though. He remembered all of the spiders he had slain. Only the vermin-kissed elves that now worshipped Viscus would accept him and he denied Viscus despising the god of Oblivion more so than he despised Na-Dene. He was truly exiled now and could never show his face for fear of a priestess chanting one of her spells that identified him as a spider killer. Aleiz turned and went back to his friends to let them know what he had found and aid them in the chasm if needed.

The chasm was crossed and the mountain was behind them. They had found a way through the mountains from the path the tunnel led them to. The cold wind howled down on them stinging their skin the farther north they went. The air was thin at their current elevation and made them dizzy at times. It took them three days before the trail led them to another cave opening and out of the blistering cold weather. They did not travel far within the cave before setting up their first campsite in three days that would keep them warm enough so they could actually get restful sleep. Only Sametria had a warm winter blanket and Aleiz and Morglum did not even have a normal bedroll to sleep on.

"We need food and furs to make winter coats and gloves," Sametria informed her friends who were well aware of their situation.

"Let me use your winter blanket to shelter me from the winds. I will track down something out there." Taegrid offered.

"You can use my blanket and I will cast a spell to protect me from the harmful cold and we will both go outside. The rest of you stay here until we return and stay warm." Sametria ordered and no one argued given the fact that they could not feel their limbs. Gilthanus and Aleiz began building a fire out of dried twigs just outside the cave and roots that grew inside. It made a lot of smoke, but it burned and helped to warm them. Sametria and Taegrid wandered outside in the cold hoping to pick up the trail of some large game animal of the cold mountains. They found no such thing, but rather they found a set of massive footprints the size of an ogre. The prints showed that it could not be an ogre because they did not wear boots in the snow and the toes were elongated like that of a large ape, almost like a pair of hands as feet.

"What's this?" Taegrid asked not having the vast knowledge of a druid.

"Yeti," Sametria answered as she began looking about. "It could be right upon us and we would not know it in these conditions." Taegrid began looking around as well, hoping that the yeti that made the prints was long gone and nowhere around them.

"We should probably give this idea up and go back to the others before we are ambushed by a whole tribe of yeti," Taegrid suggested when he realized that he could see no sign of any yeti and that fact bothered him most because the prints were fresh. Snow was falling and would have easily covered the tracks within minutes. He just did not want to tell Sametria that fact. Sametria was braver than most and would possibly want to hunt the yeti if she knew how close they were to it.

"It's that close then?" Sametria asked realizing what Taegrid was trying to hide. "I'm not a tracker like you my friend, but I understand the concepts and logic of the matter."

"Sorry," Taegrid said apologizing for his arrogance. "It is very close Sam." He warned. A roar erupted from ahead of them and they turned to see a white ball of fur leaping from out of the snow at them. The creature swung its long arms with sharp claws down as it landed at Sametria, forcing her to duck beneath them and roll in closer so that she could hit it with her scimitar. Taegrid tried to fire his bow but was forced back farther as he quickly realized exactly how long the creature's arms really were. Sametria was dangerously close to the yeti. Its arms were long enough to wrap around her and entangle her as well as crush her where she stood. Sametria tried coming in with a thrust of her curved blade, but the yeti smacked the sword aside before bashing her into the snow, picking her up and squeezing her against its body like a constrictor snake. Sametria felt her ribs crack and a lung puncture, making it difficult to breathe. The yeti even produced a cold aura that would have frozen her had she not been protected by her spell.

"Hang on Sam," Taegrid growled as he carefully aimed his bow at the yeti and let two arrows loose. Both arrows struck the yeti in the chest and knocked it to the snow covered ground. Sametria rolled free of its arms and swung her scimitar behind her in case the yeti gave chase. The yeti crawled to its feet moaning and growling in protest. It knew it was already dead from the arrows Taegrid had just put in its chest. Thick red blood covered its snow-white fur marking it so that it could not hide in the snow again. The yeti rushed Taegrid suddenly but Taegrid stepped out of its reach and fired two more arrows, but they missed this time and hit the snow wall next to the yeti. It was bleeding to death but wanted to take them with it if it could. Sametria had a dart in hand and hurled it square in its forehead. The yeti fell to the ground again. This time it had fallen unconscious from its wounds. Taegrid moved in to finish the dying creature off with his bow putting a single arrow right between its closed eyes.

"It's got to weigh at least four-hundred pounds," Sametria groaned.

"I'll drag it back to camp. You just watch my back." Taegrid said as he hung his bow over his shoulder with the other bow he had found and took hold of the yeti's arms. Sametria knew that she had been hurt badly. Every time she breathed, she felt a rib poke her from the inside painfully. She would have to take it easy for at least a few weeks if she was to heal properly. They returned to their camp and Sametria immediately tended to her wounds before passing out from the pain near the fire. The companions were battered pretty badly and needed a good time to rest. Taegrid knew as he skinned the yeti that they would not be traveling any further for some time. The fur would take some time to dry and make coats out of. That would give them time to rest and recover from their wounds fully. It also gave them all time to ponder thoughts, personal as well as their shared current situation. Taegrid was the last of his people from his home. He did not know if any other cat-folk roamed the world. As far as he knew, he was the last of his kind. He wanted revenge for that as well as the loss of his father. The perfect revenge would be the restoration of the sun to its former golden glory. That would surely force the undead back into the darkness with the rest of the evil denizens that dwelled within the subterranean realm of Athyx. How could they achieve that vengeance though? Gilthanus was limited on his spells and ability to wield the magic he possessed. He had a long way to go before he would be recognized as anything other than a sorcerer apprentice. Sametria was so utterly focused upon pleasing her father and becoming a great druid as well as avenging her people, that she did not realize she should also be training with her scimitar to become a better swordsman. Morglum seemed like a good choice for teaching them all better skill with the sword. He was savage in battle and no one among them could match his skill in melee. Taegrid was good, but his primary focus was his bow and that made him a menace to those who were well out of reach. Taegrid was not afraid of melee. He just preferred the bow to the sword.

    Gilthanus looked outside the cave they used as their shelter and felt the sting of the freezing winds on his face. He knew his father would be angry with him, but he also knew he had something more to become than just a simple wizard. He did not need to study magic books every night like his father had. He remembered his spells and how to cast them. He only needed scrolls or books to learn new spells he had not yet memorized. Staring out into the white wind-swept snow, Gilthanus saw what resembled a female wearing a nearly translucent silk own and covered from head to toe in fine jewelry approaching. His first instinct told him to run and warn his friends but he heard the sweetest and most comforting voice call out to him within his own mind. He knew that voice. There was something about it that seemed familiar. You stray far boy. The voice claimed. Gilthanus was not sure what that meant. He just watched as the woman approached closer and then suddenly she vanished for an instant, but only for an instant and reappeared right in front of Gilthanus, startling him.

"What?" Gilthanus gasped. "Are you a sorceress?" Gilthanus managed to ask.

"I am exactly that," the woman responded. Her long black hair flowed out over her shoulders streaming down her back and over her revealing silk gown.

"If it is refuge from the cold you seek, we have a fire inside." Gilthanus offered. The sorceress laughed.

"You think to become rich? Riches as you now see them are insignificant unless you gain stature and power." The sorceress balked catching Gilthanus off guard.

"Who are you?" Gilthanus asked feeling very nervous and confused.

"I am the one here to put you back on your path," the sorceress began and Gilthanus cast a wicked glare at her.

"You would be wise to hold your tongue witch," Gilthanus growled. Again the sorceress laughed. Gilthanus cast a spell and sent a fan of flames at her. The spell dissipated on contact.

"You are very important," the sorceress began, as Gilthanus looked even more confused than before. "You can serve a purpose greater than your own and gain high stature in this world and Hell. With high stature comes great power and wealth beyond your greatest imaginings." The sorceress claimed.

"Hell? Why would I want high stature there?" Gilthanus asked with complete distrust and confusion. The sorceress paced to his left and cast him a seductive look.

"You have grown and become very handsome," she purred as she examined the elf while circling him. Gilthanus never took his eyes off the witch.

"What do you want?" Gilthanus asked.

"I want this world?" the witch answered matter-of-factly as she came to a halt after completing a full circle of Gilthanus.

"The world seems to belong to Viscus at the moment," Gilthanus responded.

"But you and your friends plan to change that don't you?" the witch asked as though she already knew.

"You have been spying on us," Gilthanus accused.

"I admit I have. Would you not watch over your son?" the witch asked suddenly and Gilthanus felt the weight of a thousand bricks upon his shoulders.

"Mother?" Gilthanus gasped I question.

"Yes Gilthanus," Villisca answered. "I am Villisca, the daughter to Armco a powerful duke of Hell. I am here to put you on the path to power if you so choose." Gilthanus was not sure if he should believe the woman so easily, but it all sounded good and there was something very familiar about her. It made sense. He saw no harm in at least finding out what she had to offer him.

"How can you help?" Gilthanus asked. The woman chuckled.

"Now you sound like my son. I can offer you access to spells that would aid you greatly. I can offer you magical weaponry to help you fight the wraith forces." Villisca answered. Gilthanus looked at her curiously.

"What more can you offer me?" Gilthanus asked and again Villisca chuckled, but this time she ended it with a sudden evil glare.

"I can offer you your continuing life and the resources to become the greatest sorcerer of your time." Villisca growled. Gilthanus felt a wave of fear fall over him.

"I will do as you ask mother," Gilthanus said with devotion and Villisca again smiled. "The wraith army grows with great numbers. You must be ready for them by morning." Villisca vanished and where she stood was a small pile of gear. The medallions will protect you from the life sapping energies of the black sun. Villisca's voice spoke in his mind as she left. Gilthanus knelt down to examine the gear closely. He found a book bound with thick, rough red leather entitled The Devil's Own. Gilthanus opened it and found it to be a spell book with what seemed to be limitless spells for him to learn as he flipped through the pages. He would never be able to learn them all, but at least he had a way to study magic again. He had left so abruptly that he had not thought to steal one of his father's books. Gilthanus tucked the book away into his pack and looked at the rest of the gear. Potions of healing labeled Tears of Villisca were among the gear. Several vials of the thick and foul smelling potions were found in a sack that Gilthanus through over his shoulder. Everything there had fiendish markings or artwork on them. He was not sure if that would bother his friends. There were also five medallions, one for each of his friends if they would take the fiendish necklaces forged to resemble the face of a roaring horned devil. Gilthanus placed one around his neck. He placed the other four medallions in the sack with the potions. He knew they would need more than what Villisca, his so-called mother had given them, but it was a start. They needed magical weapons to even have a chance at hitting an incorporeal being such as a wraith. Gilthanus approached Taegrid who was now hanging the yeti fur to dry.

The skinned yeti corpse remained and it stunk but for some reason the smell did not bother him.

"I had a mysterious visitor that offered to help us," Gilthanus whispered.

"Who was it?" Taegrid asked as he finished hanging the fur and began rinsing his hands with water from his water skin.

"That does not matter. What matters is she gave us a supply of healing tonics and medallions that should protect us from life sapping energy like the sun." Gilthanus responded defensively.

"Are you certain the tonic is not poison?" Taegrid scoffed with pessimism. Gilthanus looked at the vials in the sack.

"I am certain. Only an undead wants life to end." Gilthanus claimed.

"Or an ignorant servant of an undead," Taegrid countered.

"She was no minion of the undead," Gilthanus said defensively.

"How do you know this?" Taegrid asked now giving Gilthanus his full attention.

"She was my mother," Gilthanus finally admitted.

"Your mother?" Taegrid asked taken by surprise.

"I know it's a lot to take in, but she is a high ranking fiend and fiends need souls, which means we can trust her to an extent." Gilthanus hid nothing now. Taegrid looked at the elf curiously.

"Fiend's are known to lure mortals into traps so they no longer lay claim to their own souls." Taegrid said in response.

"That is what I mean by to an extent. Just have to be careful of our dealings with her. I have signed nothing or made no fatal deals. She has simply told me of my heritage and offered assistance if we choose to take it or not." Gilthanus explained. Taegrid sighed in defeat.

"Let me have a look at this help she offered us," Taegrid demanded. Gilthanus opened the sack and revealed its contents. Taegrid saw the vials of healing tonics and the medallions. The medallions looked evil and were a symbol of destruction as far as Taegrid was concerned.

"Tell your mother when next you see her, I thank her for her generosity, but I cannot partake." Taegrid said as he pushed the sack away. Gilthanus was shocked.

"Not even if it helps us restore our world?" Gilthanus yelled and suddenly everyone else was awake and interested in the conversation.

"What is going on?" Morglum barked when he saw how badly injured Sametria was. She could not even sit up to be part of the conversation due to the severity of her wounds.

"I've made my choice Gilthanus. Perhaps they will choose differently." Taegrid ended the conversation and went back to cleaning up the yeti mess and disposing of the carcass out in the snow to keep from rotting inside their shelter and stinking up the cave. Gilthanus looked over to the others fearfully. Morglum approached fast. Sametria stared at him from her bedroll and Aleiz sat up from his spot by the fire.

"Okay, I am well aware of what risks are at hand," Gilthanus began as Morglum came to a stop in front of him. "But we want to succeed at our goals right? So why not accept help from those that have just as much to lose if not more than we do even if it means taking a chance?"

"What are you babbling about? Who wants to help us?" Morglum asked trying to catch up on a conversation he had not been a part of.

"His mother, a devil by trade has offered aid to us." Taegrid said simply. Everyone looked at Gilthanus in shock. Taegrid just dragged the carcass out of the cave leaving the elf to explain the rest.

"Help is good right?" Gilthanus said to break the silence that seemed to fall over everyone present.

"We want to save our world from the undead that have overrun it," Sametria grunted.

"I know and we can with her aid. She has gifted us healing tonics that can mend your wounds now. She claims that wraiths will find us by the morning and has also given us medallions I believe will protect us from the negative energy of the sun." Gilthanus whined. Morglum looked in the sack and took a potion and medallion in hand to examine. The medallion was wicked to the eye, but Morglum liked it just because it was different and nothing more. He hung it around his neck as Gilthanus had.

"I will trust you, but I will not trust a fiend!" Morglum barked before turning around and heading back to fire. Gilthanus moved towards Aleiz.

"Will you trust me?" he asked the vermin-kissed elf. Aleiz looked in the sack as well and then eyed the surface elf curiously.

"I will trust you," Aleiz responded as he took a medallion. Morglum drank the entire potion and felt its magic revitalize him as all of his wounds ended completely with no residual pain or side effects.

"It healed me," Morglum informed his friends with excitement. "We need to save those for our most critically wounded." Gilthanus looked at the half-orc and indeed his wounds had fully closed. The elf sorcerer ran over beside their half-elf healer and knelt low.

"You have healed me several times already and I know you will continue to do so. Will you let me help you now?" Gilthanus asked.

"I'll take the potion, but I will not take the medallion." Sametria responded sincerely. Gilthanus nodded in understanding and handed her a vial. He helped her sit up so that she could drink it. It pained her greatly to sit up the slightest, but as she drank the potion, the pain dissipated. She felt her bones mend and her wounds close. Even Sametria was amazed that a devil had helped them.

"I will do what I must to restore Athyx. If I must sacrifice my own soul I the process then that is a small price to pay." Sametria expressed her true feelings of her devotion to her religion. Taegrid returned and saw that only Sametria did not take a medallion but she had taken a potion. He sighed as though he was disappointed in her.

"So we are taking aid from devils now?" Taegrid scoffed.

"Is it not worth your own life to restore our world?" Sametria asked the cat man. The question smacked Taegrid across the face as he realized it was through self-sacrifice and not for personal gain that she had taken the aid. Taegrid looked to the floor of the cave in shame.

"I want to restore our world Sametria. I just want to make sure it doesn't fall into the hands of something worse." Taegrid admitted as he looked back to his half elf friend who obviously understood.

"I won't let that happen, my friend." Sametria claimed.

"I will take a potion," Taegrid finally said.

"I will gladly give one to you my friend," Gilthanus said as he stood up and walked over to the cat man. The elf handed a vial to Taegrid and the cat man drank. His wounds closed as the magic ran through his veins.

"So, what of these wraith forces?" Sametria asked Gilthanus. "Has this fiend offered us means to defeat them?" Gilthanus looked at the ground in defeat. He only had a book that he had yet to study and practice teachings from and what he had in the sack. The sack that was still very heavy for him. He knew that the potions would not restore his strength. How would they defeat or even defend against the wraiths? Your weapons. His mother's voice spoke in his mind once again. Then he realized.

"She enchanted our weapons," Gilthanus claimed with excitement. Sametria drew her new scimitar in hand. It did not appear anything more than it already was.

"Check the other one," Gilthanus suggested with anxiety in his voice. Sametria drew the other scimitar and its blade appeared almost translucent. She sheathed the other scimitar and touched a finger to the strange enchanted blade. It cut her flesh, but it appeared to reach out to the ethereal plane as well.

"This is different," Sametria said as she tried to fathom the power of the devil that had aided them. The unique enchantment was mysterious to the eye. Taegrid grasped his bow. He hoped it was the bow he had the strength to wield that had been enchanted. He took the bow from his shoulder and examined it. The bow shared similar traits to the blade of Sametria's scimitar. Morglum's battle-axe was also imbued with the same type of magic. Aleiz had the same enchantment on his kukri and the long sword of Gilthanus was enchanted as well. The companions smiled at one another with hope.

"We actually stand a chance now," Morglum said with glee. Sametria looked to Sadie.

"Sadie has no weapon," Sametria reminded her companions.

"I will study my book that she gave me and see what knowledge it has to offer me," Gilthanus announced before retiring.

"I would hope that you recover your strength before the wraiths find us," Sametria noted as she watched the elf struggle to carry the sack and backpack to his spot around the fire. Gilthanus studied a few pages of his vile book before turning in to sleep. Taegrid took first watch while his companions rested. He knew that any alliance was helpful. He just also knew that devils and demons were the most notorious for coming to the aid of mortals when they needed it most and striking a deal that would forever condemn their souls or misguide their paths. Taegrid took the potion to heal his body so that he could fight when the wraiths arrived in the morning. He did not want the alliance with the she-devil. Morglum awoke and relieved Taegrid of his watch duties so he too could get some rest. The half-orc stared outside as Gilthanus had before Taegrid and listened to the howl of the freezing wind and felt its bite on his thick-skinned face. It would take a while before the fur was ready to be made into coats and if they had to retreat, they had nowhere to run that would not eventually kill them because of the freezing cold. Morglum knew that Taegrid had dragged the corpse of the sinned yeti outside and buried it in the snow, but there was no sign of it anywhere. He looked to the bloody fur hanging up and suddenly got an idea. Morglum ran over to Taegrid before he could completely fall asleep and roused him. Taegrid opened his eyes to see the muscular half orc staring down at him with a wry smile on his face.

"I have an idea," Morglum whispered. Taegrid sat up.

"What is it?" he asked.

"The fur of a yeti is immune to the cold right?" Morglum had to be sure to make his plan work.

"The yeti is," Taegrid corrected. "It could have something to do with the fur."

"There is no sign of the yeti corpse in the snow where you buried it," Morglum told the cat man who understood what the half-orc was getting at.

"Let's get to work then," Taegrid said as he rolled to his feet and ran outside with Morglum following behind. The two of them dug a trench in the snow and laid out Sametria's winter blanket across the bottom. They made sure it was big enough to hold all of them, but the ceiling would have to be supported to keep from collapsing from the weight of the snow. They took Mar Doldon and the un-wieldable bow of Taegrid's, to support the bloody fur as they draped it over the trench.

"Let's get the others in here so the snow has time to hide us," Taegrid said to Morglum sounding very pleased with their work. The two of them gathered their friends and every possession. Their friends were very tired and did not even have a chance to ask what was going on before being ushered out into the cold weather and guided to a trench. Taegrid ran back inside and doused their fire before returning to the trench. Morglum pulled the bloody fur over top of them and let the snowfall upon them. They would be sealed in darkness.

"Wait," Gilthanus said as he raised a portion of the fur just enough to create a peephole and vent for fresh air. "We need to breathe you know."

"We have to be silent and out of sight when the wraiths arrive," Taegrid whispered to his friends and to Sadie who did not like being in the hole at all.

"And what if they find us?" Sametria asked her friends.

"We will fight to our bitter end," Gilthanus dared to say.

"Not me, I'll sneak out while you all die." Aleiz teased. They enjoyed their last chuckle before again laying down to sleep. This time they were all snuggled close together to keep warm while Morglum watched through the peephole and made sure it stayed clear of the new fallen snow. He watched the first dark light if it could be called that at all come over the horizon. The wind did not blow quite as hard now and the snow was not falling now. Morglum's jaw dropped wide open when he saw the shadowy bodies of thousands of wraiths heading for the cave they had once called their campsite. The first thousand or so that entered the cave resembled kobolds. The next hundred or so resembled orcs and the last two were the leaders resembling humans directing both groupings.

The number of wraiths bothered Morglum a great deal, for if they had to fight them, it would only be a matter of time before that number of wraiths overwhelmed them. What bothered him most was that among the orc wraiths was one that resembled the orc that sired him, Chief Gaji Bloody-Knucks. Morglum was certain that it was him. He must have come after Morglum and the army they had seen passing through the lower pass apparently ambushed the orcs. Morglum felt dishonor fall over him. Him killing his fellow orcs was one thing, but for his brethren and father to be drained forever of their souls and risen as wraiths was not a fate he would have wished upon them. This was exactly what he wanted to stop from happening to their world. It was why the companion had united. There were just too many wraiths for the six of them to stand a chance, even with their new weapons. Morglum just watched in silence as the wraiths examined the cave.

"Yeti's must have dragged them off to be eaten," one of the wraiths hissed to the leader. It looked around and seemed at one point to look right at Morglum before turning back to his armies.

"We march to the orc caves," the lead wraith hissed and in moments, the thousands of wraiths flew out of sight. Morglum slumped to the floor and sat beside Sametria who was starting to rise.

"Are they here?" Sametria asked daring not to whisper too loudly.

"They have come and gone," Morglum meant to whisper but instead groaned. Sametria sensed the agony her friend felt.

"What troubles you?" She asked sympathetically. Morglum looked to the half elf sadly.

"My people I meant to slaughter have lost an army and their chief, my father to the wraiths." Morglum answered.

"So you?" Sametria was uncertain what Morglum wanted to do about it.

"They left to go back and finish off the orcs in the orc caves. If they do that, the army of thousands I just saw will turn into even more." Morglum tried to explain even though Sametria knew by now he could not count passed twenty. Sametria smiled in understanding.

"We will go back and see if we can aid the orcs," Sametria assured Morglum.

"It's our best shot at defeating the army of wraiths that size," Morglum claimed and Sametria nodded in agreement.

Chapter Six:

The wraiths swarmed the orc caves, but this time they all entered together like a blanket of darkness coming to fill the orcs with dread. Calvin the Mad was enjoying his victory over the orcs. He would be held in the highest status with Viscus. His former master no longer mattered to him. The one called The Servant of Viscus had abandoned him. He wanted that label now and he would rightfully earn it as his former master had. The wraiths launched through solid rock walls and struck from the shadows before the orcs knew what hit them.

Even when the orcs realized what was happening, there was little they could do but fight to their ends. Chief Foogart cut down wraith after wraith with the Pride of the Bloody-Knucks Chief. They all seemed to resemble kobolds with their grotesque shadowy features. Even Faerxerous his green-scaled dragon friend fought at his side. The wraiths would not win over the orcs as easily as they might have believed too.

Chief Foogart roared in battle after every wraith he hacked obliterated into oblivion. The orc younglings could not defend themselves and the wraiths went for the defenseless first, knowing that very few orcs had the means to even harm them. The wraiths did slaughter many orcs quickly, but there were more orcs than they had anticipated with the means to hurt them. One orc in particular was a priestess of Bolnarg called Gelona. She now fought beside Chief Foogart and Faerxerous casting what few spells she could to aid her chief. She was savage for a female orc and Chief Foogart liked what he saw displayed in her. She was loyal to him as he had been to his father. He did not want to be chief. It was forced upon him.

They roared out cries to Bolnarg together as they fought against the wraiths. The wraith numbers never seemed to diminish and they seemed to come from every direction when they attacked. Gelona used her divine energies to destroy as many of the wraiths as she could before her power diminished and she was forced to only fight in melee against the wicked foes.

*****

Thortwerg woke up in a panic, kicking the dead yeti off him. His back still hurt and he had thought that he was a goner. His spear was deeply imbedded in the chest of the yeti. He must have found the beast's heart with his spear. He looked to the sky with thanks.

"The fallen gods be watching over me dumb-ass," Thortwerg spat as he rolled to his feet and walked over to retrieve his spear. Thortwerg yanked the short spear free of the yeti corpse and wiped it off on the fur. Its stomach was bloated with gas that formed during the decomposition of the body and some of it escaped and found its way to Thortwerg's nostrils.

"Disgusting!" Thortwerg barked. "I better get going before that smell attracts scavengers." The lone barbarian of the north began following the pass to the south again. He was not sure how long he had been out. The yeti fur had sheltered him from the cold after the beast died and kept his body warm while it began to heal. He was far from being completely mended though. His ribs hurt and his back ached. The pass was long and narrow and it was constantly winding this way and that, but it kept him sheltered from the worst of the freezing winds. The trail of the army was long gone, but he knew they had to of gone this way, because there was no other way to go but up and mindless skeletons would not have done well with such a climb. There would have surely been some evidence of some of them falling if they had taken to the higher pass trail. Thortwerg trusted his instincts and continued on his path to the south, hoping to find a settlement that he could find a port at and take to the seas. He had but one gold coin, but he was not looking to be the captain just yet. He would start as a crewmember and learn how to sail first. Then he would eventually save enough booty to buy his own ship. That was his dream and that was what drove him.

*****

Morglum led the way with Gilthanus' gear, his own belongings and the rolled up yeti fur strapped to his back. They had already passed back through the dwarven carved tunnels where the kobolds had dwelled before the wraiths came. Even the spiders were all dead within the mountain. Now they were close enough to here the screams of dying orcs and the hissing of the ghostly wraiths. The companions had their weapons, as they came down the mountain trail and cut to their right, never slowing their pace. Several of the kobold-wraiths emerged from the mountainside and swooped down at the companions.

"Ambush!" Morglum roared as he dove to the side and raised his enchanted battle-axe in defense. The kobold-wraiths swooped down at the surprised companions with their shadowy claws extended and ready to strike at their very souls. The grouping of kobold-wraiths focused on one target at a time to quickly bring down their enemies. It was a tactic that benefited them greatly. Nine kobold-wraiths swarmed down at Morglum to devour his life energy. Taegrid Prowler the cat man archer put two arrows through a kobold-wraith and it dissipated into Oblivion. Aleiz leaped at one of the kobold-wraiths focused on Morglum and cut through it with his newly enchanted kukri. The kobold-wraith dissipated instantly from the vermin-kissed elf's accurate attack. Morglum hacked his enchanted battle-axe right through one of the small wraiths that swarmed at him and it seemed to be absorbed by the unseen air that surrounded them all. It was how wraiths died. The life sapping energy that empowered them was released and unable to remain in the material world. It was instantly forced back to the plane from whence it was forged from, Oblivion. Sametria, Gilthanus and Sadie stood together in case any other groupings sighted them and attacked. The wraiths were still focused on the half-orc barbarian and tried to claw out his soul. Morglum was ready for them and managed to keep them at bay with his battle-axe. Morglum cut down a second kobold-wraith and Aleiz followed his example and destroyed one of the vile beings with his enchanted kukri. Taegrid put two arrows through one and popped it out of existence. Three of the kobold-wraiths remained and still targeted the mighty half-orc.

"I am Morglum," the half-orc roared in defiance of the undead forces they now battled. The kobold-wraiths flew in and passed Morglum again trying to claw out his soul. He rolled out of their reach, came back up behind one, and hacked it in two before it dissipated. Aleiz moved beside Taegrid as the kobold-wraiths turned their attention towards the cat man who fired his enchanted bow at them. Taegrid Prowler destroyed one before they could reach him. The final wraith hissed as it came in at Taegrid with its claws extended. The vermin-kissed elf stepped in front of the cat man and cut his kukri through the ghostly being like it was made of solid matter.

"These were the kobolds that we encountered in the mountain," Taegrid noted to his friends.

"This is why our people preferred suicide over death by wraith," Sametria said matter-of-factly.

"It makes sense to me now. I would not want to go out by the hands of a wraith." Taegrid claimed.

"I would not want to come back as a wraith either," Sametria agreed.

"I would gladly kill you before the wraiths got their chance to," Morglum offered.

"No time for joking around Morglum. Your people scream their final war-cries'." Aleiz reminded his friend.

"You don't have to come and help," Morglum said sincerely to his friends as he took a deep breath.

"Who will kill you to keep the wraiths from making you one of them?" Gilthanus responded sarcastically.

"No more goofing off, let's get this over with." Sametria growled as she moved up by Morglum with Sadie. Morglum growled as he sped off in the lead with his loyal friends in tow. There were thousands of wraiths attacking the orcs and few had enchanted weapons to use against the wraiths. Even the orcs that possessed enchanted weapons did not wield anything with the enchantment that they possessed. They knew that it was not going to be pretty inside. Most of the wraiths they would face from here on out would not be the weaker wraiths like the kobold infantry they encountered just moments ago. They would face actual wraiths. The brunt of the infantry would be battling the orc forces inside and that meant that the high-ranking wraiths would be in the rear waiting to strike.

"Will these medallions protect us from the touch of a wraith?" Aleiz asked Gilthanus as they entered the orc caves. Gilthanus chanted a light spell on his enchanted long sword to illuminate their way. Sametria cast a light spell upon her enchanted scimitar in case they had to spit up.

"I don't think so," Gilthanus finally answered.

"Why are we helping the very orcs that wanted you dead?" Taegrid asked as they moved through the caves.

"They are life aren't they?" Morglum spat. Sametria smiled wryly at Taegrid who simply shrugged in defense. Lifeless orc bodies littered the caves they passed through. It seems that the wraiths killed their victims very fast. The main forces were ahead in the great chamber and Morglum was leading his companions towards the sounds of the screams and war cries'. They rounded a corner and peered into the great chamber where the orcs all dwelled together and saw wraiths by the hundreds swarming orcs and clawing out their souls. The only wraiths they saw attacking were the small kobold-wraiths. Where were the orc wraiths and the leaders, Morglum wondered.

"Keep your eyes open, these are just the kobold forces." Morglum pointed out and the others understood that the threat of the more powerful wraiths still lingered in hiding. Taegrid saw wraiths swarming near youngling orcs that could barely run and put arrows into motion at the wraiths that threatened the orc children. Morglum ran into the great chamber roaring out in defiance the name of his tribe.

"Bloody-Knucks," Morglum cried out to rally his people. Morglum saw Gelona, a well-known priestess of Bolnarg among their tribe battling beside a green dragon that stood the size of a man and Foogart a great warrior among his people and one of many sons of Gaji. Foogart wielded the Pride of the Bloody-Knucks Chief. It was obvious that he had replaced Gaji. The three of them looked sickened from the touch of the wraiths that clawed at their bodies and souls. Morglum hacked through a kobold-wraith along the way to his half brother's side. Morglum charged towards his brother hacking through any wraith that got in his way. Taegrid, Sametria and Sadie tried creating a perimeter around the younglings, cutting and shooting at the wraiths that tried getting near them. Sadie kept the younglings herded in the perimeter while Sametria and Taegrid defended them. Aleiz and Gilthanus stayed in the cave entrance and defended against any wraith that came their way. The wraiths slaughtered the orcs and grew in numbers. The wraiths were too dominant for the orcs to defeat alone. Foogart shouted out orders to his orcs as he fought among them. The chamber was cold and full of the life sapping energy that fed the wraiths.

*****

Calvin the Mad watched from the cavern ceiling as the tide was turned. His forces suddenly fell faster than they slaughtered the living. He looked to see who it was that had come to the orcs rescue. He saw a half-orc charging towards the new orc chief and cleaving down his infantry along the way. A half-elf and cat man, stood guard with a mighty wolf over the young orcs.

"What are your commands, master?" a wraith hissed at Calvin the Mad. These must be the heroes that had destroyed Dax, Calvin the Mad thought. He saw that the thousand kobold-wraiths they sent in were all but lost.

"Send in the wraiths," Calvin the Mad hissed and the wraith led the charge with the orc wraith army. They were specters of their former selves hollowed out and empty of anything they once were. They were minions of Viscus now and Bolnarg if he could see them would have been angered greatly, for these were his worshipers. The wraiths swarmed down upon every living being they saw. One wraith approached Chief Foogart slowly and when the young orc chief saw the wraith, he froze in panic. It was his father, or at least it resembled his likeness.

"Father?" Foogart whimpered. The wraith smiled insidiously before lurching at the orc chief. Morglum shoved his half brother to the ground and out of the path of the wraith.

"He is not our father anymore. We have to destroy him." Morglum said to Chief Foogart as he lay on top of his back. Foogart's face was pressed against the rock floor when he heard the familiar voice.

"Morglum," Foogart growled through clenched teeth before rising up and tossing him off his back. "He was never your father.' Foogart roared as he grasped the Pride of the Bloody-Knucks Chief in a threatening manner.

"My friends and I came to aid you and our people." Morglum claimed to try to calm Foogart. "We are allies." Foogart was angry and still an orc, but he was no fool.

"We are allies for now, Morglum." Chief Foogart growled. The two of them fought against the wraiths back to back. They saw their father again and he swooped in at the two of them. They broke their stance for only an instant so that the both of them could free the soul of their father. They struck home, but Foogart's enchanted weapon passed harmlessly through what had once been Gaji. Morglum's battle-axe sunk into the wraith as though it was made of solid flesh. Gaji felt the sting of Morglum's enchanted battle-axe and clawed at him. Morglum hopped back and the claw missed passed by harmlessly.

Calvin the Mad recognized the cat man and half-elf as survivors from two of his recent raids and wanted to kill them personally. He summoned the eldritch fire that he as a warlock possessed and sent it streaking down at Taegrid. The cat man saw the flash from high above and dove to the ground in a roll. The wicked magic acted like flames that burned hotter than normal fire and seared the rock floor where Taegrid once stood. The rock floor glowed orange to reveal the dangerous heat and potency of the eldritch blast.

"Taegrid," Sametria called out in fear for her friend. She could not see if he had dodged the blast. She was busy fighting a wraith that was ripping away at her soul and sickening her spirit. Taegrid came up from his roll and fired his bow at the wraith that Sametria struggled with and popping it out of existence. Taegrid barley dove out of the way of another eldritch blast sent down from above. Calvin the Mad circled the heroes and cackled wickedly.

"I killed your people and your families. Now I will kill you as well." Calvin the Mad hissed. Sametria heard the wraith hiss at them from above and turned her attention on it. Taegrid put two arrows into the air at the wicked wraith, but he dodged them easily. Sametria wanted to hack the wraith out of existence, but it fought fearfully from a distance sending down its eldritch blast at them. Calvin the Mad was breaking down Taegrid's defenses fast, cornering him against a wall. Sametria heard a voice in her mind, but she could not make out the words it spoke. That did not bother her at that moment. Her power suddenly grew and a spell was granted to her from the forces of nature that she had not known before. She chanted it out of instinct and touched a stone on the ground that instantly erupted with a great and powerful yellow light. It was as if the sun had been restored and shone down brightly in the orc caves. The light was limited with its radius, but it was enough to frighten the wraiths and send them in retreat. Calvin the Mad hissed as he vanished from view through the stone ceiling. Taegrid turned and looked at his half-elf friend touching the bright shining rock that emitted the bright daylight they were all too young to know. The orcs in the radius of the bright light covered their eyes to shield them from its intensity. The wraiths were gone and all that remained was the cold and empty bodies of the fallen and the few that still lived. Morglum and Foogart looked at one another. Morglum offered an open hand of friendship. Chief Foogart smiled and reached out to grasp his half brother's hand but the hands never touched. Darkness fell over Morglum followed by a severe pain in the back of his head.

"Good job, now take his weapons and bind his feet and hands." Chief Foogart barked to Gelona who stood over the fallen Morglum with a large bloodied rock she struck him with.

"You don't want him dead?" Gelona asked her chief. Foogart looked at the motionless half-orc.

"He came back to help us," Chief Foogart informed the priestess.

"But he is a traitor," Gelona reminded her chief.

"Then he should become a slave of his people. Take him to the slave pits." Chief Foogart ordered.

"As you wish my chief," Gelona responded. Chief Foogart left Morglum to his priestess and turned to see the allies that had come with Morglum to aid them against the wraiths. It was only because of them that they were still alive, but this was the caves of the orcs and they were still enemies according to law, if they had any. One of them was the vermin-kissed elf that they had captured before and Morglum helped to escape.

"Take them prisoners," Chief Foogart barked to his orc army. The companions were surprised that the orcs had turned on them after they had come to their rescue. The orcs swarmed them where they stood and surrounded them from all sides to prevent their escape. Sametria lowered her scimitar and glared at the chief that had sent the orcs upon the very ones who had come to their aid.

"You would assault the ones who just saved you?" Sametria asked loudly so every orc in the chamber heard her. The orcs sopped and looked to their chief for guidance.

"You are trespassers and allies to an exile." Chief Foogart saw what the half-elf was trying to do. She was attempting to put doubt in the minds of his people and loyal followers.

"If Morglum had not returned from his exile, you all would surely be wraiths right now." Sametria spat her words in defiance. The orcs lowered their weapons and looked again to their chief.

"We have no allies, we are orcs." Chief Foogart roared.

"He would gladly go back into exile again if given the opportunity. Morglum just could not stand by and allow his people to be slaughtered even if it meant his own death." Sametria pointed out and the orcs felt shameful, including Chief Foogart.

"Lower your weapons," Chief Foogart commanded to his people and they obeyed. "Cut Morglum loose." Foogart instructed Gelona who had just finished tying up the half-orc. Gelona complied after nodding to her chief.

"The wraiths will surely return and they will not show you mercy next time." Taegrid warned the orcs. Aleiz and Gilthanus never lowered their weapons. They stood ready to attack at any moment. Chief Foogart looked upon his people and then to the cat-man and half-elf.

"If that is to be our fates, then so be it. If Morglum wants to end his exile and return to his people, I give him this one chance. Bring back the head of the Master Vampire that had once enslaved us under the rule of Gaji and his exile will be lifted." Chief Foogart offered before his people.

"We will leave and never return," Aleiz spat in retort to the foolish orcs.

"If that is what you wish," Sametria added.

"Take this half-breed with you and inform him when he awakes of my offer. If ever I see his face again, he had best be carrying the head of the Master Vampire to throw at my feet." Chief Foogart declared and the orcs shouted in agreement. Morglum's exile would be lifted if he took the head of the Master Vampire and presented it to the chief of the orcs for all to look upon and be reminded of what their tribe had been lowered to and risen above. The orcs parted and allowed the heroes passage to Morglum and out of the caves. Taegrid slung his bow over his shoulder and approached his unconscious friend cautiously. Sametria and Sadie followed close behind in case it was a trick of some kind. Taegrid knelt low and scooped up his heavy friend and all of the gear that was strapped to his back and lifted him up like a baby being cradled by its mother. Sametria picked up Morglum's enchanted battle-axe, knowing that he would need that again.

"Now go," Chief Foogart, ordered as he pointed a finger towards the cave that led outside. Sametria and Taegrid nodded and took their leave. Aleiz and Gilthanus waited for their friends and joined them by the cave, leaving together. Aleiz cast a constant glare at the orcs as they left, wanting to spit more insults for their foolishness. He did not say a word though, knowing that it would only make things worse for them and especially for Morglum if he ever wanted to return to his people from exile. The companions made their ways back out of the orc caves cautiously. They kept a constant watch for the wraiths that Sametria had frightened off with her newly acquired spell. It was amazing, and though none of them said a word about it yet, they all thought it. Was that what the sun was supposed to make things look like? Was that the light the sun once covered the world with? It cast such a bright light over things that color was enhanced in everything. It made sense if it were the light the sun once cast over the world, because the wraiths were said to have feared the light of the sun and they feared the light that Sametria had summoned. It had weakened them and made them powerless. Sametria was proving to be a powerful druid. Nature was blessing her with many gifts that many would have overlooked as being vital weapons. The orcs watched as the trespassers left.

"Should we send a death squad to slaughter them?" Gelona asked her chief after the intruders were gone. Chief Foogart contemplated the idea for a moment.

"No, I made a deal and I will honor it." Chief Foogart declared. The companions exited the orc caves and the black sun sickened Sametria and Taegrid once again with its life sapping rays. It was as Viscus himself rained down the energy of Oblivion upon them. Taegrid nearly fell over and dropped Morglum on the rocks, but Aleiz grabbed him and helped support his weight.

"We must find shelter from the sun." Sametria groaned.

"You would not need to if you wore one of the medallions." Gilthanus reminded them. Taegrid and Sametria looked at each other and then to Gilthanus.

"Alright then," they both agreed. Gilthanus reached into the sack that Morglum carried for him and took out the last two medallions and hung one around each of their necks. Sadie felt the reprieve from her masters medallion as tough she also wore one. The black sun could no longer harm them as long as they wore their medallions.

"They may be evil, but they lift a great burden." Sametria said in defeat.

"Where shall we go?" Taegrid asked Sametria.

"How about back to the den in the plains," Sametria suggested. No one argued and Sadie led the way this time feeling renewed with vigor now that the black sun no longer sickened her.

The companions reached the den and made certain that it was still clear of any creatures natural or tainted. Gilthanus studied his book with great determination with hopes of not just learning new spells, but finding some way to make his dreams come true without offending his friends. His companions trained, prayed and meditated over the next week. Sadie had grown magically enhanced by Sametria, who had become quite the beast master. Her bond with nature was intensified and that meant her bond with Sadie had been empowered as well. Sadie was the size of a bear and had oversized jaws with large and very sharp teeth. She was not a natural wolf that you would come across in the wild. She had been battle hardened and enchanted with nature magic. Sametria knew that other gods still existed. They just needed to find them and restore them to power. She wanted nothing more than to bring Tevlos back into his rightful place among the Athyxian Pantheon. She had to find him and was determined to do so.

Taegrid trained and disciplined his body so that one day soon, he might wield his new bow. He could almost draw back the string now, but his strength was not quite good enough. He had seriously thought of offering the bow to Morglum who had the strength to wield it, but he felt that it was a prize he deserved and would prove it in time. He saw Sametria in deep meditation a great distance away from the rest of them. Aleiz trained with a fighting style so foreign to everyone that they often observed him just to try to learn it. Morglum had trained with Taegrid and Aleiz to better his fighting style. The half-orc wielded the lighter than normal mithral great-axe called Mar Doldon in one hand and his enchanted battle-axe he had named Wraith Defiler in the other. Many rangers and warriors used a devastating fighting style. It was not often used by orcs, who preferred to wield two-handed weapons. Morglum just happened upon a light two-handed weapon he could wield with one hand as easily as if it were crafted as a one-handed weapon. He had also learned to read over the last week thanks to Gilthanus. The elf sorcerer found time in his busy schedule of studies to help Morglum learn how to read and write. He still needed a lot of practice, but understood the basics and would get better with practice. Gilthanus came out from his studies for a moment to watch his friends train and get some fresh air.

Sametria had meditated and prayed about her newfound sword that spoke the name of Tevlos whenever she swung it in battle.

"Tevlos," Sametria called out kneeling out in the open plains and holding her newfound sword up to the sky with her head bowed low. "If you can hear me, I pledge my life to your service and restoring Athyx to what it once was. I vow to slay every undead being and unnatural creature I come across in order to accomplish the rebirth of Athyx. Bless this blade as it was meant to be blessed. It cries your name I battle my patron." Sametria cut the palm of her hand drawing her own blood to seal her blood vow. With her bloodied hand she grasped the enchanted medallion crafted by the wicked and otherworldly beings known as devils and ripped it from her neck snapping the chain. She suddenly felt the sickening effects of the black sun again and Sadie who laid nearby her master cringed as well as both feeling nauseated.

"This self sacrifice is how I prove my word to you," Sametria claimed as she tossed the medallion on a flat stone she had laid out earlier and then brought her enchanted adamantine forged blade that spoke the name of Tevlos when it was swung down upon the wicked medallion and destroying it with a flash of magical light. Her vision was blinded for a moment and then slowly returned, first to a blurry view and then it cleared to her natural sight. She sat down her sword and bandaged her fresh wound. Sametria did not know it yet, but her minor ceremony and sacrifice had unlocked a hidden blessing in the enchanted sword. The sword had a history that was to be discovered. Tevlos had forged the blade before his death to defend Athyx from such a terror as had destroyed it, but no wielder had taken the blade and taken the time to discover and unlock the hidden magic it contained.

"It is time Sadie," Sametria said to her wolf as she finished bandaging her hand and picked up her blade. "We have to leave the others to find their own paths. We have one of our own and I am going to start with the forest we once called home." Sametria spoke to her wolf as if it was a person that understood her. She was certain that even though the wolf did not speak back to her, that it understood her. Sadie followed close by her master as she walked over to her friends. Sametria looked to the ground once she approached her friends.

"We saw you destroy your medallion. Is there something we should know?" Taegrid asked curiously. Gilthanus glared at her with disrespect.

"I have a calling. I am going to find a way to restore Athyx to its former glory that we are all too young to have ever seen except for Aleiz and Gilthanus. You all have paths of your own to follow. Perhaps our paths will cross some day, farewell my friends." Sametria said and immediately she turned and began walking to the south with Sadie following. Taegrid ran up to stop the half elf and blocked her path.

"You would leave us now?" Taegrid accused more than asked.

"I would have you at my side if it is your path to follow," Sametria answered. Taegrid was taken by surprise.

"Where are you starting your quest?" Taegrid asked with a serious demeanor.

"Our forest home," Sametria answered matter-of-factly. Taegrid looked at their friends and then back to the half-elf.

"I hope to do the same thing you want to do, but I feel that our friends can help and so I will remain with them. I pray our paths cross again someday Sam." Taegrid said with passion and hugged the half-elf goodbye before running back to the others. Morglum was speechless. He wanted to say something, but no words came to mind.

"Bye," Aleiz waved to their friend as she and Sadie left them and headed back to the south to the Great Forest. They all watched her leave and never look back. They were hypnotized by the sight of one of their friends leaving them and stared until she was over the horizon and out of view.

"Wow," Morglum gasped in disbelief.

"What, did you think that she would really stay with the likes of us?" Gilthanus balked before storming back inside the animal den they used as shelter.

"She thinks she can really change things back to the way they were before the cataclysm?" Aleiz asked Taegrid. Taegrid looked to the dark elf with a serious expression.

"We all can make a difference. In fact we have already made a big difference." Taegrid answered.

"How? We still live in a world of darkness. What exactly did we do to make a difference?" Aleiz retorted.

"Where most have been slaughtered, we stood and survived. We slew a great number of undead and still live to destroy more. That is how we made a difference. We got the attention of the wraith that is sent out by the Servant of Viscus to raid any surviving settlements of living beings. He will be hunting us." Taegrid responded with pride. Aleiz gave him a look of confusion.

"You want him to come after you?" Aleiz asked in confusion. Morglum understood.

"He wants revenge on the bastard that slew his people," Morglum explained. Aleiz nodded in understanding.

"I can do revenge," Aleiz said as he nodded. "Revenge would be good."

"What do we do first?" Morglum asked gaining the attention of his two friends.

"What do you mean?" Taegrid asked caught by surprise by the question.

"He wants to know if we are going after the wraiths or the Master Vampire first," Aleiz explained. Taegrid pondered the thought.

"The Master Vampire is not hunting us yet, so it would be best to go after the wraiths first don't you agree?" Taegrid asked. The logic made sense. Aleiz and Morglum shook their heads in agreement after looking to one another.

"What about Gilthanus? He seems distracted." Taegrid wondered.

"Let me talk to him," Aleiz offered and strolled into the den after the sorcerer. Morglum and Taegrid went back to practicing their melee drills with one another. Aleiz entered the den and saw Gilthanus reading something from his book and making strange gestures with his hands.

"Are you learning new spells?" Aleiz asked rhetorically. He just wanted the sorcerer to realize that he had come inside to talk. Gilthanus stopped his studies and looked up to his friend.

"Do you require my assistance for something?" Gilthanus asked sounded quite annoyed. Aleiz was shocked that the sorcerer would even consider speaking to him that way after everything that they had been through together and scoffed.

"I thought you might want to talk," Aleiz said evenly. Gilthanus sighed in defeat and suddenly began to sob.

"Is it not enough that we have to fight undead on a daily basis to survive? Is it not enough that we have to wear magical protection to walk outside under the rays of the black sun?" Gilthanus began running through a vital list of issues that apparently bothered him very deeply. Aleiz never interrupted the elf sorcerer. He just listened to his friend vent. "Is it not enough that I am a cursed offspring of some devil bitch? Now we are shunned by orcs that we saved from certain doom. We are hunted by wraiths and a Master Vampire is a mark for one of our comrades and now Sametria has left us." Aleiz understood. The elf felt abandoned and overwhelmed. It was just too much to have to take at once.

"Sametria walks the straight and narrow path my friend," Aleiz reminded Gilthanus of the druidic code that the half-elf lived by. "She wants us to survive and live well, that is why she goes. She goes to find the answer, the way to make the world right again as you remember it. I was still beneath the surface, but I remember what my people lost after the cataclysm. We lost contact with our goddess and priestesses went mad with the loss of their powerful spells." Gilthanus wiped the tears from his eyes.

"Can you believe that I am the son of a devil?" Gilthanus gasped again. Aleiz managed a slight chuckle.

"I cannot my friend. With a frail body like yours, I would think you to be the offspring of a kobold." Aleiz shared a moment of laughter with Gilthanus.

"I have recovered my strength completely," Gilthanus said when he finally stopped laughing.

"That is good my friend. We have been discussing our next move." Aleiz informed Gilthanus.

"What is the plan?" Gilthanus asked.

"It seems our wisest choice would be to take out the wraith forces first and then the master vampire." Aleiz shared what they had discussed outside.

"I wouldn't mind to square off against another wraith," Gilthanus growled. "I have a new arsenal of spells that will aid us."

"Come outside and join us then," Aleiz held out a hand of friendship and Gilthanus took it. Aleiz helped his friend stand up and together they went back outside the den and practiced with Taegrid and Morglum. The four friends trained for an hour or so and then stopped to eat and rest. As they were, eating and sharing laughs with one another the mysterious woman appeared before them all. Everyone but Gilthanus drew their weapons when she appeared in a flash of red flames.

"I am Villisca," the woman said. Her voice was very powerful when they heard her speak. "I am the one who aided you. I am here to aid you further now."

"Hi Villisca," Morglum said flirtatiously. Villisca ignored the half-orc.

"What aid do you offer us now mother?" Gilthanus asked. Calling someone mother that he did not truly remember was awkward for him, though her voice was very familiar.

"Viscus is not the only god still in power. He has an opposite that he holds imprisoned, for if one of them dies, they both would die says the prophecy." Villisca began. "Viscus created a prison somewhere in Oblivion. It is there that he holds the many gods prisoner. Only Enamor and Viscus still have their godly power. The others have been stripped of their power by a powerful relic known as the Marble of Godly Doom."

"So why does Viscus and Enamor have their powers?" Aleiz asked curiously. Villisca nodded to the vermin-kissed elf for his intuition.

"The relic can only be wielded by mortals. Gods for mortals to keep the gods in line forged it. There was a curse however. In case any mortal servant of a god attempted to use the relic for such a purpose as Viscus did, that mortal would be forever turned into a wraith under the control of the deity that commanded it." Villisca continued her story.

"So if only a mortal can wield the relic, where is it now?" Gilthanus asked and impressed his mother with his intuition.

"It resides on the Ethereal Plane in a hiding place called Eye of the Gods," Villisca claimed.

"How do we get there?" Gilthanus asked.

"And who is crazy enough to wield it?" Aleiz added.

"That is for you to figure out," Villisca said coldly before disappearing in a flash of red flames.

"So that's your mom eh?" Morglum scoffed. "I'd do her." Aleiz and Taegrid laughed and caught dirty glares from Gilthanus.

"That's my mother you guys," Gilthanus said in protest.

"She could be the mother of a kobold for all I care so long as she looks like that," Aleiz said laughing in between words. Gilthanus joined the humor and laughed. She was very attractive. Gilthanus realized that his mother even aroused him and he blushed when he realized that she might be watching them.

"Does that book of yours tell you how to get us to the Ethereal Plane?" Aleiz asked Gilthanus bringing their laughter to a serious halt.

"It does, but I have a long way to go before I am ready for a spell like that," Gilthanus admitted.

"Well you had better get started on it if you ever want to see Sametria again." Morglum barked as he looked to the south where their friend had gone and was long out of sight.

"That can wait until after we destroy those wraiths and the Master Vampire," Gilthanus argued.

"If that's how you feel about it my friend," Taegrid said as he stretched. "I think I am going to turn in for the night." The cat man yawned.

"I'll take first watch," Morglum offered.

"Wake me for second shift," Aleiz offered. Morglum nodded and the others grabbed their gear and went back into the den where they could safely sleep. Morglum followed but sat in the doorway and watched the landscape and the sky as the dark and eerie glow of the black sun dissipated when it set over the horizon. The sky turned a dark black and stars of white and yellow appeared throughout the sky.

"I wonder if that's the Ethereal Plane out there," Morglum mumbled to himself in contemplation. He stared off outside keeping vigilant and watching for anything that he could see moving across the landscape. He thought he saw a silhouette outside and squinted to adjust his vision. He did see someone. It was a lone bearded man carrying a spear and looking like he was lost.

"Aleiz, get your ass over here. I see something." Morglum barked. All of his friends roused, but only Aleiz hopped up and strapped on his weapons.

"Do you need us as well Morglum?" Taegrid asked in a half sleep state.

"Roll your fury ass over and get your shut eye friend," Morglum said in response. Gilthanus was already back asleep and snoring. Aleiz ran over to the half-orc with his kukri in hand.

"What is it?" Aleiz asked.

"There is a man strolling out in the open. Keep watch while I go and see what he is about." Morglum instructed. Aleiz nodded and watched his friend as he strolled out into the darkness with his axes in hands. Aleiz laughed to himself. If Morglum wanted to see if the lone man was friendly, he was not going to make a good first impression.

"What are you about?" Morglum called out to the man who spun around defensively and faced the half-orc with his spear at the ready.

"Half-orc," Thortwerg growled having run into a few of them as a child.

"That is right; I am a half-orc." Morglum said matter-of-factly. "I am called Morglum. Who are you and what are you doing wandering the lands alone?" Thortwerg was not sure about this half-orc. He carried a great axe in one hand as if it was a twin to the battle-axe in his opposing hand. His posture was relaxed though and he did not seem aggressive. He was just armed. Thortwerg understood. Do not approach someone you do not know unarmed unless they too are unarmed and Thortwerg carried his spear in hand.

"I be Thortwerg, a barbarian from the north." Thortwerg said proudly.

"What is a barbarian of the north doing this far south?" Morglum asked.

"That's me own business," Thortwerg spat. An eerie sensation fell over the two of them as they stood there conversing. Morglum instinctively looked about and Thortwerg did not understand.

"What are you doing?" Thortwerg griped.

"Shush and follow me quickly if you want to live," Morglum whispered before running back to the den with his friends. Thortwerg looked around and saw nothing, but the hairs on the back of his neck stood up tall. He followed the half-orc to see what he had to offer. Aleiz saw what looked like a dark blanket come over the horizon. The vermin-kissed elf quickly stamped out the campfire inside their shelter, but he did not know if it would be enough or if they had already seen the light within the cave.

"Wake up, wraiths are coming," Aleiz whispered as he stamped out the fire. Morglum and Thortwerg ran inside the dark cave.

"I can't see a thing," Thortwerg whispered.

"Then that means the wraiths might not notice us," Morglum whispered in response.

"Let's hope not," Gilthanus whispered as he roused along with Taegrid and readied their weapons. They all heard the shrieks of angry wraiths outside and knew at that moment that the army of undead had indeed spotted them. Morglum could see the human barbarian looking quite panicked in the dark, though he could not see any of them.

"You are not prepared to face these. Stay here." Morglum ordered the barbarian as he stepped out of the den. He saw the wraiths swoop down and clash with something he had not noticed before. A group of ghostly looking knights wielding ghostly swords fought against the wraiths as equals of the incorporeal realms. The wraiths outnumbered them, but the ghostly knights seemed to be more savage in battle and cut many of the wraiths down, obliterating them. Morglum did not know what to think. Part of him wanted to go and help the ghostly knights, but something deep inside him warned against the idea. Taegrid, Aleiz and Gilthanus came out to back up their friend ready for battle and saw exactly what held their friend in a trance.

"I don't think they saw us after all," Aleiz said breaking the silence.

"Slaughter the spectral riders of the Servant of Viscus. He has sent them upon us." One of the wraiths hissed. Taegrid recognized the wraith as the same wraith that he and Sametria faced in the orc caves. It wielded a power so deadly that it burned hotter than normal and magical fires. It was known as an eldritch blast. It was forged out of raw magic and wielded as a deadly weapon second only to Hellfire. The spectral riders as they were labeled destroyed many wraiths, but they were outnumbered and eventually they were destroyed. The companions stood in awe and watched the wraiths battle against their own until the confrontation had finally ended. Six spectral riders stood against a hundred wraiths and slaughtered nearly half of them before they were destroyed.

"We found the wraiths. Should we attack them before they notice us?" Morglum asked his friends who still stared in confusion.

"They are too many," Gilthanus warned.

"Back into the den quickly," Taegrid whispered and the companions ran back inside to hide as quietly as they could and as quickly as they dared. They watched from the shadows until the wraiths left. They seemed to be heading back towards the mountains and the orc caves. Morglum looked to his friends.

"You are not to return until you have the head of the master vampire," Aleiz reminded the half-orc.

"Well I guess they are on their own this time," Morglum whispered sarcastically.

Chapter Seven:

Sametria wanted to be alone and was happy that none of her friends joined her. She returned to the Great Forest and the place where she stood when she heard her father's final cry. It had been three days now since she left her friends and she knew that the place where her father and Dillveign had fallen was near.

"Come on Sadie," Sametria said as she felt her tears begin to swell up in her eyes. It had been nearly a month since her father fell. She hoped to say a few words over the sight of his death if there was anything left of his body. When she arrived to the sight, Sametria was surprised. There were two graves and they were unmarked. Someone had buried the bodies out of respect, but whom? Sametria looked all around her and wondered who else could have possibly survived the assault of the wraiths. Sadie sniffed the air around them but could smell nothing out of the ordinary. Sametria knelt at the foot of the grave that was obviously her father's.

"I miss you," Sametria sobbed. Sadie sat down near her master and watched her sympathetically. "I wish you were here to guide me, to see what I have done and how fast I have risen in my devotions to nature and Tevlos. You cried out that name and it stuck in my mind. Now I have a sword that speaks that very name every time I swing it. It has made me think of you. Are you in my sword and trying to lead me somewhere?" Sametria remembered how her father must have died and answered her own question.

"No," she began. "You couldn't be. Your soul was devoured by the wraiths and forever lost." Sametria whimpered in sadness.

"No it isn't," an unfamiliar deep voice claimed. Sametria stood to her feet and drew both of her blades instinctively. Sadie also leaped up and looked about sniffing the air and growling. Neither of them saw anything.

"Who is there?" Sametria asked.

"Vortis is what I am called," the deep voice spoke from somewhere in the trees. Sametria and Sadie looked all around and then in the direction they thought the voice came from.

"Are you some sort of wizard? Show yourself!" Sametria barked.

"There is no need to be hostile. I'm right here." Vortis said trying to calm the visitors. Again, Sametria looked all around, but Sadie stayed focused in the direction they believed the voice was coming from.

"I only seem hostile because you do not show yourself to me," Sametria explained through nervous teeth.

"But I am right here," Vortis said and branches rustled above her dropping leaves to the ground. Sametria looked up in the tree and saw no one.

"I have a couple of friends that play games like this. You are trying to confuse me to catch me off guard." Sametria scoffed as she put her back to a tree. A loud crackling noise issued from above and the tree bent down revealing a rough face in its bark.

"I told you I was right here," Vortis said again and frightening Sametria. Sadie backed up in a defensive position next to Sametria.

"Wow," Sametria managed to gasp. "I uh-, didn't realize."

"I saw your father first kill the bear so that the wraiths could not feast upon its spirit and then he took his own life. I waited until the wraiths were gone and buried them where they died. The wraiths do not know I exist or any of my kind. I am the first of my kind to reveal myself in years." Vortis said as he lowered into what appeared to be a sitting position for him. Sametria sheathed her swords.

"Heel Sadie," she instructed her wolf and the wolf calmed. "Why do you reveal yourself now? Why did you bother to bury my father and Dillveign?" Sametria asked sounding completely confused.

"He wanted to save our world but did not know where the path began." Vortis claimed.

"Do you know where the path begins?" Sametria asked. Vortis smiled and leaned what appeared to be his chin in branch fingers of his leaf-covered hand. He was a tree to the naked eye, but held faint features of sentience. Sametria could not believe that she was speaking to a tree.

"Many will misguide you and easily so given the desperate times we are faced with. Even if you mean well, the choices you make can make things worse if you are hasty." Vortis warned.

"I think I understand. A friend of mine was offered aid from a devil," Sametria informed Vortis.

"That's never good," Vortis warned.

"Where would my path begin then?" Sametria asked feeling as though their only chance at restoring Athyx was just a false hope.

"There is a gate to the Ethereal Plane in a temple hidden deep within the Swamps of Mordakai. On the Ethereal Plane, there is a place called the Eye of the Gods and there lies a relic of great power. It is called the Marble of Godly Doom. Only a mortal can wield it." Vortis claimed.

"What does it do?" Sametria asked.

"It was created to keep balance in the pantheon. However, because only mortals can wield it, the balance is not always upheld. Through mortals, it steels the divine power from gods at the beckoning of whatever mortal wields it, but at a great cost. The wielder becomes a wraith afterward under the control of the deity he worships, never again to be mortal. Not even the power of the gods can change that. So as you can imagine, not very many people would want to wield it." Vortis explained.

"So if I find this marble, I could theoretically restore the world to the way it was?" Sametria asked.

"Yes you could, but at the cost of your own life," Vortis warned. "We only learned of the legend when the Servant of Viscous returned to Athyx as a wraith and then his minion Calvin the Mad followed in his fate." Sametria absorbed the information carefully.

"Swamps of Mordakai, where is that?" Sametria asked sounding very hopeful.

"The Swamps of Mordakai lie further south of the Great Forest. Terrible monsters still reside there. The wraiths terror has not reached that far yet as far as I know." Vortis answered.

"Do you want to come with me and help me restore Athyx?" Sametria asked Vortis. Vortis sat up and shook his head. Leaves fell upon the ground.

"I wish I could, but I am forbidden to leave the forest. The elders say that the black sun will taint our kind as it does the wild animals that roam the world." Vortis responded.

"Has it tainted my kind?" Sametria found herself asking.

"Oh no," Vortis answered with a slight chuckle. "Your kind is sickened by it because it feeds on your souls, but everything else it seems to taint."

"How will I find this hidden temple in the swamps?" Sametria asked hoping that Vortis could help her more in some way. Vortis reached his branch fingers to his side and ripped a piece of bark away from his trunk. Sametria grimaced believing it to have hurt him.

"Take this map, it will guide you." Vortis offered as he handed the large piece of bark to Sametria. Sametria examined the bark and saw that the underside of it was indeed parchment with a map. She peeled the parchment off the bark carefully and rolled it up.

"Thank you for all of your help Vortis," Sametria said with a bow as she placed the rolled up map in her pack.

"It is your destiny to restore nature according to your father. I often heard his prayers to Silvanus and he truly believed that it would be you that made a difference and ended the darkness." Vortis told the enthralled half-elf.

"Thank you Vortis, for everything." Sametria was almost in tears.

"I will leave you to your privacy with your father now," Vortis offered as he stood up and seemed to blend back in with the forest. The ground seemed to shake as he walked away and disappeared in the forest. Sametria was filled with hope. She returned to her father's grave and again knelt at the feet of his final resting place. Sadie watched Sametria from where she still sat. She cried different tears now. She seemed happy.

"I do not know if I will fulfill the destiny that you dreamed father, but it is my goal to make the attempt. Rest in peace." Sametria said before standing up straight and turning to face Sadie. "Come on girl. We will need our friends help for this." Sametria and Sadie took off running to the north as fast as they could. They had run for several minutes when she stopped dead in her tracks suddenly. Behind her, she thought that she heard the voice of her father cry out her name.

*****

Villisca watched as the living tree left and the half-elf said her final farewells at the grave sight of her father. Sametria left and seemed to head back to the north. Two hulking fiends covered in metal plates bolted directly to their flesh. The nails that fixed the plates in place, dripped blood that stained the armor and bodies alike. The creatures resembled orcs with their monstrous features. They had rotten tusks that dominated their mouths and maggots wriggled within the wounds created by the bolts that mounted the armor plates.

"Kill the living tree and then kill the half-elf," Villisca instructed the war devils.

"Yes Villisca," they grunted in the infernal language. The war devils took off running after the living tree and Villisca approached the graves. She stood over the grave of Gilthiam.

"I have come to collect," Villisca said over the grave as she held out a rolled up vile looking scroll. The soul of Gilthiam rose from the grave.

"You cannot have my soul Villisca. You have not kept your end of the bargain." Gilthiam resisted the hold of the vile scroll. Villisca knew that she had violated their deal when she ordered the war devils to kill the half-elf as well as the living tree.

"You asked me to keep her safe from harm long enough to fulfill her destiny. Just because you believe that she is to restore Athyx, does not make it her destiny. You only want me to make sure that it happens." Villisca scolded the soul.

"I love my daughter," Gilthiam pleaded.

"Which do you love more, your daughter or your world?" Villisca asked diabolically. "Would you have your world lost in darkness forever or have it restored at the mere cost of your daughter's life? It's not like I get her soul." Gilthiam knew he should never have made the deal with the diabolic devil daughter of Armco all those years ago. She was well within the rights of their contract. She manipulated him and caught him at a weak point in his life where he made a foolish decision and what made it worse was that he did not realize that his contract was so well worded that she could get away with this. Gilthiam would have cried tears if he could. He moaned in sadness. Without his world, Sametria would struggle for the rest of her life and possibly be devoured by wraiths. However, without Sametria living Gilthiam's legacy would end his legacy that he started when Sametria was born. He wanted her to save the world and put her on the path to do so. She was only twenty-eight years of age and had never before looked upon the yellow sun. A thought came to the soul of Gilthiam.

"You cannot have my soul," Gilthiam growled. "Send your minions after my daughter and see what happens to them."

"Very well," Villisca said calmly and the contract erupted into flames, disintegrating before their eyes. "Your soul will go to Viscus now."

"What?" Gilthiam moaned as he felt the grasp of the dark deity on his soul. "I thought that suicide protected our souls from the devourer."

"From the devourer as you refer to him, that is somewhat true. Your souls are not devoured, but imprisoned in darkness for eternity." Villisca explained.

"But that is not fair. That should only be for the wicked." Gilthiam whined.

"You know all too well that life is not fair Gilthiam," Villisca scolded.

"But good souls deserve to go elsewhere. Viscus should have no dominion no matter how powerful he is." Gilthiam dared to argue.

"There is nowhere else for your souls to go unless you make a deal with a devil to take your soul by contract." Villisca cackled insidiously. It seemed that no matter what Viscus and Villisca would win out in the end. Wraiths swooped in out of the shadows and clutched a hold on the soul.

"Sametria!" Gilthiam cried out as the wraiths dragged his soul into the shadows and disappeared. Villisca laughed before vanishing in a flash of flames.

*****

The war devils ran with their heavy feet sinking deep into the soft earth. They followed the tracks that the living tree had left in its wake, but had to take the time to find the tracks and make sure that they had not lost sight of their target. They knew that they had to be getting close. The war devils were surprised when a massive branch swung down and slammed dangerously close to one of the war devils and indenting the ground. The war devils held their hellish spears out defensively and spotted the living tree.

"What do the forces of Hell want with me?" Vortis asked the fiends but they did not understand him. They lunged in with their vile looking barbed spears. Vortis realized that the war devils could reach him as well, even though he stood well over ten feet away. He hopped back as the spears came close to hitting his bark skin. One of the war devils rolled back and strapped his hellish spear to his back before drawing out a fiendish crossbow that had hot flames dancing where a bolt should have been loaded. The second war devil kept the living tree occupied in melee with his hellish spear. Vortis tried to crush the spear-wielding fiend, but it smacked aside the attack with ease. The crossbow eliding war devil fired a stream of Hellfire from his weapon and singed leaves and branches from a nearby tree. The tree began to smolder.

"What have you done?" Vortis gasped as he tried to smash the war devil closest to him. The war devil used its spear and smacked his attack out wide again. The barbs on the hellish spear ripped bark away from his hand and exposed his unprotected wood flesh. The crossbow wielding war devil fired a second stream of Hellfire and singed the leaves on Vortis. He panicked as he patted them out on the ground.

"Who commands you?" Vortis roared in defiance, as he swung his flaming branches at the spear wielding war devil again. It laughed as it smacked the living tree's attack down low with its spear. A third stream of Hellfire caught several surrounding trees on fire and the heat became unbearable very quickly for Vortis. Vortis tried to escape the war devils, but the range of that fiendish crossbow was a greater distance than Vortis could cover before the war devil fired it again. Vortis felt its sting as the

Hellfire ignited him. He roared out in pain as the unnaturally hot flames burned him into cinders. The living tree fell to the ground smoldering as hot coals among the savage forest fire.

"Now we find half-elf and kill her," one war devil grunted to another in their infernal language.

"Let's have more fun with this hunt," the second war devil suggested. The two war devils set out to pick up the trail of Sametria, but when they returned to the grave where she last stood, they found no prints anywhere.

"How is this possible that she leaves no tracks?" one of the war devils asked.

"She might not, but her big wolf does." The second war devil pointed out Sadie's large paw prints leading to the north. The war devils smiled at one another wickedly, exposing their rotten tusks even more with their wide smiles before taking off after the trail of the wolf.

*****

Sametria and Sadie ran through the forest. She never turned back around after thinking that her mind had played a dirty trick on her when she thought she had heard her father cry out her name. Sadie stopped and sniffed the air looking around.

"What is it girl?" Sametria asked as she scanned their surroundings as well. Sametria drew out her adamantine forged scimitar when she spotted a mound of vines and mutated plant life shambling toward them. Sadie leaped at the plant monster.

"Sadie wait!" Sametria yelled. The ferocious wolf nipped at the massive mound but found that it was difficult to latch onto. Sametria followed in after Sadie to help her against the living shrubbery. The living shrubbery whipped plant tendrils made of thick vines at Sametria and Sadie to try to keep them back. Sametria was struck and wrapped up so fast that before she could defend against the attack, the living shrubbery had her entangled and squeezed her within the vines that wrapped around her. She felt pain all through her body as the vines squeezed the life out of her. Sametria found it very difficult to breathe. Sadie bit onto a part of the plant monster that was just too big for her mouth and her teeth slipped free harmlessly. She panicked as she saw her master suspended helplessly in the air above her by the living shrubbery. Sametria managed to cut herself free with her scimitar and fell to the ground gasping for air.

"Drop it!" Sametria heard a voice roar out as a beam of flames streaked passed her and hit the living shrubbery. The flames seemed to do little, as the moisture within the plant monster seemed to protect it a little from the fire. She heard arrows streak by and lodge into the monster as two dark-skinned humanoids ran passed her. She rolled over to her back and forced her eyes to clear. It was her friends. The living shrubbery slapped its heavy vines at Morglum, but the half-orc held his axes up to block. Morglum buried Mar Doldon deep into the mound of living shrubbery, spewing out the moisture that gave it life. Aleiz sunk his kukri into living shrubbery as deep as he could force it. The living shrubbery slumped over motionless. Sadie growled and barked at it before running over to Sametria's side.

"Are you alright?" Taegrid asked reaching down to help Sametria stand. Sametria took her friend's hand and stood up with his help. Her body hurt from the battle with the mound of living shrubbery.

"I'm fine thanks," Sametria managed to gasp as she noticed a new member in their group. A man with long red hair and beard braided together and brandishing a short spear in hand.

"We came after you when we found out there is a way to put things right," Taegrid told her with some excitement.

"I found a way as well. Before we discuss this though, who is that?" Sametria groaned in pain. Taegrid knew without looking, who she was referring to.

"That is Thortwerg. He is a barbarian from the north with dreams of sailing the open seas. We didn't have the heart to tell him that we have ever seen the ocean either." Taegrid responded quietly.

"You have to admit, that is a pretty good dream." Sametria said pondering the thought of open seas and salt-water air in her face. "After we put things right, I might have to go with him."

"It does sound like an adventure doesn't it?" Taegrid joined in the dream.

"Thortwerg set up camp," Morglum barked as he came stomping back wiping Mar Doldon clean of the liquid. "Did you miss us?" Morglum asked with a smile. Sametria returned the smile.

"I did indeed. I was on my way to rejoin you in fact. I found my path and will need your help to restore Athyx." Sametria claimed.

"Uh, we were also told about how we could restore Athyx, but have no means to travel to the Ethereal Plane." Gilthanus informed Sametria as he joined the conversation.

"Who told you?" Sametria asked sounding as though she was accusing him of something.

"My mother," Gilthanus answered defensively.

"For a devil, your mother seems very helpful." Sametria warned.

"I take no offense, but until she crosses the line I think we can trust her." Gilthanus suggested.

"Well she doesn't seem to be steering you away. I was told that what I was looking for was on the Ethereal Plane as well. It's a relic called the Marble of Godly Doom." Sametria shared.

"Well talk some more after we set up camp," Taegrid offered before turning to help Thortwerg. Sadie sniffed the air and started whimpering. The air smelt like smoke and suddenly everyone smelt it.

"Fire," Taegrid warned. Dancing flames could be seen burning in the distance beyond a tree line of the clearing they stood in. The fire was just ahead of them, but before they could do anything about the forest fire, two hulking figures the size of ogres came running out of the flames. They both wielded twenty-foot long spears with razors running down half of its length to the tip where it held a fine sharp, barbed tip. Gilthanus handed Sametria a potion.

"You might want to drink this," Gilthanus warned and Sametria drank without hesitation. It closed her wounds completely and revitalized her stamina. There was something off about these large monsters. They looked like orcs the size of ogres. Maggots crawled on their bodies beneath their armor, which was tacked on with bolts right to their flesh. The monsters seemed to be masters with their Hell-spears and rallied into a tactical formation as the companions charged in to meet them head on. Gilthanus cast a spell and sent several magical projectiles streaking at one of the foul creatures. They struck its armor and burst harmlessly on impact. Taegrid's arrows could not pierce the armor either. Morglum ducked under one of the dangerous spears as he came I full force and battered his axes against the monster's armor plates, putting dents in the plates. Aleiz performed a series of flips and handsprings until he came into range and leaped over the spears, before stabbing his kukri through the exposed flesh on one of the fiends. It did not go deep, but the blade still managed to hit a vital artery. Blood poured out, but the maggots devoured it before it reached beyond the armor plating and almost landed on Aleiz as if they were looking to feast upon him as well. Morglum had to dodge a burst of maggots that poured from the wound Aleiz created. It seemed that the maggots were almost symbiotic to the war devils. Aleiz clung to his kukri as the fiend collapsed to its knees cursing the vermin-kissed elf in its native infernal language. Gilthanus recognized these monsters from some of his readings in his new book. They were war devils, fiends bred for war in Hell. Why would devils be attacking them, when his mother was trying to help them? Gilthanus wondered if his mother was trying to misdirect them in some way. Thortwerg rushed up before he realized how dangerous the battle was and roared as he stabbed his spear at the second war devil. He was caught out of nowhere by the war devil's hellish spear and was knocked aside with a bloody shoulder.

"Stay Sadie," Sametria ordered and her wolf obeyed. The brave half-elf ran up to help the wounded barbarian. She came up under the spear of the war devil and sunk her sword blade into its lower abdomen. It collapsed to the ground as it clutched its wound. Maggots seemed to eat the blood, stopping any fatal bleeding instantly. Several maggots burst from the wound towards her. She felt the maggots land on her flesh and begin to devour her skin, before they died and fell from her body. They chewed at her flesh and wounded her and that was enough to panic the half-elf. Both of the war devils stood up wounded and struck down with their hellish spears at the foes that stood before them. Sametria rolled out of the way and helped Thortwerg to his feet.

"Get out of here now," Sametria barked at the man she had yet to meet. The other war devil tried to run the razor covered haft of his spear down across the dangling vermin-kissed elf's body, but he was wrapped in shadows from his cloak, vanished from the war devil's body, and popped back into view a short distance away. The war devil could still reach Aleiz and lunged with his spear at him once again, but the vermin-kissed elf was wrapped in shadows from his cloak and disappeared again, popping back into view in a different location right behind the war devil. Aleiz continued to beat at the war devil armor with his spells. Morglum pounded the armor and still could not find a weak point as Aleiz had. Thortwerg was not a coward, but he knew when he was of no use. He took off running back to Gilthanus with his spear in hand. Aleiz dug his enchanted kukri in flesh exposed near the war devil's lower back and watched as it exploded in a burst of maggots and fire, being banished back to Hell. Again, the maggots nearly covered Morglum and Aleiz. However, the two of them rolled out of the way and readied to face the next war devil. Taegrid charged up to help Sametria with his sickle now in hand, but the war devil caught him with the end of his spear and knocked him to the ground short of reaching the fiend. Luckily, Taegrid had his sickle up and it took the impact from the spear, protecting him from the razors and spear tip. Sametria rolled behind the war devil as she cast a revitalizing spell on herself. The war devil knew that the half-elf he fought was his mark. He would please Villisca even if he fell this night. He spun around and stabbed his spear through the body of Sametria, impaling her to the ground. Her body would have fallen if the spear let her, but she remained supported in an upright position, unconscious and blood running down the spear to saturate the ground. Her sword fell from her open hand. Sadie no longer stayed where her master had instructed her to remain. She roared to life and leaped in at the war devil, but the fiendish monster kicked the wolf aside with a heavy boot.

"Sam," all of her friends cried out as they saw the horrible sight of their ally impaled to the ground motionless with a hellish spear. Gilthanus bombarded the second war devil with his spells, blasting away at its armor as he had the first. Morglum saw exposed flesh and clove at it with both of his axes, spilling maggots by the hundreds and even thousands out on him as the war devil burst into flames and vanished, banished back to Hell. Morglum shook the dead maggots from his raw, bloody body and watched as the spear vanished. Sametria fell to the ground, but Aleiz was there to catch her and ease her to the ground gently.

"Taegrid," Morglum called hoping that the cat man was already on his way to save Sametria from her wounds.

"I need fire to cauterize this wound," Taegrid shouted as he ripped a bandage to place over the wound. He chewed some herbs in his mouth to saturate and mix their contents as Gilthanus chanted a spell that scorched the flesh of his friend and stopped the bleeding that would surely kill her, first on her chest. Taegrid took some of the herb and covered the chest wound before bandaging it. He carefully rolled her over to inspect her back. Taegrid made sure that her spine had not been pierced first before letting Gilthanus cast his spell again to stop the bleeding. When Gilthanus had stopped the bleeding on her back, Taegrid smeared the remaining chewed herbs over the wound and bandaged it as well.

"Give me a potion as well. I will force it down her throat." Taegrid commanded his friend. Gilthanus promptly pulled out a potion and handed it to the cat man. Taegrid carefully forced it down her throat and into her stomach. It was a long moment until she took a breath. The companions had just found her again. They did not want to lose her already.

"She will live," Taegrid said as he laid Sametria down flat. "Now we must tend to this forest fire."

"How, we have no water and the fire is too great?" Gilthanus asked, as he looked around frantic. Sadie lay next to Sametria and stared at her as she rested. Taegrid looked around at what they had and thought quickly of how they could save the forest.

"Morglum cut down the trees that are already on fire. Do not stop until they are all cut down low to the ground. The rest of you start digging a trench around the burning trees." Taegrid ordered and they all followed. It took them hours of work to get the fire under control. Finally, as the black sun began to rise over the horizon, they had it in a controlled burn. They all passed out from exhaustion beneath the blanket of trees to protect them from the sun or view of any undead minions that passed overhead.

Taegrid awoke a few hours after they had passed out from exhaustion in a panic. The smoke had to of attracted the attention of someone. What were his options he wondered? He could lead his friends to the ruined village in the trees that Sametria once called home and hope that no one would think to search there. It was the closest option and possibly their only option.

"Everybody up now," Taegrid ordered as he roused his friends. "Morglum you need to carry Sametria, but carefully." Morglum nodded as he shook the cobwebs out of his head and rubbed sleep from his eyes. The companions gathered their belongings and packed them up. Thortwerg grabbed Sametria's pack and slung it over his back while Morglum gently picked up the half-elf.

"The rest of you, form a perimeter around Morglum and follow me." Taegrid instructed. His friends knew not to argue and followed the ranger's instructions. Taegrid led them around the smoldering area of the forest that was now a very large clearing where smoke spewed into the sky. They moved cautiously and carefully through the undergrowth of the forest for several miles. Taegrid led them to an area within the forest and stopped, looking up into the trees. He had found it, the ruined tree village that he was on his way to warn about the wraiths, and the home of Sametria. No dead bodies littered the area. It was as if something had devoured them entirely. Taegrid led his companions up a spiraling staircase that wrapped around the base of a wide tree, leading up in to the canopy of the tree. Catwalks and bridges stretched out to other trees and a shelter was at the center, constructed around the tree itself. Sadie looked around and sniffed the air. It was her master's home. She smelt familiar scents in the air. She remembered this was the place she came to when a friendly voice had called out to her in the forest. Taegrid opened the door and checked it for any lingering traces of the wraiths. It was dark. Gilthanus spoke a single word and his sword illuminated the inside of the tree house like a torch. Taegrid moved around and lit candles and lanterns to light the whole house.

"Lay her on the bed in here," Taegrid instructed after he finished checking the house and lighting every room to make sure no wraith hid within the shadows. Morglum entered the room with their badly wounded friend and laid her on the cozy bed. Taegrid unstrapped her weapon belt and hung it on a bureau within her reach. Taegrid and Morglum made certain that Sametria was comfortable before leaving her to rest.

"Where are we?" Gilthanus asked as he noted every cupboard in the kitchen was full of tree bark, roots, fruits and vegetables. Taegrid smiled. The druids, at least most of the druids had been vegetarians. Meat was a rare think to eat for them having so few untainted animals left in the forest, they tried to preserve the life that did remain and chose not to eat meat. It was no wonder that the druids were not physically strong. Sametria should have been physically stronger than she was having a human mother. Her diet prevented it. If ever she ate meat, her muscles would properly develop and store energy that would serve her well in combat. The companions made themselves at home in the tree house. Aleiz stared out the window in awe. How could such a place as this be a ghost town he wondered? He left the house where his friends rested with Gilthanus in tow.

"Wait for me," Gilthanus called as he followed the vermin-kissed elf. Together they scouted the tree village. There was no sign of any life here. There were not even any dead bodies to prove someone had lived here in ages other than the fact that the houses were clean and food was not all rotten. Only a little dust covered tables. There were several tree houses and places of business all built within the canopies of the trees. Aleiz and Gilthanus wandered through several of them hoping to find something, anything that would help them keep their sanity. All that they wound up finding were homes that housed the druids and rooms where children and adults once dwelled. The wraiths were completely evil. Vermin-kissed elves had slaughtered children before, but luckily, Aleiz had not ever had to kill a child. After everything he had experienced, he did not think that he had it in him to commit such an evil act of violence.

"What does your mother say about the devils we faced?" Aleiz asked his friend suddenly when they were alone. The question put Gilthanus on the defense. He suddenly felt that the vermin-kissed elf might not be as good of a friend as he had hoped.

"She has not spoken to me since the last time we saw her." Gilthanus answered truthfully.

"What do you think she would say if you asked her about the devils?" Aleiz asked. Gilthanus watched his friend carefully. He seemed to be inching his hand towards his kukri. Gilthanus did not want to hurt his friend but if he had to, he thought of a spell right away that would keep the vermin-kissed elf from hurting him but not kill him.

"I am sure she would try and deceive us if they were indeed her minions." Gilthanus again answered honestly.
"If she set them upon us, whose side would you be on?" Aleiz dared to ask. Gilthanus was certain that the vermin-kissed elf meant to end him here and now if he did not answer carefully.
"If she sent them upon us my friend, I would have no choice but to choose your side. You are all my friends." Gilthanus responded. Aleiz turned around with his hands upon his hips.
"If she was testing you at our expense, would you still share those feelings for us if it meant great power and wealth as you desire so much the same as I?" Aleiz asked seriously and ever so intently.
"Even if she never again helped me or recognized me, I would choose you first Aleiz." Gilthanus answered wholeheartedly.
"Me? What about the others?" Aleiz gasped in confusion.
"I feel closest to you for some reason. They are my friends, but I would kill them for you if I had to." Gilthanus answered and shocked Aleiz. The vermin-kissed elf did not know what to say next, but he understood what Gilthanus meant. They had bonded more so than any of the others. It was not anything other than two good friends bonding more like brothers. They shared a laugh and relaxed. They had no idea that Villisca was back in Hell within the castle and lands that she ruled sitting in her throne pondering her next move to gain the devotion and loyalty of her son. With Viscus in power, no good deity held the dark planes in check by sealing the gates to the world of Athyx. Villisca could come and go as she pleased, as so many devils and demons did. It was a world of souls for the taking and not even the celestials could stop them from making their enticing deals. The celestials only seemed to get involved personally when the beings of the lower planes traveled to Athyx with an army. Small numbers never gained their attention and that was how the fiends continued to go unnoticed.

Chapter Eight:

Calvin the Mad and his small army of wraiths saw the black plume of smoke rising from the Great Forest far away, from where they now resided. They pondered attacking the orc caves again after their foolish retreat from the daylight spell, but had decided against it after losing so many wraiths the last time they had faced the orcs. They had foolishly believed that the daylight spell was a sunbeam spell. The smoke however had gained his full attention as a possible sign of life in the Great Forest. He knew that there were still animals untainted by the black sun that dwelled within the forest. The wraiths often hunted such animals, even the tainted ones.

"Wraiths," Calvin the Mad hissed. "We go to the Great Forest to hunt." Calvin the Mad commanded and flew off in the lead with the sixty plus wraiths that followed him in tow. They flew in a formation that created a blanket of darkness in the sky.

The wraiths flew for hours and what would have taken anyone else days without a horse to travel. They were tireless and constantly on the move. The smoldering clearing in the forest was about a hundred yards in diameter, and almost a perfect circle. Fallen trees still smoked and burned hot, but they did not expand their borders of destruction any further. A trench had been dug and many trees had been cut down to prevent the flames from continuing their path of destruction.

"Someone prevented this fire from spreading further," Calvin the Mad hissed to his minions. "Scour the lands and find whoever did this the wraith ordered and his minions scattered in all directions entering the Great Forest and searching for any life that it might be hiding. Calvin the Mad remembered the druid village nearby. He flew off to investigate it for any surviving inhabitants. Five wraiths followed their master, passing through the trees as though they did not even exist. The six wraiths sped through the forest with nothing to slow them down and halted suddenly. Ahead of them in the trees were the homes of the druids that Calvin the Mad had led the slaughter on nearly a month ago. They began swooping around the area and checking the tree houses for any sign of life. The village was small and would be completely checked in a short time at the rate the wraiths moved. A distant light caught their attention and the wraiths shrieked their hideous call that would summon the rest of their forces in a matter of minutes before swooping in towards the tree house.

Aleiz and Gilthanus heard the shrieks and ran over to a window to peer outside. Six dark ghostly figures swooped in at the tree house where their friends remained. It was lit up bright so no wraith could sneak up on any of them.

"We have to help them," Aleiz gasped and took off running towards the well-lit house with his kukri already in hand. Gilthanus shrugged and followed his vermin-kissed elf friend as he drew his enchanted long sword. The two elves would not reach the house before the wraiths and hoped that their friends had heard the shrieks of the wraiths as well. Two arrows flew out of an open window to answer that concern and struck one of the wraiths. They had no vital organs keeping them alive. They were made of raw negative energy and it would take a lot to bring them down, unlike the minor kobold wraiths, they faced a few days ago. Until the wraiths got closer, only Taegrid could harm them. Five of the wraiths continued their charge from the air, streaking into the tree house and passing through the walls that sheltered the companions. Two wraiths came in clawing at Morglum and Thortwerg. They seemed to take away a piece of their souls as they clawed them. The fifth came in at Taegrid, but the sleek cat man rolled to the side and let it pass by. That was the defiant cat man from the orc caves Calvin the Mad recognized him and aimed an outstretched shadowy hand out towards him. A fiery blast was unleashed and streaked down at Taegrid. Taegrid saw a flash of light in the corner of his eyes and rolled forward as the eldritch blast struck the floor where he had been standing and singed the boards. Taegrid smiled without even looking out the window, he knew it was the wraith that they had encountered in the orc caves that claimed he had been responsible for the destruction of Taegrid's and Sametria's villages. He spun around and released a barrage of arrows at Calvin the Mad. Thortwerg did not have an enchanted weapon that allowed him to even stand a chance of defeating the wraiths. These foul creations were devouring him and there was nothing he could do about it. Morglum hacked at a wraith as it clawed him and ripped away some of the negative energy that fueled it. Aleiz rounded a corner and came to the catwalk that led to the tree house where his friends battled for their lives. Gilthanus was close behind and sent three magic missiles at Calvin the Mad, but they passed through his incorporeal body harmlessly. Calvin the Mad laughed at the elf, taunting him.

Morglum and Thortwerg were nearly falling over drained from the life robbing claws that ripped away at their souls. Calvin the Mad sent his eldritch blast down at Gilthanus as he ran towards the tree house for cover. It struck the catwalk behind him and blasted through the planks. Taegrid continued to fire his bow at Calvin the Mad, blinded by hatred and completely unaware of the danger his friends were in. A bright light suddenly erupted within the room and Sametria stood in the door of the bedroom leaning on the doorframe, which now illuminated both rooms like the sun they longed to have again. The wraiths inside shrieked in pain and sunk through the floor unable to move or fly until they were outside the house and the radius of the bright light. They hissed as they recovered and flew to their master for sanctuary. Aleiz dove in through the open window and rolled to his feet with kukri ready to cut down any wraith that might remain, but none did. His eyes stung from the bright light coming from the doorway where Sametria stood leaning. Thortwerg and Morglum fell to their knees vomiting from the wounds bestowed on their souls from the wraiths. Gilthanus stopped outside and focused his attention on the lead wraith that taunted him and sent the eldritch flames at him. The sorcerer sent a ray of scorching heat at the wraith and this time the spell took hold, singing the energies that manifested the wraith.

"Kill the sorcerer," Calvin the Mad hissed to his minions and the five wraiths suddenly lurched in his direction.

"Get inside Gilthanus," Aleiz shouted in panic. The five wraiths struck their claws at the sorcerer as they passed by, but some sort of ectoplasm surrounded his body from their incorporeal touch. Gilthanus smiled at Calvin the Mad and returned the taunting laugh. He had chanted the spell on himself when they head the wraiths shriek before he started running after Aleiz. The spell he learned from his new book that now aided him from their enemies made him feel very powerful in the eyes of his companions. Calvin the Mad sent another stream of eldritch fire down at the mocking sorcerer, but Gilthanus rolled out of the way before it ripped through the planks he stood on. Taegrid put two more arrows into the wraith, weakening its hold on reality even more. Calvin the Mad knew he was defeated and had to retreat.

"Kill them all," he hissed as he took flight up through the trees and out of sight of any harmful projectiles.

"I will finish you!" Taegrid roared as the wraiths circled Gilthanus. He was the only victim they could target outside the harmful magically summoned daylight. Sametria felt the cries of the tree as the wraith began to fly through its branches as though it was not there. The tree felt the coldness of the wraith and somehow sent the empathic cry to her. She instinctively chanted a healing spell and palmed the tree, discharging the positive healing energy. It passed through the tree like electricity through metal as the wraith passed through its canopy. The energy wrapped around the wraith as it tried to escape and wracked it with pain. Taegrid saw the positive energy outline the entire tree that supported the house they were in and he heard the final shriek of the wraith that he hated so as it was ripped into Oblivion by the spell Sametria had cast. The loss of their master confused the five wraiths that circled Gilthanus and with a shriek that sounded more like a baby's cry for its mother, the wraiths retreated.

"He has been destroyed Taegrid," Sametria claimed as she collapsed from the pain of her wounds.

"Sam," Taegrid gasped as he dropped his bow and ran to her side. He picked her up gently and carried her back to the bed. Sadie returned to the floor at the foot of the bed where Sametria slept. Taegrid covered her up and made sure that her wounds did not rip open before leaving the room. Gilthanus joined his friends inside the tree house with his chest puffed out with pride.

"You did real well," Aleiz said with a smile to his friend. Taegrid came out of the room and checked on Thortwerg and Morglum.

"I'm sorry I let my anger blind me. I should have targeted the wraiths inside the house first." Taegrid apologized to his sick friends as he helped them one at a time into chairs.

"Will I recover from those damn things?" Thortwerg asked feeling as if he was on the verge of death.

"In time Thortwerg, your health will return." Taegrid answered truthfully.

"Good," Thortwerg moaned as he passed out where he sat. Morglum fell asleep as well as soon Taegrid sat him down. Taegrid looked to Aleiz and Gilthanus.

"What were you two doing?" Taegrid asked the suspiciously.

"We were searching other houses," Gilthanus answered honestly.

"And making sure that Gilthanus didn't need to be killed," Aleiz added catching a humorous look from Gilthanus. Taegrid, Aleiz and Gilthanus stood watch all night while their friends rested. Only one person on watch would be a foolish. If any wraiths were brave enough to return, they would be ready. Sametria's spell lit the two rooms for over an hour before it dissipated back to the normal illumination of the candles and lanterns.

"I'm going to tend to our friends. Keep your eyes peeled." Taegrid said as he turned to check their wounded friends. Gilthanus and Aleiz looked at one another.

"Would you really kill me?" Gilthanus asked sounding hurt by the notion. Aleiz smiled at the surface elf.

"I would hope you would do the same for me," Aleiz chuckled. Gilthanus smiled at the chaotic black skinned elf.

"In a heartbeat," Gilthanus claimed. Taegrid returned after he tended to their friends, his tail waved gracefully as he approached as though he was relaxed.

"I think we are going to be alright. If the wraiths have not returned yet, then they probably will not at all. You guys can get some rest. I'll keep watch." Taegrid offered.

"I could use the sleep. I don't really feel too well." Gilthanus said suddenly feeling very nauseous.

"What's the matter? Are you bothered bout what I said? I was just kidding you know." Aleiz claimed as Gilthanus staggered outside to get some fresh air. The nausea suddenly stopped and instead he felt pain all over his body as though his skin was drying out and crackling. When the pain stopped, Gilthanus looked at his hands. They were almost as rough as leather to the touch.

"What is this?" Gilthanus asked in confusion as Aleiz approached him.

"Are you alright?" the vermin-kissed elf asked as he saw his friend shaking.

"I don't know. It is as if my body just altered itself in some way. My skin seems rougher to the touch now, almost like leather." Gilthanus claimed. Aleiz took his hands in his own and felt them. Gilthanus was right. Aleiz looked to his friend as he let go suddenly.

"It's your devil blood coming into play." Aleiz gasped.

"Am I going to grow horns and wings as well?" Gilthanus asked almost ready to cry.

"I'm not sure. I have never encountered one such as you that develops this slowly. I have only heard of those that are born with deformities. They are known as half-devils, half-demons and half-celestials." Aleiz answered honestly.

"Will the others kill me because of this?" Gilthanus asked suddenly paranoid. Aleiz wondered that as well.

"We should leave," Aleiz suggested. "Together. We can hunt for treasure together." Gilthanus looked at his dear vermin-kissed elf friend.

"Should we tell them why or at least say goodbye?" Gilthanus asked. Aleiz looked back and saw Taegrid eyeing them curiously.

"I will tell them something. Wait here." Aleiz instructed as he turned around and began approaching the cat man. What would he say to make them understand, but not come after them he wondered? Aleiz entered back into the tree house and looked the cat man in his eyes.

"We won't kill a friend Aleiz," Taegrid said with promise.

"You heard?" Aleiz asked sounding panicked.

"I hear a lot my friend," Taegrid answered with a calming smile.

"I'll go tell Gilthanus then," Aleiz said with a slight stutter.

"Make sure to tell him that whatever changes he goes through, that we are here for him." Taegrid assured the vermin-kissed elf. Aleiz nodded and left to inform Gilthanus of the good news. They were friends. They had bonded through several battles already. Most warriors did not see as much action as they had in such a little time as they had.

Over the next few weeks, the companions recovered from their wounds, spiritual and physical. Taegrid developed some sort of an affinity with felines and found that he could sense them when they were near. It was as though he was becoming what his people called a cat lord. Many non cat-folk have developed the bonds with specific animal types and become a lord of that grouping of animals, even having conversations with the animals at times. Taegrid wondered if that was what might be happening to him.

They were all going through changes in some way or another. Sametria had a growing bond with her wolf, Sadie. Morglum had practically begun to worship his mithral great axe. The wraiths touch had caused him a great amount of suffering for nearly two weeks. Thortwerg suffered about the same amount of time from the emptiness they felt inside. The seven friends seemed to feel happy for those few short weeks as they recovered and bonded. None of them knew where their path was going to lead them exactly, but they knew that danger and adventure was a way of life to them now. They knew that they had to travel to a strange plane now and after all of them knew the information that Villisca and Vortis had shared, they were aware that what they did not know was what the true anger was. Sametria had Gilthanus examine her sword and study it while they were healing. What the elf sorcerer had discovered was astonishing. He sat down with her in private on one particular day when the others were outside training or gathering food.

"Your sword is imbued with a great amount of magic. Strangely enough, as far as I can tell it has to be unlocked by its wielder as your bond with it strengthens and you build a legacy with it. Your legacy to defend Athyx is what seems to fuel it." Gilthanus explained to her.

"Why does it speak the name of Tevlos whenever it is swung?" Sametria asked the sorcerer.

"It was forged by Tevlos to defend nature," Gilthanus answered matter-of-factly. Sametria took the adamantine forged blade and looked at her friend.

"I vowed to protect this world form unnatural beings that do not belong here. You belong here Gilthanus. I will not kill you." Sametria promised and caught a confused look from the elf.

"Taegrid told all of us that you feared what we thought about you possibly changing into a devil of some kind and because of that we might want to kill you. Understand this, my friend, just because a devil took part in your conception, does not mean you do not belong here. You are an elf first because you were born an elf of Athyx. You are changing now for some reason because of who your mother is, but she has only what dominion over you, you allow her to have." Sametria stood up and rested a comforting hand on his shoulder before leaving him to absorb it all. They were truly his friends and Gilthanus knew that without a doubt now.

Sametria came down the stairs that spiraled around the massive tree to the forest floor where the rest of her friends were. Gilthanus had followed her down a short distance behind. There they practiced with their weapons. They all stopped practicing when Gilthanus and Sametria arrived.

"Are we leaving soon?" Taegrid asked the half-elf. She smiled as she was taken by surprise.

"Who all is going?" Sametria asked, thinking that everyone had other personal goals.

"We are like a family of orphans. We have decided that we are better off sticking together." Morglum barked.

"We have a very long journey to the south that we have to make on foot. I have no issues moving through the thick underbrush, but the rest of you do and that will also slow us down. Not to mention the dangers of the wilds we will face along the way." Sametria sounded like she was trying to dissuade everyone from going.

"It sounds like a challenge," Gilthanus said as he returned the friendly hand on her shoulder now.

"It sounds like fun," Morglum barked.

"Hoo-ha!" Thortwerg shouted.

"Get your packs ready and I'll have a look at the map," Sametria instructed her friends. With several nods, the companions began preparing their backpacks, filling them with food, bedrolls, water skins, tools and other miscellaneous supplies they might need that they scavenged from the empty tree houses. It took them a while to pack their backpacks and make sure that they were not forgetting anything. The companions were heading south and following the map to their destination marked as the Ethereal Temple deep in the Swamps of

Mordakai. The Great Forest was called the Great Forest for a very good reason though. It was massive in size, stretching for miles in every direction. They were nearest to the northern borders that met with the open plains and then the mountain range of the north. Beyond that was the Great Frozen Wastelands. According to their map, the Great Forest stretched so far to the south that several lonely mountains were surrounded by the forest. Taegrid guessed that it would take them a month to reach the edge of the Swamps of Mordakai and then another week of travel through the swamps before they reached the temple. They were well aware of how long their journey was. There was no open road or trails to ease their trip. They had to cut a path the whole way it seemed. The good news was that as far as they knew, nobody hunted them any longer. The Great Forest was once full of life from elves to animals and even humans and satyrs and centaurs. There were once so many different beings dwelling within the Great Forest that they had many prospering communities. Now, if they came across any life of any kind, they considered it a blessing. Sametria and Taegrid sighted a deer on their first day of travel. Morglum wanted to hack it down and feast, but Sametria and Taegrid advised against it if ever he wanted to taste deer on a regular basis again. They were so rare that if they had killed that one, it was possible it would be the last in a long time if not ever. The wraiths had done a great job at slaughtering everything they found within the Great Forest. It was rumored by Vortis that they had not yet reached beyond the Great Forest. It would be a long time before the companions could know. Their second day out was even less promising. They did not even see a chipmunk along the way; the forest was so empty of life. It was not until they had been for their first week that they came across a thunderous noise.

"What's that?" Thortwerg growled as he clutched his spear tightly.

"The river," Sametria answered.

"A river?" Morglum gasped. "No one said anything about a river."

"It's alright Morglum. We plan on keeping it to our left as we continue." Sametria explained.

"We don't have to cross it," Taegrid assured the half-orc.

"I'm not scared of the damned thing," Morglum growled feeling quite insulted. "Why don't we use the river to cut our travel time down?" Morglum made a suggestion that blew the druid and ranger away.

"That is a very good idea Morglum," Taegrid said sounding quite enthused.

"But we don't know the river. It may be full of rapids and waterfalls." Sametria warned.

"That sounds like a lot of fun Sametria. Thanks for telling us." Taegrid said as he patted the half-elf and moved ahead to investigate. Sametria was silenced with confusion.

"Yes Sam, that truly sounds like a lot of fun." Morglum agreed as he followed Taegrid.

"Are they crazy?" Sametria managed to ask as she turned to Gilthanus and Aleiz. Sadie looked up at her master, feeling her confusion and seemed to smile. Gilthanus and Aleiz shrugged before following after them and leaving Sametria to her personal thoughts. She looked at her wolf, which now stood as high as her chest from the ground, without standing on its hind legs.

"What, you think it would be fun too?" Sametria gasped as she realized Sadie was smiling at the thought of playing in the water. "Alright, but I have a bad feeling about this." Sametria and Sadie moved through the underbrush with ease and caught up to their companions as the forest seemed to open up and part to allow the life giving substance to pass through. With the tree line behind them, they moved easier. They stood twenty-feet above with a sheer drop from a rock face that they were now standing upon. Below them was the rushing river that they heard just a short distance away. A light mist was felt on their faces, but Sametria and Sadie did not enjoy it as much as the others did, because she had chosen to suffer from the black sun's ill effects by sacrificing the magical medallion that had been given to her to protect her. With the parting of the trees, the sun's rays reminded her of why they were on their journey to begin with. She had developed a strong fortitude and resisted the sun's ill effects because of her constant exposure to it. Sadie had also developed this and because of it, they were not sickened most of the time. However, they did feel its drain as though it wanted to devour the entire planet within its constant darkness forever.

"Anyone got a boat?" Morglum asked, hoping that one of them at least knew how to make one. The sudden excitement was brought to an end with the fact that they had all overlooked until now. None of them had a boat.

"Damn!" Taegrid growled in defeat. Sametria saw the sudden displeasure upon everyone's faces.

"Go find a large log and make sure it's at least thirty feet long," Sametria instructed her friends. Morglum glanced around looking as though he was going to state something obvious.

"Could I just cut down a tree and cut it to size?" Morglum finally asked.

"Yes but you won't have to cut it to size," Sametria answered and the half-orc sped off to find a suitable tree that he hoped would not be missed.

"Cut one down where we can access the river," Sametria added. Morglum followed the river south until he could finally reach the river bank without climbing down a cliff and began hacking away at a tree that stood near with Mar Doldon. His friends had followed close by and watched as the half-orc took out his aggression on the poor, defenseless tree. The tree finally gave and the sound of wood crackling as it fell seemed to bring life to the forest where there was none. The sounds of the wild were nowhere to be heard in this area of the forest. The tree slammed to the ground with a loud thump and hit a couple of other trees along the way snapping branches from their lengths.

"How's that one?" Morglum asked as he turned to face Sametria and rested the head of Mar Doldon on his shoulder.

"It will do nicely," Sametria responded as she approached the fallen tree.

"Are you sure? I can do it again if you like." Morglum offered.

"It's quite fine Morglum," Sametria assured as she kneeled low and chanted a spell. Taegrid stepped up close to the half-orc and leaned in.

"You would be wise not to offer to waste trees or anything nature related around her," the cat man whispered. Morglum looked over at Taegrid with a look of ignorance.

"Oops," was all that Morglum could manage looking quite embarrassed. Sametria placed her hand on the fallen tree as she finished her spell and the wood began to alter its shape. Branched fell off as the log itself hollowed out two sections and formed into two canoes. Other portions of the log fashioned into paddles.

"That's a nice spell Sam," Taegrid complimented the half-elf as she stood up.

"I thought it would come in handy. Let's get them into the river." Sametria instructed as she picked up the paddles and placed three in each canoe. Morglum, Aleiz and Gilthanus grabbed one while Taegrid, Sametria and Thortwerg grabbed the other. They waded out into the river shin deep. The water was swift and cold. They sat their canoes down in the water and made sure that Sametria's magic had fashioned leak proof canoes before they climbed in them. Sadie tromped through the water and hopped in the back of the canoe Sametria held and the canoe seemed to sink slightly in the rear. The current grasped the canoes before the last person had even climbed in. They were nearly flipped as Thortwerg climbed in his and Morglum in the other. The water seemed grab them and pull them down the length of the river. It seemed as though the river was alive as it pulled them towards rocks and rushing white water that sounded like thunder.

"Paddle!" Sametria shouted, but only those in her canoe could hear her. Aleiz saw what the others were doing with the paddles in their canoe and grabbed one out of his canoe as well.

"Do what they're doing." Aleiz instructed as he tried digging the paddle into the rushing water. It felt as though the water wanted to take the paddle out of his grip. He clutched it tightly and tried to keep them from running into any rocks. They all felt rocks bounce off the sides of their canoes and grind the bottoms as they traveled the length of the river with such speed that it would take a horse to keep up on land. It was tiring and the water was cold. Their muscles seemed to ache from the new motions that they were unfamiliar with. The river tossed them to the side as it curved around a bend and they were flung towards the shoreline. The companions paddled their canoes away with ease and kept within the current until finally the river seemed to calm as it widened and slowed a bit. They could relax for the moment, it seemed and let the canoes just carry them with the peaceful river flow. They were wet and cold and had gone several more miles than they would have on foot.

"Let's pull out soon and set up camp," Taegrid called over to the other canoe and Aleiz nodded that he had heard his instructions. The two canoes finally came ashore and were pulled far away from the cold river water and flipped upside down to dump the water they had taken on. Taegrid had a fire built quickly and they sat around it warming up for a long while before they finished setting up their campsite. Their muscles were sore from the workout of the river. It was as though they had competed against the river in some sort of contact sport and they had lost the first round. Thortwerg had enjoyed it a great deal and studied what they had done wrong. He realized that how they held their paddles and slapped the water was making them work harder. He figured if they dug the paddles into the water rather than slapping them down and then pushed the water behind them, that it would be less of a strain. Thortwerg shared his thoughts with the others as they sat around the fire eating. They all thought that for a barbarian, Thortwerg had a knack for water related subjects. He had the heart to be a sailor and the mind to go with it, it seemed. Morglum knew that they needed meat to go with the nuts and berries they ate.

"You think there are any fish in the river?" Morglum asked Taegrid quietly. The thought sent more hope into Taegrid's heart. He loved fish.

"Let's go and see," Taegrid offered as he stood up and walked out to the river. The cat man waded out into the cold water about waste deep. Even the calm current seemed to try to pull his legs out from him. He took his cloak and tried to use it like a net in the swift water. He felt nothing collect but small gravel that the current carried. Taegrid turned towards Morglum who stood on the shore with a dry blanket for Taegrid when he returned and shook his head. Morglum slumped. Taegrid felt something else hit his cloak and the power of it almost ripped the wet cloth out of his hands. Taegrid lost his balance and fell over, splashing into the water and beneath its surface. He held the cloak tight as he closed it off and stood back up before he was carried too far out.

"We have fish," Taegrid roared as he rose from beneath the water. That night, they feasted. Sametria ate fish for the first time ever and enjoyed its taste. It fed them the protein that their sore muscles needed to recover. It filled their bellies as well and helped their bodies stay warm as they slept.

The friends traveled for weeks down the river until it branched off to the east. Taegrid pointed to the channel that continued south. Fish jumped here and wildlife still existed this far to the south. The sight of the wildlife, such as the bears swiping at fish that jumped up river filled Taegrid and Sametria with hope, that they still had a chance to restore their world. The channel south ran for several miles before the water turned murky and seemed to run over the landscape like floodwaters. Trees and undergrowth grew from beneath the waters and the small amounts of land that barley stood above the waters of the swamps.

"This must be the Swamps of Mordakai," Sametria whispered. There was an eerie feeling about the foreign landscape. They ran out of river and ran their canoes ashore.

"We're on foot from here," Sametria said as she hopped out of the canoe. Sadie leaped out and sniffed the air.

"They were some nice boats. It's a shame we have to leave them behind." Morglum stated as he hopped up and out of his canoe.

"Actually they are canoes and with a canoe, you can paddle up river so long as the current isn't too terribly strong." Taegrid claimed. Thortwerg absorbed the information like a sponge. He wanted a great ship some day to sail out in the open ocean and explore the world over. The companions all left the canoes behind with the paddles resting inside their hulls.

"How much farther?" Thortwerg asked. He was not close to any of them except Taegrid. He was just another companion along for the adventure as far as the rest of them felt. Everyone else had seemed to bond in some way or another. Morglum was good friends with Sametria, Aleiz and Gilthanus. Taegrid more or less just spoke to everyone. His only close friend was Sametria. Gilthanus and Aleiz were nearly inseparable. Thortwerg just spoke when he needed to and hung around to help when he was needed.

"Another day perhaps," Sametria answered as she looked at her map.

"We have to be cautious here. The ground could swallow you up in a bog or some quicksand if we aren't careful." Taegrid warned as he looked around. The sound of nature sent Taegrid and Sametria into a state of bliss for a moment as they heard the frogs croaking around them and the growls of nearby crocodiles. They could not see any of the crocodiles and when the swamps suddenly grew silent except for the croaking frogs, the companions looked around and saw nothing, nothing but a frog or two hopping from the muddy landscape to a lily pad in the murky waters. Sadie sniffed the air, but all that she smelt was unfamiliar to her.

"Let's move," Taegrid suggested as he and Sametria led the way through the treacherous landscape. The bogs slowed them down a great deal. Aleiz and Gilthanus had difficulties spotting dangerous obstacles such as quicksand and deep bogs, but the others were careful to point them out to one another. They did not want to lose anyone when they were this close to reaching the Ethereal Temple. The map labeled it as such and the only reason they figured was the fact that it was said to house a gateway to the ethereal plane. They waded through a waste deep bog. The water was slightly warmer than the river water because it was not constantly moving, but it was still cold just not cold, enough to cause hypothermia like the river that led them to the swamps. Aleiz felt something brush his leg and hopped to the side as a crocodile passed by him.

"Something big and rough just tried to bite my leg," Aleiz warned his friends as he drew out his enchanted kukri. Sametria knew she would not be able to calm such a creature. She was not familiar with their habitat or ecology.

"Maybe they taste like fish," Morglum chuckled as he spun Mar Doldon in his hands. Sametria looked at Morglum curiously.

"I'm not familiar with them. Perhaps they have enough meat to feed us longer than a single salmon." Sametria wondered.

"You want me to hunt it?" Morglum asked sounding excited.

"Sure," Sametria answered. "Taegrid find us a dry spot to make camp soon. We should get dry." Taegrid nodded and trekked off ahead leaving the others. Morglum moved close to Aleiz.

"Where is it?" The half-orc asked. Aleiz looked all around him and saw nothing. He had only felt it come close to snapping at his leg, but he never saw it.

"I don't know where it went," Aleiz said honestly, as he helped Morglum look around. Sadie started barking at the water suddenly as she felt something come close to seizing her as well. The companions looked at the wolf.

"It must be hunting us," Sametria warned her friends.

"We should probably get out of here then," Morglum suggested, suddenly losing interest in the hunt. They all rushed after Taegrid with hopes that they would be out of the bog soon. The crocodile was hungry and getting frustrated. It had missed its prey twice now. Taegrid felt a clamp on his legs and suddenly he was ripped beneath the waters of the bog with nothing but a ripple to warn his friends.

"Taegrid," Aleiz called out as he witnessed the devastating sight from afar. The companions rushed to the last spot that their friend had been seen. The crocodile held Taegrid beneath the water and tried to thrash him and drown him. Morglum tossed his great axe to Aleiz, who caught it as a reaction. The half-orc dove beneath the murky water and swam until he found the thrashing crocodile that held his friend beneath the water. Morglum swam in close, grabbed a tight hold on the crocodile, and squeezed it until the crocodile let go of his friend. Taegrid swam to the surface with wild splashing movements.

"I can't swim," he cried out a short distance away from his friends. Aleiz tossed Morglum's great axe to Gilthanus, who promptly caught it. The vermin-kissed elf dove out into the water and swam to the panicking cat man.

"Calm down and relax, I got you." Aleiz said as he swam in and grasped a hold of Taegrid. "I'm beginning to wonder how many of us can swim." The vermin-kissed elf's words were heard from those in the shallow water.

"I can't," Gilthanus admitted.

"My back pack weighs me down," Sametria confessed. Everyone knew that the half-elf needed to eat more protein from meats rather than nuts and her other vegetarian sources. Her strength would improve greatly as far as they were concerned.

"I can swim, but my armor isn't the best to be wearing if I do." Thortwerg offered as Aleiz reached them with Taegrid.

"Take him so I can go help Morglum," Aleiz barked as he helped Taegrid to the others reach. Thortwerg took the cat man's hand and Aleiz dove back out into the water with his kukri still in hand. He swam beneath the murky water where he saw the crocodile spinning and thrashing about, stirring up mud and making it difficult to see. The water suddenly turned red within the mud and the thrashing stopped. Aleiz got as close as he dared to and waited for the muck to clear. He saw something rise up from the murky water and followed it up to the surface. Morglum swam back to the others with a dead crocodile over his shoulder with a battle-axe still sticking out of the top of its head. Aleiz saw his friend climb out of the bog and plop down upon the muddy land nearby. The others made their way over to the shore and their panting friend. Aleiz swam gracefully and came right up to the half-orc. Morglum sat in the mud panting with the crocodile still over his shoulder.

"Are you alright?" Aleiz asked as he came up out of the water.

"I gots dinner," Morglum gasped and Aleiz chuckled. They sat around a fire warming their bodies and cooking the crocodile meat that Morglum had wrestled into submission and finished with his battle-axe. The hide was thick and rough and made it difficult to get to the meat, but Morglum managed to skin it and save the hide. Taegrid hung the thick hide out to dry.

"So maybe tomorrow we will reach the temple?" Aleiz asked curiously.

"The temple should be close," Sametria answered. "I dare not split us up again and send a scout after what happened to Taegrid."

"That's understandable now that we know so many of us can't swim," Aleiz scoffed.

"Hey, that's enough. Not everyone has training in as many areas as you or me," Morglum scolded his friend.

"My apologies," Aleiz offered. "I guess what I mean is that this expedition is turning out to be more dangerous than hunting the wraiths."

"We haven't even reached the temple either," Gilthanus added.

"You two are pessimists," Sametria pointed out. "You don't even see the things that we have conquered in such a short time. We have found a chance to make a difference and along the way we have encountered many dangers foreign and domestic that we have survived and conquered."

"She's right," Morglum agreed. "We braved rapids and conquered that cold river."

"And we found wildlife to hunt and use for food and clothing." Taegrid added.

"What will we find inside the temple?" Aleiz asked.

"And what will we find on the ethereal plane?" Gilthanus added.

"You two are pessimists," Morglum spat.

"You should tell us what we should watch out for Gilthanus. You are our arcane source of knowledge. Sametria and I are the nature and survival experts here in the wild." Taegrid pointed out.

"Me, Thortwerg and Sadie are the muscle," Morglum boasted easing the tension from the conversation and sparking a laugh from everyone.

"That is true for you most certainly Morglum," Taegrid said as he held up a portion of the crocodile meat they had cooked. Morglum smiled. He had found a purpose for himself. All his life his father and brethren had called him a half-breed. Now he found his place in the world he believed. He was an adventurer.

"The way you took down that croc was pretty crazy. I think we should call you Morglum the chaotic." Aleiz laughed. Morglum liked the sound of that and smiled yet again.

"I can live with that," Morglum said as he absorbed the name with a sense of pride.

*****

The wraiths scattered across the lands in confusion when their master, Calvin the Mad had been destroyed. One of the wraiths instinctively headed to the west for days, wandering the lands until it came across a small village of hobgoblins. The wraith swooped down and began draining the life form them as they slept, moving from shadow to shadow and assaulting them when the hobgoblins least expected it. The hobgoblins were battle-hardened soldiers and often ready for combat. They did not have the keen senses of the elves however and the wraith seemed to kill them all easier than a defenseless child. The wraith had the entire village drained of all life within a few hours and the hobgoblins never even knew what happened to them. The wraith felt powerful as all of the souls it had devoured empowered it. It seemed to remember that it had training useful for war and how to focus extra power in the assault of an attack. The wraith did not remember where or how he had learned the special training with weapons. He also seemed to be a natural leader of some kind. The wraiths of his slaughter seemed to feel his powerful presence and were drawn to him over the next few days. Of all the wraiths that rose from the drained hobgoblins, only a small number were his slaves. One wraith that had risen and not been enslaved by its creator destroyed another wraith that had risen and absorbed the negative energy, evolving in power. It remained in the area watching its creator from afar as its creator also watched it. With its slaves, the emancipated wraith swarmed an undead settlement of wights that roamed the lands it now resided in. They slaughtered the leader of the wights and many of its loyal underlings. The wraith master suddenly recalled who he had once been in the middle of his slaughtering of wights. He was a great orc chief before he was slain by a wraith he was forced to call master that has since been destroyed. His anger took him now. A primal rage that once filled him with vitality and renewed strength in life, now simply guided his actions as he, Gaji Bloody-Knucks slaughtered wights. He had been a chief of orcs before, now he was a master to wraiths. He wanted to be a chief again, but no orc would serve him truly. It would be as if the master vampire had returned in their eyes. He was smarter in his afterlife. The wights would serve him, Gaji thought.

"Stop the slaughter," Gaji hissed with his otherworldly voice, still sounding somewhat like an orc. The wraiths obeyed their master.

"Wights of the land," Gaji shouted gaining the attention of the remaining wights. "I have a proposal for you. Make me your warlord, your chief and serve me, and I will keep you around to feed on the living."

"You serve Viscus," one wight hissed and a wraith swooped over it to silence the undead being.

"Stop," Gaji ordered and the wraith held its place near to the wight. "I never served Viscus. In life, I served Bolnarg. In death, I served my master wraith who served Viscus. Now I serve myself." Gaji looked out over the wights and wraiths who listened to his words. They seemed to be enticed by his charisma and natural ability to lead.

"Who are you?" the wight dared to ask with the wraith minion hovering near.

"I am Chief Gaji," Gaji responded proudly. The wight looked around at its fellow undead brothers.

"All hail Chief Gaji," it shouted. The many other wights joined in the shouts and praises to their new leader and chief. Gaji was a chief again and it made him feel a certain glee that filled the void of who he had once been in life. Now he was immortal and he could conquer all who opposed him. His first rival and nemesis as he remembered was his son Chief Foogart Bloody-Knucks. He remembered a problem. When he was a slave to his former master wraith Calvin the Mad, he recalled that Chief Foogart had a priestess with enough power to harm his minions.

Even with a fallen deity, she still managed to wield a divine power strong enough to battle undead forces. Chief Gaji would have to think his attack through very carefully before he led his troops to their dooms.

Chapter Nine:

   The companions had broken camp early and set out together in search of the Ethereal Temple. They hacked a path through some thick undergrowth so they could continue in the direction that their map was leading them. The ground had risen a bit and was dry enough to take refuge. They came across random bogs, but for the most part the ground was dry here. Sadie halted first as she smelled something ahead and looked to Sametria.
  "What is it girl?" Sametria asked as though the wolf could answer her. They all heard something ahead and drew their weapons at the ready.
  "Be cautious," Aleiz warned having keen senses. He thought that he heard the cracking of a whip. The sound brought back terrible memories of his home and the vile priestesses of Na-Dene who tormented the males who failed them.
  "I'll scout ahead," Taegrid whispered.
  "Watch out for crocodiles," Morglum whispered back playfully. Taegrid shook his head and smiled as he took off quietly, leaving his friends while he scouted ahead. Taegrid Prowler moved through the swampland quietly, taking refuge behind trees and undergrowth as he approached the sounds. He peered over a shrub and saw what looked like a village of humans working farms and what looked like humanoid lizards standing over them with whips like slave drivers. He saw farther out beyond the farms what looked like a broken down keep. The lizard men were obviously in charge over the humans. Taegrid ducked down behind the shrub to think for a moment. He thought about returning to get his friends at first, but then he got another idea. Taegrid kept low and moved quietly around the outer perimeter of the village, taking great care to stay out of sight of the watch that had elevated positions on the walls of the keep. Taegrid circled the opposite way from the keep and moved to get a different vantage point. The village was made up of mud and brick structures that seemed to be more like holding cells than anything as well as storage houses for food and supply stuffs. Taegrid was about to go and get his friends when he saw a young boy thrown out of one of the structures and a whip crack across his back while he was face down in the mud. A lizard man cracked his whip at the boy from the doorway and hissed at him threateningly.
  "It's my sister," the boy cried out defiantly and the lizard man whipped him again as two other lizard men exited the holding structure. One of them carried a small girl who cried and looked frightened. The

other blocked the doorway so no other slaves could get out. Taegrid grabbed his bow from his back and notched two arrows. What should he do he wondered? If he took the time to run and get his friends, these children might come to some unknown harm. He figured he had to do something now and if he was overwhelmed, his friends would understand and come for him or avenge him. Taegrid put his arrows into motion with deadly accuracy. The two arrows split off at the perfect angle to hit two different lizard men, the one holding the girl and the one cracking a whip at the boy. The arrows struck them in their chests and dropped them to the ground clutching the arrow wounds. The little girl was loose from the dying lizard man's clutches and scurried to her cowering brother who risked his life to protect her. The third lizard man closed the door and locked it so none of the slaves could get out.

"We are under attack," it shouted with a hissing voice. Taegrid sent two arrows at the lizard man to silence him, but he ducked and they shattered against the stone structure.

"Help," the lizard man hissed as it dove upon the two children and grabbed them. It rolled up right and used them as shields. Taegrid saw several lizard men approaching from a distance and he was certain that several others that he did not see were coming as well.

"That was a mistake," Taegrid whispered as he sent a flurry of arrows at the lizard man. One struck the left shoulder and the second the right shoulder causing it to release its grasp on the children and the third struck clean between the eyes, killing it instantly. The children stood up and pulled away from the dead lizard man's hands as Taegrid rushed towards them.

"Come with me now," Taegrid instructed as he sent an arrow at an approaching lizard man wielding a whip. The boy had never seen a cat man before, but he looked like a man tiger and he had saved them.

"Come on sis," the boy said as he grasped his sister's hand and led her towards their savior. Taegrid thought to lead them away, but several lizard men had come up behind them and blocked their escape route.

"Stay close to me," Taegrid instructed as he sent several arrows at the approaching lizard men. The lizard men cracked their whips at the cat man who appeared to have no armor protecting his body, but the whips cracked harmlessly off the invisible barrier of magic that acted like armor over his body. Taegrid dropped another, hoping to create an escape route for the children, but the whips did harm them. Taegrid knew that he could not take them all alone and that reinforcements would soon come to aid the many that already surrounded him. He flung his bow over his shoulder and scooped up the children. The whips cracked all around him as he used his own body to protect them, the cat man rushed forward and slammed the lizard man aside that blocked his escape.

"After him," one of the lizard men shouted as Taegrid rushed into the swamplands with the children in arms. The lizard men were fast a foot and trailed him quickly, but even while carrying the children, Taegrid was still ahead of them. He knew he was close to where he left his friends.

"Morglum-, Thortwerg-," Taegrid called out as he came crashing into view of his friends carrying the two children.

"What have you done?" Sametria gasped as Taegrid came into view with the children in his arms. Taegrid grimaced at her question and looked behind him to see how close the lizard men were.

"We got company," Taegrid warned as lizard men surrounded them from all sides. Sadie growled threateningly. Only a few carried whips now at their sides while the many others that backed them up wielded javelins and clubs. The companions stood ready with their weapons in hand as the lizard men stopped their rush a just out of reach. They seemed to be waiting for instruction

"Put the kids behind me and take out your bow," Morglum growled as he whirled his two axes in a threatening gesture to the lizard men. They stood back to back in a circle with the children behind them.

"Those are our slaves," one lizard man said as he pushed forward through the crowd. Two others followed him closely. They were obviously the leaders of the bunch. It appeared that the entire tribe had come after Taegrid minus a few slave drivers that tended to the farm slaves.

"And how would you like to be slaves of mine?" Morglum threatened. The lizard man cast the half-orc a wicked glare as it barred its teeth at him.

"We are slaves to no one, but we do serve one greater than you have ever known." The leader of the lizard men warned. "Surrender and he will only have us make you slaves. Fight us and you will surely die at our hands or his claws."

"And who exactly do you serve?" Sametria asked curiously, as she whirled her scimitar over her wrist.

"Why the master of these swamps, we serve Mordakai." The leader of the lizard men answered matter-of-factly. The companions figured that they were in for it either way. The fact that they may face the one called Mordakai, the one the great and treacherous swamps were named after brought the fear factor even higher than they would have imagined.

"See what I mean? We still haven't even reached the temple and we are going to die." Gilthanus moaned.

"Listen to your friend. He knows what you are up against." The leader of the lizard men hissed. Morglum shrugged before rushing up at the loud mouthed lizard man leader and bearing down at him with Mar Doldon.

"Time to put up or shut up," Morglum growled as the battle went into motion.

"Attack!" the lizard man leader roared and the lizard men swarmed in at their prey. The leader faced off with Morglum with his two lieutenants at his side. The half-orc found that he was over matched as long as he faced off with the three of them alone. The lizard man leader blocked Mar Doldon with his shield. To Morglum's surprise, the shield was not even dented from the great blow he struck it with. The lizard men rushed back at Morglum, surrounding him and striking at him fiercely. Morglum slapped aside the leader's battle-axe only to find two short spears come in at him from opposing sides. He stepped out of the way of one and slapped the other down with Mar Doldon. Gilthanus backed off several of the lizard men with a fan of flames that burned their flesh. Taegrid put several arrows into one lizard man before he was forced into melee. The battle was intense and none of them could get to Morglum to help him. The lizard men came in like a massive wave of green death at the companions, the entire tribe against the seven of them. Sadie latched a hold of one lizard man and bit his head clean off. Morglum followed Sadie's example and used Mar Doldon to sever the head clean from the lizard men's leader, severed the head from one of his lieutenants with his enchanted battle-axe and then the arm from the other lieutenant. The bloody sight of their fallen leaders struck fear in the hearts of the lizard men and they backed off cautiously, helping their wounded as they left. Morglum kicked the dying lieutenant to the ground and finished him off with a quick swing of his enchanted battle-axe. Taegrid and the others watched as the lizard men backed away into the swamps.

"We are coming to free the other slaves you hold, so you would be wise to find a new home." Taegrid warned. The lizard men did not respond, but rather they ran back to the village and retreated within the walls of the keep. Sametria wiped her blade clean before sheathing it and then turned her attention to the children.

"Who is Mordakai?" Sametria asked. The boy looked to his sister fearfully.

"The Oblivion Dragon," the boy answered after turning his face back to the half-elf. Sametria looked at Taegrid with anger.

"What? They needed our help." Taegrid groaned in defense.

"And they are children," Morglum added.

"I know they need our help. I am sorry. I am just too distracted with anxiety from what awaits us at the Ethereal Temple and beyond." Sametria explained feeling quite foolish.

"We aren't dead," Thortwerg claimed happily.

"Yet," Gilthanus added.

"Have you ever faced a shadow dragon before?" Aleiz asked gaining everyone's attention including Morglum's.

"No have you?" Morglum spat as he stepped forward.

"No, but a young dragon of any breed is nothing to trifle with. This is a dragon of the shadow realm. That makes it worse as far as I'm concerned." Aleiz responded.

"I know where the temple is," the boy claimed quietly and the attention of the companions was now upon him.

"You will show us?" Sametria asked.

"If you kill Mordakai and free my village," the boy offered and then cringed in fear of retaliation. Sametria sighed and then looked to her friends. Morglum, Taegrid and Thortwerg nodded right away. Sametria looked to Aleiz and Gilthanus. Gilthanus crossed his arms and looked over to Aleiz who looked away. The sorcerer looked back to Sametria.

"I'll help. With dragons there is usually quite the hoard of treasure." Gilthanus answered and Aleiz through his arms up in defeat.

"Alright, I'll help to." The vermin-kissed elf said finally. The children looked happy

"You hear that Coralline? They are going to free us?" the boy said, as he looked his little sister in the eyes. He was covered in wounds from the whip that had struck him and appeared tougher than the average child. Morglum wandered over to the boy and looked him over carefully.

"How old are you?" Morglum asked as Sametria tended to the children's wounds.

"Twelve," the boy grimaced as Sametria cleaned his wounds.

"Where is the shadow dragon hiding?" Taegrid asked abruptly as he heard the sound of a loud and deep horn blowing.

"Beneath the ruined keep," the boy responded.

"We haven't much time then," Taegrid warned.

"Take shelter with your family," Aleiz instructed the children as he tossed a ring of keys to the boy. He got strange looks from the boy and his own friends in response.

"Where did you get those?" Thortwerg asked. Sametria and Gilthanus suddenly erupted with a slight laugh.

"He lifted them off a lizard man when we were fighting," Gilthanus chuckled, but the laughter stopped suddenly when they all heard the loud roar of Mordakai from the distance.

"Run," Taegrid groaned with fear in his tone and the boy led his sister away as a black plume of shadows erupted from the center of the ruined keep up into the sky.

"So that's an Oblivion Dragon," Thortwerg gulped as he saw the long mass of darkness rise up high into the sky before it rolled and spanned out its wings to glide down towards them. It was not the largest dragon of legend, but it was large, well over thirty feet long and a wingspan a little wider than it was long. Taegrid did not wait for the dragon to come into range, and began firing arrow after arrow at it as it flew towards them at high speed from above. The arrows lost momentum by the time they struck the dragon's scales and they could not penetrate the thick hide that protected Mordakai. Weapons were drawn into hands as Mordakai swooped down and opened its maw wide, unleashing a plume of billowing smoky shadows over the companions as it passed by over them and then landed a short distance away from the lingering black smoke. The plume did not even dissipate and five of the seven companions charged out of the black cloud at the dragon.

"Interesting," Mordakai mumbled as it enacted one of its innate magical abilities and made five duplicate dragons appear out of thin air. They all roared in unison. The cloud seemed to cling to Sametria, Thortwerg and Sadie as they charged forward. The cloud seemed to drain the energy from the three of them, but not enough to stop them. The mere presence of the Oblivion Dragon was menacing, but the companions fought against the fear of the dragon and pushed on. Morglum rushed head on at one of the Oblivion Dragons and swung his great axe with all his might. The image seemed to pop out of existence when Mar Doldon struck it. The same thing happened to Sametria and Sadie when they charged a separate dragon together.

"What is this?" Morglum balked.

"A spell known as Duplicity," Gilthanus answered from the dissipating cloud before he began to chant a spell. The spell seemed to be ineffective against the dragon as it simply dissipated with a soft eerie glow upon contact. Thortwerg dared to rush up to one and strike it with his spear, but it was a false image of the dragon as well and popped out of existence. After Aleiz rushed in and struck at one image with his enchanted kukri, he seemed to have found the real dragon. His kukri twanged off the thick hide.

"I found the real Mordakai," Aleiz shouted and Taegrid put three arrows into motion, streaking at the image in front of the vermin-kissed elf. Two of which shattered upon impact with the dragon's hide, but the third took hold and found flesh. Mordakai roared as it snapped its maw down upon the vermin-kissed elf and clenched down, sinking its teeth deep into the flesh of Aleiz. Aleiz could not call out for help. His lungs were forced to expel all the air from the massive pressure that squeezed down on his body. He looked to his friends in pain as he stabbed his enchanted kukri into the one of the eyes of Mordakai. The Oblivion Dragon roared in pain and dropped Aleiz in reaction to its new wound.

"I will devour you alive so that you suffer slowly within my stomach acid," Mordakai roared at the wounded vermin-kissed elf that rolled to his feet and ran for his life, leaving his enchanted kukri behind within the eye of the shadow dragon. Sadie bit the Oblivion Dragon and found that it was the final false image of Mordakai. It popped out of existence and only the real Mordakai remained. Sametria rushed up with her adamantine scimitar, but Mordakai forced her charge into a swift retreat with a snap of his maw. Sametria rolled to the side to avoid the massive mouth of the Oblivion Dragon. Morglum hacked away at the dragon scales, trying to expose more flesh to cut open. Mordakai roared its final roar of agony as it slumped to the ground and died. It was not Thortwerg or any other trained and skilled in the ways of combat that struck the fatal blow. It was Gilthanus. The elf sorcerer had grown outraged when his spell failed and drew his enchanted long sword out and charged at the chest of the dragon while his friends distracted it. His sword had found a soft spot in the underbelly and sunk in deep to pierce the dragon's heart. His battered and fatigued friends stared at the elf sorcerer in awe as he pulled free his enchanted long sword in self-amazement. Gilthanus looked around at each of his friends, all of them awe struck including him from what they had just faced and who had struck the killing blow.

"I thought you were a sorcerer," Thortwerg managed to grunt breaking the silence.

"Are we all alive?" Gilthanus asked as he looked over to his badly wounded friend. Aleiz had deep teeth marks upon his body, but luckily, for him, the wounds were not fatal, just very painful. They were all alive and a sudden rush fell over them, as they were victorious over such a mighty foe as Mordakai the Oblivion Dragon.

"We are all fine it seems," Sametria answered and they all cheered, even Aleiz who was the worst off from the battle.

"I'll grab the elf and carry him back to the village," Thortwerg offered.

"Okay," Sametria gasped. "Taegrid scout ahead and help free those enslaved people." Taegrid nodded and took off running. He wanted to make sure that the children he had saved were still all right and be the first to let them know that they were free and Mordakai was dead. Thortwerg carefully picked up Aleiz and carried him off towards the enslaved village. Sametria looked around and absorbed what they had jus accomplished. She looked to Gilthanus who wiped his sword clean with his cloak.

"You still think we can't restore Athyx?" Sametria asked rhetorically with a smile wide across her face. Gilthanus smiled back at the half-elf.

"I don't believe I ever said we could not do it. I simply said that we are going to die during the process." Gilthanus claimed and then broke out into laughter with Sametria and Morglum. Sadie sat near Sametria and panted with a happy expression upon her wolfish face.

'Let's get to the village," Sametria said putting their laughter to an end and she began walking with Sadie and Gilthanus towards the village.

"I'll catch up," Morglum said and halted Sametria and Gilthanus for a brief moment. "There is something I want to do first." Sametria looked to Gilthanus and they shared a look of disgust before continuing their walk to the village with Sadie. Taegrid found the boy and his sister and many freed slaves that were already helping the children free the rest of their people. Taegrid felt good about himself. The freed slaves cheered and greeted their saviors well that day. A great feast was prepared that night in their honor and celebration of their freedoms. Morglum returned a few hours after the others with the usable equipment from the slain lizard-folk and what he called a souvenir from the Oblivion Dragon.

"To whom do we owe our thanks to?" one villager asked loudly.

"I am Sametria and these are my friends Taegrid Prowler, Gilthanus, Thortwerg, Aleiz, Morglum and my wolf companion Sadie." Sametria answered as she pointed to everyone individually as she said their names. The man's eyes seemed to widen in surprise when he saw a vermin-kissed elf and a half-orc among their saviors. The man seemed to direct everyone to duties of celebration.

"We would like to hold our celebration inside the safe guarded walls of the ruined keep. Would you be kind enough to make sure that none of Mordakai's minions remain?" The man pleaded more than asked.

"I will. Our friend here needs his wounds attended. Are any of your villagers healers?" Sametria asked hoping to take a break from her healing duties.

"Yes, I will gather our healers at once and have your friend Aleiz tended to. Vermin-kissed elf or not, he is one of our saviors as well and they will gladly accept that." The man responded, easing any suspicions of them being prejudice towards him or Morglum. Many healers tended to Aleiz while the others cleared out the ruined keep so the villagers could clean and cook in preparation for their celebration. What they found deep inside a large chamber that was obviously the den of Mordakai astounded them. There was a mound of gold and a collection of precious and semi-precious stones.

"I bet Aleiz wishes he was here right now," Gilthanus gasped as he looked at the treasure hoard of the slain Oblivion Dragon. Taegrid eyed the wealth, saw a single ring, and scooped it up. He dusted it off revealing its true beauty and tossed it to Gilthanus who promptly caught it.

"I think the others will agree that you deserve that, on top of your share of the rest of this for striking the killing blow." Taegrid said hoping that no one would argue. He looked at each of his friends and no one contested. Gilthanus looked at the ring and he felt the powerful magic within it.

"You do realize this is magical?" Gilthanus asked his friends trying not to hide the value of the ring as he normally might.

"We do not care Gilthanus. If it aids you then that is a good thing for us." Sametria responded.

"Who else do we have that can cast arcane magic?" Thortwerg asked.

"We have to keep you safe as we always have tried," Taegrid said in offering.

"I don't rightly care for any other arcane casters at this point. You're one of the few I don't want to kill." Morglum balked and they all shared a laugh before gathering up the hoard.

They feasted within the walls of the ruined keep where the best of all their foods were stored and could be prepared. The freed people danced and celebrated while those with the skills prepared the food for the entire village. The heroes of the village seated their saviors around a great table fit for a king if it were restored along with the two children that had aided them.

"Who is in charge here?" Sametria asked one of the village-folk as she sat in wait for her meal.

"Nobody now," the villager replied as he began plating out food to the heroes. It made Sametria think. She wanted to restore Athyx and this was as big a part of that as traveling to the Ethereal Temple. They needed leadership so that they would not again be enslaved. The lizard men were sill about in the Swamps of Mordakai. Morglum sat next to Taegrid who was seated next to the boy. The girl was beside her brother and Sametria next to her ending that side of the table. Gilthanus sat on the opposite side with Aleiz and Thortwerg. Sadie was even given a place at the table. They all feasted in celebration. When the feast was over, the dancing continued and everyone began to join in dancing around a massive bonfire.

"What is your name boy?" Taegrid suddenly asked the brave child. The boy wiped his face clean with the sleeve of his shirt and looked up at the cat man.

"I'm Gareth," the boy answered after he had finished swallowing his last bite. "My sister's name is Coralline."

"Well met then Gareth and Coralline," Taegrid said as he placed a proud hand upon the boys shoulder and patted him. The celebration lasted late into the night until many simply passed out on the floor or wandered off into an empty room to sleep. Taegrid and Morglum noticed that the boy and girl passed out on a thick carpet near a stove that still burned warmly from the cook who had used it, but no adults seemed to claim them as their own. They both began to wonder if the children were orphaned.

"We should find out who their parents are," Taegrid suggested. Morglum agreed with a nod and the two of them began questioning any of the villagers that still had not passed out from drunkenness or exhaustion. Morglum had not even partaken in the drink that night. He knew as his friends did that danger still lurked outside the walls and if it was to come at them, they needed to be ready to defend the villagers until they could defend themselves. After a long night of questioning the villagers, Taegrid and Morglum had discovered that he children were indeed orphans.

"Watch over the children Morglum. I'm going to take watch on the walls tonight." Taegrid looked as though he was in deep thought.

"Wake me if you get tired. I'll take over for you." Morglum offered as the cat man walked away to the stairs that led up to the catwalk and battlements. "That's one selfless cat man." Morglum whispered. Aleiz and Gilthanus had passed out by their mounds of treasure in the dragon den. Sametria and Sadie had gone to the other side of the keep to patrol the walls. Taegrid would not be alone. Thortwerg had drunk himself into such a drunken state that he had bedded three of the village women. When he awoke, he might not be so popular Morglum thought. He had taken the gear he had recovered from the dead lizard men and placed it in the den for now with the rest of their things. His souvenir was a chunk of bone from the dragon, the pelvic bone to be exact. Morglum went to get it from the den. He had a lot of work to do. Morglum gathered everything he would need for his task and placed them all under his head as a pillow before he went to sleep.

Everyone awoke to the sounds of a weapon smith at work. Taegrid, Sametria and Sadie now slept. Thortwerg had awakened with a puddle of drool on the bed where his face rested. He realized he was without clothing and quickly raised his face off the bed and looked around. A large fur covered him and three of the village women. Normally he might have bragged about the whole ordeal, but after noticing that the women were not exactly the best of looking, Thortwerg carefully crawled out from beneath the fur and grabbed his clothes. He had his clothing back on in a hurry and found Aleiz, Gilthanus and Morglum together. Morglum was working the forge and Gilthanus and Aleiz sat nearby watching the half-orc work. Sametria and Sadie slept outside on the wall and Taegrid had slumped against a battlement on the wall that he patrolled and fallen asleep. The villagers had begun to stir because of the ruckus that Morglum was making. There was work for them to do as well. Their quest to find the Ethereal Temple had to be put on hold. Sametria roused with that thought in her mind and woke Sadie.

"Come on girl, we have a lot of work to do." Sametria said to her wolf companion. Sametria waited until the villagers had begun to rouse and then called for their attention. She hopped up on the table she had dined at the night before.

"Good villagers here me," Sametria called out loudly as the villagers began standing up and many were still waking. "You need the means to defend yourselves."

"We have you," many villagers replied. Sametria cast them all a look of confusion.

"I am no slave of yours," Sametria gasped.

"No," one village began to correct the wording. "We thought that you were staying." Sametria understood and shook her head regrettably.

"I am sorry, but I cannot. We stumbled upon your situation and made a minor detour form our true quest." Sametria explained.

"What is more important than protecting what little life remains on our world?" a female villager asked.

"It goes hand in hand with our true quest," Sametria responded. "We seek the Ethereal Temple. It is said to have a gateway to the ethereal plane where we can find an ancient relic that can restore our world to the way it once was, before I was even born."

"The Ethereal Temple is a cursed place a few miles from here that we have always avoided and have taught our children not to go there." Another villager claimed.

"We will need a guide to show us how to get there when we are ready to go, but for now we must get you all established." Sametria informed the villagers.

"We are not skilled with weapons like you and your friends," a villager who spoke up more often than others said loudly.

"That is why we remain here for a time. We will teach you what you need to know before we go. I believe I have already found you your village leader." Sametria sounded promising with her words as she eyed the villager that spoke more than any other. He was the one that would lead them and guide them. Sametria rallied Aleiz, Taegrid and Thortwerg. She would have asked Morglum to help, but he was preoccupied with making a lot of noise and working hard on whatever he was creating out of the shadow dragon's pelvic bone.

Morglum worked the forge for three days before his masterpiece was finished. The half-orc lifted the great sword high with one hand for Gilthanus to see. It was amazing to look at with two violet garnets they had found in the treasure hoard mounted in sockets like eyes of a dragon upon the guard. The guard, hilt and pommel resembled the face of a dragon and the blade was shaped wide like a sharpened body of a dragon that ended in a fine point. The violet garnets accentuated the black bone that the sword was crafted from. Gilthanus stared in amazement.

"What do you think, keep in mind this is my first?" Morglum asked with hopes of getting an honest opinion from the elf sorcerer. Gilthanus stood up and stepped forward with his hand outstretched as though he wanted to touch it.

"It is absolutely magnificent," Gilthanus gasped as he ran a finger along the blade and cut a tiny drop of blood from his fingertip as he checked its sharpness. "It's a fine piece of work. I would like to enchant it someday."

"I made it for Gareth," Morglum said.

"Who is that, a village warrior?" Gilthanus asked curiously. He was not part of the conversation with him and Taegrid.

"Gareth is the boy," Morglum informed his friend. Gilthanus looked puzzled.

"You crafted this masterpiece for a boy?" Gilthanus balked.

"He will grow into a fine man. I plan on training him to be a great swordsman." Morglum said, sounding quite defensive. Gilthanus realized he had crossed a line and put his hands up in front of him.

"I'm sorry my friend. He is a good boy. I just thought that it was for one of us." Gilthanus explained.

"Maybe he will be one of us some day," Morglum growled as he laid the sword down on a table.

"If he does become one of us, I would gladly adventure at his side." Gilthanus claimed with a bow. "The others have been training and preparing the villagers to fight, defend and grow as a community." Gilthanus changed the subject.

"Yes. It will be a shame to leave them soon." Morglum said in response.

"Right, our quest still remains ahead of us." Gilthanus remembered. "Let us enjoy the time we have left then."

"We will survive our quest, and perhaps we will return here and make it our home." Morglum pondered.

"Life in the Swamps of Mordakai, it is rather peaceful for a swamp setting now." Gilthanus thought. "I think it's a great idea to establish ourselves here before we leave." Morglum looked at his sorcerer friend.

"You mean build homes?" Morglum asked curiously.

"Yes, then we will have a comfortable and safe place to return to and recover from our ordeals. I plan on taking a long vacation afterwards and perhaps enchanting your sword and any other item you fashion." Gilthanus said with all seriousness. Over the next two weeks, along with training and preparing the villagers to run their community successfully, they had all discussed making homes for themselves at the village to return to when they were finally finished on the ethereal plane. The villagers began construction of a wall that surrounded the village and the keep. It would be some time before it was finished due to the number of able bodies that had working on the project. The heroes of Mordakai, as they had been dubbed remained longer than they had planned, finding comfort in the community. They did not have to run or hide here. It was peaceful, except for the occasional run in with a local wild denizen.

Lizard men had been sighted a few miles out by scouts as well as trolls and dangerous wildlife.

The heroes had constructed homes for themselves and found they liked it there more than they had thought they would. Thortwerg practiced with the use of spears primarily and was given three spears that Gilthanus had identified as enchanted weapons along with an enchanted battle-axe, shield and bracers. Some other weapons were nicely crafted, but not enchanted. Thortwerg took a couple javelins as well. His home was full of weapons he enjoyed using. As for his armor, he had decided to be done with the bulky suit of chainmail. For the life of someone who wanted to eventually go out to sea, it was not a good choice. He presented it to the captain of the village guards. Gilthanus eventually wanted to add a tower to his single level brick home. For now, it was adequate. The captains and lieutenants of the watch were given fine armor and weapons that the heroes had found and had no other use for to help defend their village, the Village of Mordakai.

When finally, the village wall was finished and the next project would be restoring the ruined keep, the heroes made their plans to leave. A caring family adopted Morglum and Taegrid spent a lot of quality time with the young boy Gareth and Coralline who they had made certain. The family had only one child of their own, a young boy they simply named Kid. The father was called Travis Orman and his wife was a loving mother named Violet. Morglum approached the couple as he and his companions prepared to leave carrying a large wrapped object as long as a man.

"When the boy is old enough, I made him a sword. He will need to have a reasonable amount of strength to wield it so it probably would not hurt if I gave it to him now. Do you mind?" Morglum asked the family that had taken in the two orphaned-children.

"Only because it is from you Morglum," Travis said as he gestured the half-orc to enter their home. Morglum entered the house with his head low as he approached the saddened boy.

"You're leaving," Gareth sobbed. His sister did not mind. She figured that they would return someday and just played happily with Kid.

"We have to make the world safe for you and any other survivors out there," Morglum claimed with all honesty.

"I know," Gareth groaned as he wavered from side to side.

"I have something for you," Morglum said as he held out the wrapped object that was almost twice as long as Gareth. "You can't wield it now, but someday you will and I will return to teach you how to use it." Morglum removed the cloth that was wrapped around the sword. The sword was made from a dark colored bone. Morglum had forged the bone into a great sword and Gareth's eyes lit up as he saw the magnificent gift being handed to him. Gareth looked at Morglum as he took the heavy sword in both hands. It was lighter than he had thought it would be and designed of bone rather than steel. It was like a sword that one would practice with or display as a decoration. Gareth never thought he could use the sword in actual battle for fear that it would be destroyed. It was a gift from one of his heroes and he would cherish it for as long as he owned it.

"Thank you," Gareth managed to say between sobs.

"You're welcome," Morglum responded as he patted the boy on his shoulder and then turned to take his leave. Gareth watched as one of his heroes left, possibly forever. He meant to travel to another plane of existence to attempt to restore their world to its true beauty.

"You're going to be a great hero someday too Gareth," Coralline said to her brother from across the room as she played with Kid. Gareth looked to his sister in confusion and then to his ornamental sword created of Oblivion Dragon bone.

Taegrid and Sametria prepared their packs and their guide was ready to take them out. Aleiz and Gilthanus locked up their homes before they joined Sametria, Sadie and Taegrid. Morglum was already prepared and arrived with tears in his eyes and looking back towards the home of the Orman Family, where Gareth and Coralline now lived.

"They will be fine," Taegrid assured the half-orc when he noticed the sadness in his expression.

"Yes they will," Thortwerg reassured. "Because I'm staying here until ye return." The companions all turned their attention to the barbarian of the great north.

"Are you sure?" Taegrid asked.

"Bah, I am certain. I want to live to see the oceans and set sail. If you guys aren't back in a month, I'm leaving without ye." Thortwerg grumbled.

"I'm sure if we are coming back that we will be back in less than a month," Aleiz balked. His wounds from Mordakai had healed well with the help of the village healers.

"We don't think any less of you for staying behind Thortwerg," Sametria said sincerely.

"I know. I want to go and help, but I'm afraid of never seeing the open sea before I die." Thortwerg admitted.

"What if I assured you that we would return and the sun would burn bright yellow once more, illuminating the world as it was meant to and chasing the minions of darkness back into the bowls of the world?" Sametria asked. Thortwerg looked the half-elf into her eyes. She looked as though she truly wanted his company with the rest of them.

"You promise?" Thortwerg asked.

"The only other option is eternal darkness, and I'm not meaning a black sun." Gilthanus balked.

"I promise," Sametria vowed.

"Then I guess I'm going," Thortwerg said. "I better hurry up and pack." The barbarian of the great north sped off to pack his things and join his companions on their journey to the Ethereal Temple. If it was going to be their last adventure together, then they wanted it to be just that, together.

Chapter Ten:

The Servant of Viscus hissed in anger when he saw within his scrying pool the destruction of his once faithful minion, Calvin the Mad. He hissed again when he saw his former minion develop a mind of his own and remember that he was once an orc chief. What set the Servant of Viscus off and into a complete rage was when he saw a village of people far to the south, within the Swamps of Mordakai named after the Oblivion Dragon that ruled the land. Mordakai ruled those lands and the servant did not ever cross the dragon, but he did plot. Now with the dragon's untimely demise from heroes that should have been slain long ago by his failed minion and fallen outcast, the Servant of Viscus could make his move on the swamplands and continue to the south, wiping out all life in the name of Viscus. The absence of life fueled the void of life sapping energy that was Viscus. The Servant of Viscus was again angered when he saw the heroes had discovered the relic and how to reach the plane where it remained. They had not yet reached the Ethereal Temple. When they did, he hoped they met their dooms.

"Soul Hunter Wraiths," the Servant of Viscus called. An uncountable number of powerful wraiths known as the soul hunter wraiths circled the Servant of Viscus suddenly, passing through solid walls around their master. "Rally your troops. You will soon feast upon the living, far to the south beyond the Great Forest is a land called the Swamps of Mordakai. Mordakai can no longer prevent us from entering those lands." The dread wraiths hissed and bowed before streaking out to gather their armies. The Servant of Viscus knew how treacherous the ethereal plane was for the living or any visitor that was not a natural denizen of the plane. He knew that its inhabitants if not other dangers would surly kill the presumed heroes, if they even survived the swaiths that guarded the temple gate. The mighty wraith cackled with glee as he plotted and pleased himself with every thought that he conjured. He was an ultimate nemesis. He always used his minions and never anything living. That was why wraiths and other undead dominated the Frozen Wastelands of the north, the mountains that divided the plains from the frozen tundra, the Great Forest and soon the Swamps of Mordakai. The insidious wraith was a perfect servant of the dark god, Viscus and such was why he laid claim to the title.

Sheets of darkness that were actually hundreds of wraiths with their dread wraith masters flew through the sky to the south through the frozen winds of the great north. They had one task, to annihilate all life they came across. That was what their master instructed and that was what they meant to do. They would let nothing or no one get in their way of achieving the goal of Viscus, the complete annihilation of all life.

*****

Orc scouts laid low in the mountains and froze in terror when they saw the great multitude of wraiths fly overhead. It was a massive army, greater than even the one they had faced. They headed south beyond their lands, but the fear remained. Was it a trick? Would they turn back around and swoop in upon the orcs? An orc scout dared to sneak down to the cave entrance and warn their chief of what they had seen. Even with their great numbers, they did not stand a chance. They did not have the means to create the weapons they needed to destroy incorporeal creatures. None of them had the potential to become practitioners of the arcane arts. Few could even master the divine arts. Most orcs simply studied the arts of war. It was what they were bred for after all. The orc was a war machine. They just needed someone else to create the right weapon for the job when theirs were not good enough to complete the task. The scout ran into the main chamber where Chief Foogart sat and looked quite bored.

"Chief Foogart," the orc scout called out as he approached with all haste. "An army of wraiths passes us by as we speak and heads to the far south." Foogart sat up and leaned forward looking curious as he rubbed his chin.

"The time will come when we will come out of hiding. But it is not today." Chief Foogart grunted before he leaned back in his chair and closed his eyes in great thought.

*****

The village guide led them as far as he dared before pointing the way and speeding back to the safety of the village. Beyond an area full of overgrown foliage was a foreign temple that had been erected by a very different culture long ago. The temple was an open design with vines and other foliage twined about the structure. The open temple had a roof of a strange design that the companions had never before seen. It had one main floor with a massive statue at its center, reaching up to just short of the ceiling. The first level was walled around three sides with the front open and a flight of wide stairs leading up to the main floor. Pillars supported the second floor, which was a terrace. Beyond the first terrace was a second terrace for three levels in all. On the second terrace, a faint glow emanated from the center near the statue.

"That must be the gate," Sametria whispered to her friends.

"I'm surprised we have gotten this far to be completely honest," Gilthanus admitted.

"We are almost to the gate Sam. What next?" Morglum asked.

"Taegrid and Aleiz scout out the temple before we go inside." Sametria directed. Taegrid Prowler and Aleiz complied and kept to the shadows as they approached with caution. Taegrid and Aleiz moved cautiously to the wide stairs that led up to the open temple. Undergrowth covered parts of the stairs and the temple as well. From their new vantage point, Taegrid and Aleiz could see what looked like several figures inside the temple moving about like soldiers on guard duty.

"What is this?" Aleiz gasped to Taegrid. Both of them saw the dark figures pacing and neither of them could decide whether it was safe for them to continue.

"Let's go tell Sam," Taegrid suggested quietly. Aleiz agreed and the two of them returned to their comrades to report their findings. They moved back through the undergrowth ducking and hiding along the way until they reached their companions.

"What did you two find?" Morglum asked as Taegrid and Aleiz came into view. He had not thought to whisper. Whether or not that mattered was beside the point. It could have simply been that they had set foot on sacred ground and some sort of magic had warned the guardians of the temple. From out of the ground several dark figures arose, mud falling from their rotten bodies as though they had been laying there for a very long time.

"Those," Taegrid warned his friends as they saw the dark figures rise up with black swords and armor. Their skin was an off gray color and their eyes burned an eerie orange. The companions turned to face the several figures as they drew out weapons. The temple was so sacred, that its creators hired a group of mercenaries so devoted to defending it that after they died, they continued their service as swaiths. Unlike the standard wraith that was incorporeal, these had bodies of decayed flesh. They brandished long swords and shields and wore breastplate armor, all of which bore an insignia of foreign nature that none of the heroes had ever come across before.

"We only wish to pass through the gate to the ethereal plane," Sametria pleaded with hopes that she could reason with the undead beings. The dark figures did not seem to care as they charged forward at the trespassing companions. Aleiz struck first, swiftly moving to engage one of the swaiths and plunging his enchanted kukri deep into flesh through a seam in the armor it wore. Aleiz was not surprised to see the undead being not fall from the wound or even cringe. He was surprised that the swaith had struck back so quickly with a wide cut aimed right at his neck. Thortwerg rammed his spear at a swaith, only for it to glance off the armor harmlessly. Even Taegrid's arrows could not penetrate the shields or armor of the swaiths. The swaiths moved quickly. Aleiz's cloak enacted its magic and teleported the vermin-kissed elf directly behind the savage foe. Thortwerg smacked his shield out wide to block the swaith's counter attack. The blade barley touched his shoulder, not even cutting the skin and Thortwerg felt his strength begin to diminish.

"They be strength suckers," Thortwerg warned his friends. Sametria and Sadie blocked the path of the swaiths to Taegrid and Gilthanus to better enable them to use their ranged assaults. Morglum also was engaged by a swaith. Morglum knocked his opponent's sword and shield out wide, exposing its chest and brought his enchanted battle-axe down through the black armor, striking its rotten flesh.

"They don't die easily," Morglum barked as he yanked free his axe.

"They're undead. We have to ruin the bodies beyond use to force the life sapping energy to leave it." Sametria said as she and Sadie assaulted their opponents. The swaiths were skilled and parried well with swords or blocked with shields. The attacks that did get through their defenses seemed to barley harm the husks that the life sapping energy fueled. Gilthanus chanted a spell that harnessed a small amount of life giving energy into an arcane ray and sent it at the swaith Aleiz battled. Only five swaiths had risen from the mud to assault the, but that did not mean there were not more and these five seemed to take a lot out of the heroes already. Aleiz cut his foe deep in its back after plunging his kukri through a seam in its armor, but again the swaith did not slow in any way. Thortwerg dropped his enchanted spear and quickly pulled out his enchanted battle-axe as he roared to life into a furious rage. Thortwerg hacked at the swaith in a fury matched only by Morglum and nearly wrecked the body fused with the life sapping energy in an instant. The undead were resistant to specific assaults and had no critical organs to wound like the living. Taegrid didn't want to waist anymore arrows on the swaiths and slung his bow over his shoulder before pulling out his sickle in hand and moving up to help Sadie. Aleiz's shadow cloak wrapped him in shadows and teleported him behind after the swaith spun around and plunged its sword at the vermin-kissed elf's heart. Thortwerg was furious and smacked the swaith's counter attack away. Sametria was forced on her heels as the sword wraith she fought came in with great force and skill. Sadie was more agile than her master and evaded her opponent's assaults. Morglum did not care for the fact that Thortwerg was dominating their foes more so than he did. He was in fact Morglum the mighty and Morglum the chaotic and he meant to keep both of those titles. He let loose with his anger and in a violent rage like Thortwerg, Morglum felt his adrenaline rush through his veins and pump his heart faster, fueling and oxygenating his muscles more. He dropped Mar Doldon on the ground only because it did not seem to be as effective against the sword wraiths as his enchanted battle-axe was. It seemed to take magic to penetrate its rotten flesh without resistance. The wild, raging half-orc hacked down the sword wraith, cutting it until it fell to the ground and the vile black and purple energy dissipated from the lifeless husk it possessed.

"I am Morglum," the half-orc roared as he turned to help Sametria. The half-elf was moving a little sluggishly with her strikes, but seemed to be more dominant than her foe for the moment. Gilthanus sent a second ray of positive energy at the foe of Aleiz, blasting a chunk of flesh from the rotten body and draining the life sapping energy from the empty vessel. The swaith still remained and fought like a skilled warrior. Taegrid came up to help Sadie, but his sickle could not pierce the armor of the swaith.

"Help us," Taegrid groaned to his friends when he realized he was useless against their new foes. Aleiz cut free the shield arm of his foe and the severed limb fell to the ground opening up the swaith's defenses more. Thortwerg ravaged the swaith that dared to stand in his way and then turned to help Sadie and Taegrid. The swaith was getting frustrated with his vanishing opponent as it spun around and cut a powerful strike down at Aleiz, the vermin-kissed elf again vanished in a puff of shadows and reappeared behind the swaith once more. Aleiz laughed mockingly at the swaith. Just battling with the swaiths seemed to sap at the heroes strength. Sametria was beyond sluggish when she parried her opponents strike aside. She was getting sloppy like her sword was becoming too heavy for her to swing. She felt the pain in her muscles from the weakening the swaiths had done to her and tears filled her eyes.

"I am not done yet," Sametria growled in defiance. Sadie sensed her master's sadness and anger. Morglum came in roaring and brought down the swaith with his enchanted battle-axe with a blinding assault. Gilthanus sent another ray at his best friend's opponent and this time the swaith wavered. Sametria chanted a spell that filled her muscles with magical energy and strength to remove the pain that she now felt. Her strength temporarily returned and enhanced, so that her sword did not feel so heavy to her. Sadie kept snapping her maw at the swaith, but it always managed to get its shield up just in time to block the wolf's savage bite. Aleiz stabbed his kukri through the helmet of the undead guardian and severed its connection to the life sapping energy plane. The empty body collapsed as he pulled free his blade. Thortwerg slammed the swaith back from Sadie and Taegrid with the power of his tremendous strike. His battle-axe ripped a large gash in its armor. The last swaith did not care that it was the last to still stand. It held Thortwerg at even ground for the moment as it sapped his strength during the battle. Morglum was done with these foul creations. He brought is battle-axe down and split the helmet and skull of the swaith, severing its tie to the plane of Oblivion and ending its duties as a guardian. That was the last of them for the moment.

"We saw more of those things inside the temple," Taegrid warned his friends.

"A lot more," Aleiz added as he panted for breath. Thortwerg and Morglum began to calm a bit and slumped to the ground feeling overwhelmed with muscle atrophied and winded. The swaiths had weakened them, but not defeated them.

"I guess we need to take the temple and then recover our strength before we can go to the ethereal plane." Sametria admitted. "My spell will fuel me long enough to do so." Sametria claimed as she chanted a second spell that seemed to revitalize her body.

"We will have to do things a little differently when we try to take the temple," Gilthanus suggested to his friends.

"What's your plan?" Taegrid asked feeling quite defeated as he put away his sickle. Morglum forced himself up to his feet and walked over to retrieve Mar Doldon from where he had dropped the great axe.

"Sametria and I will use our magic while Thortwerg, Morglum and Aleiz rush in." Gilthanus responded tactically.

"What about Sadie and me." Taegrid asked.

"For obvious reasons, you two will remain in the rear to watch our backs for anyone or anything that might try to take us from behind." Gilthanus answered. Taegrid sighed as he looked to the powerful wolf.

"If these are the kinds of things we are going to be fighting, then I am worthless to you then." Taegrid complained.

"If you want to go home running then get the Hell out of here already. We don't have time for your whining." Morglum scolded the cat man. Taegrid felt foolish.

"I'm sorry, let's get this temple." Taegrid said with a sudden change of heart. Six heroes and a wolf approached the temple where a single swaith stood at the top of the stairs leading to the entrance, several others stood behind him on the main level, and many more stood with crossbows aimed at the heroes from the two terraces above. The heroes of Mordakai froze where they stood after noticing all of the crossbows that took aim at them.

"You would be wise to turn around and go back the way you came. This is a forbidden and sacred land." The swaith warned. It was wearing armor crafted from bones different from the other swaiths and wielding two strangely crafted curved swords familiar only to the elves and oriental lands. His swords were family daisho, a set of oriental blades called a Katana and a Wakazashi. They were quite similar to the bastard sword and short swords known in the world, but with narrower blades that curved slightly away from the edge. Sametria looked at the number of swaiths that poised their weapons at them and knew that they could not win out the day without severe losses. She suddenly feared that she would lose her friends and never achieve her goal of restoring Athyx. She was about to lead the retreat, but she was not the only one taking count. They all counted except for Sadie who did not know how and Thortwerg who could not count more than what his fingers and toes would allow. They counted ten on each level of the temple plus the leader, making the count thirty-one against their seven. They were already fatigued from the first five swaiths they had faced. Now more than six times that amount stood before them ready to attack.

"We would except that we need to pass through the gate to go to the ethereal plane in order to complete our quest." Taegrid admitted hoping that the intelligent undead would make an exception.

"The swaiths you faced in the surrounding lands were just a taste. If you thought they were difficult then proceed and find out what awaits you." The lead swaith warned again. He did not make the first move. He simply warned them. He was without a doubt evil, but he was giving them a chance as though he followed a strict code of some kind.

"We respect your warning, but in order for us to restore our world we have to go through the gate," Morglum protested trying to be diplomatic along with Sametria.

"If you refuse to leave then you will die," the swaith leader threatened.

"We run that risk either way. I choose the road that might change our world for the better." Sametria shouted and the chaos began. Crossbow bolts rained down at them as they leaped to the sides and those who were instructed to charge in did just that. The swaiths primarily targeted Sadie, because she was a larger than normal wolf and appeared very threatening to them. Not a single bolt hit its mark as the heroes moved out of the way evasively. Aleiz rushed up and engaged a swaith that met him halfway up the stairs. Thortwerg and Morglum went into a fury causing their hearts to pump the blood through their veins at higher velocity and fueling their strength with adrenaline as they charged up to meet the swaiths halfway up the stairs with Aleiz. The swaith's had the higher ground and the heroes knew that they could be biting off more than they could chew.

Taegrid disobeyed Sametria and rather than remain with Sadie in the rear, he took off into the undergrowth leaving Sadie alone. The swaiths on the upper levels were reloading their heavy crossbows while the melee ensued. The mere sound of the battle echoed across the landscape almost as loud as thunder. Gilthanus chanted a spell and pointed two fingers at one of the swaiths preparing to charge down at his friends. Two rays surged from his fingertips and blasted two holes clean through his target and destroying the body beyond use. The life sapping energy dissipated from the body and it collapsed to the stairs, sliding down with a clunk-clunk-clunk all the way to the ground. Sametria noticed that Taegrid had left them and her heart sunk. The lead swaith was nowhere to be seen either.

"Sadie attack," Sametria ordered before she began focusing on her spell and chanting. Sadie ran up the stairs and nipped at one of the sword wraiths. Sametria stared at the sky and her arms moved in an intricate pattern as she chanted and called to nature in her druidic language. The clouds overhead seemed to darken and then the sky flashed as a bolt of lightning came down upon one of the many swaiths, searing it badly, but nothing more. Sametria remained focused. Aleiz was working hard to keep his opponent on the defensive. Thortwerg felt the strength being sapped from him the longer he fought against the swaiths. Aleiz was the first of all of the heroes to be wounded by one of the swaiths. He thought his cloak would have saved him, but it did not teleport him out of the way this time. The vermin-kissed elf began a continuous back handspring down the stairs, hoping to escape with his life. Bolts rained down from above and dropped Gilthanus and Sametria where they stood. Their bodies were pierced multiple times with the crossbow bolts. Aleiz stopped his back handspring and picked up his friend, flinging Gilthanus over a shoulder and running for their lives. Sadie sensed the fall of her master, looked behind her to see the bloody body of Sametria, and ran down the stairs towards her. The large wolf bit down on her leather armor and dragged her off after Aleiz.

"Our friends are wounded," Morglum barked. He and Thortwerg turned together and retreated from battle with the deadly blades of the sword wraiths swinging after them. The swaiths chased after their retreating foes. Morglum scooped up Sametria so that her wounds did not worsen and hoofed as fast as he could. The swaiths chased them but stopped when they reached the borders of the temple grounds. The swaiths could go after them, but for some reason chose not to. This was almost like a game to them. Unlike the true guardian of the Ethereal Temple, they were not bound to it. Its ancient creators simply created them to protect it. They could go as far as needed to hunt and kill the trespassers. They decided against it. This was the most fun they have had in centuries. The swaiths returned to the temple with hopes that the intruders would recover and try again so they could again do battle.

"They're dying," Aleiz cried as he ran cradling Gilthanus in his arms. He was covered in his friend's blood and could not tell where Gilthanus' began and his ended. Morglum was covered in Sametria's blood as well. He looked over his shoulder and saw that they were well out of crossbow range and that the swaiths for some reason or another could not continue their pursuit.

"Stop here and tend to them," Morglum barked. Aleiz looked to Morglum over his shoulder.

"But they'll catch us," the vermin-kissed elf protested.

"No they won't, but if we don't stop soon, they will die in our arms." Morglum argued. Aleiz knew that he was right and slowed his pace to a stop. Thortwerg and Sadie stopped and watched their backs while Aleiz and Morglum tended to their wounded friends.

"Where is Taegrid?" Thortwerg asked as he looked around and saw no sign of the cat man.

"We don't have time to worry about someone that abandoned us right now," Morglum barked as he removed the many bolts from her body. Aleiz did the same to Gilthanus. Both of them were covered with a lot of blood that was not even their own. They had their friends bandaged and stabilized, but they could not move them for fear of tearing open their wounds again. When they were done, Morglum slumped back and Sadie plopped near to her master and whined.

"She'll be okay girl," Morglum said putting the wolf at ease.

"Looks like we are camping here tonight," Aleiz complained.

"What happened to Taegrid?" Thortwerg asked again now that their friends were stabilized.

"I don't know Thortwerg. You are more than welcome to go looking for him if you desire." Aleiz responded, sensing Morglum's annoyance with the whole issue. Thortwerg looked back to see that the swaiths had gone back to the temple.

"I hope he's alright," Thortwerg whispered to whoever cared enough to listen.

Chapter Eleven:

Taegrid ran through the thick brush taking branches in the face until he reached the back of the temple. He grabbed a handhold on a solid vine and began climbing up the backside of the temple. He figured if he could not fight the evil undead guardians, then he would bypass them if he could. He heard cries, shouts, and sounds of battle. He saw a flash of light overhead and then a loud thunder clap boomed when a lightning bolt struck down just on the other side of the temple. Taegrid made certain to stay out of sight as he climbed up the outside wall. Every now and then, he looked around the corner after he reached the first terrace where the temple was open. He saw the ten swaiths loading their heavy crossbows and wanted to rush up and push them over the edge. That would be foolish though and so Taegrid shook the thought from his head. He reached the second and final terrace and saw ten more of the swaiths preparing to fire their crossbows. He reached the top terrace and stepped in quietly and spotting his goal ahead. The terrace surrounded the massive stature. At this height between the statue and the terrace landing was a shimmering light of white and gray spiraling like a whirlpool over open air. Taegrid knew that his friends were in danger, but now was his chance and he darted for the gate. The swaiths fired their crossbows down upon his friends like a rain of doom. He knew that they might die, but his best friend wanted this more than anything did and they both knew that she was willing to die to make it happen. Taegrid was willing to die for anyone of his friends and this was his proof. Taegrid leaped for the gate and slammed against what felt like a hard suit of armor in the shadows of the temple. It was like magic as the lead swaith stepped from the shadows with his arms crossed over his chest. His armor was similar to a suit of breastplate, but created from the bones of a skeleton to fashion a sort of exoskeleton. The swaiths facial features were those of an oriental man, but they were distorted from the decomposition of his long dead body.

"You can hide from my fellow swaiths, but not from me. I am Shang Tao, the one true guardian of the Ethereal Temple. You have violated the sanctity of this temple and trespassed where you do not belong. Prepare to die." Shang Tao growled simply staring into the eyes of the cat man but not moving at all. His swords hung at his waste and his arms remained crossed at his chest as Taegrid took a chance and attempted to charge passed the swaith and through the gate. Taegrid moved fast and as he approached the swaith, it still appeared to stand with its arms crossed over its chest until he began to pass by. In a blinding motion, the swaith drew out both of its unique blades and struck fiercely. Taegrid spun at the last minute as he passed by the swaith, avoiding most of the flurry of whirling sword. He felt a sharp pain near his lower right side and the warmth of his blood run thick into his fur. Taegrid leaped towards the gate and looked back just before he passed into the white and gray whirl pool to see the swaith standing with his arms crossed over his chest and watching with anger as Taegrid vanished from his view through the gate. Taegrid felt a dizziness fall over him and a rush of energy and then instantly he was on a misty gray setting with shadowy versions of the landscape he had just been at on his own plane. He had landed on the floor harmlessly as though gravity had no relevance on the ethereal plane. The temple reached into the ethereal plane the statue seemed more menacing here than in the material world. One the floor across the terrace he saw a small marble of red, black and purple spun together in its sphere. His side ached and the warm blood soaked his fur. The wound had clotted, and was not fatal but the pain remained.

"The relic," Taegrid gasped as he stood up from the floor and moved towards the relic. He heard something behind him and turned suddenly to see the swaith standing before him with his arms folded in front of him.

"You have no power here," Taegrid roared defiantly as he reached down slowly and grasped the Marble of Godly Doom.

"I am the warden of the Ethereal Temple, but not the guardian of the relic. He was destroyed long ago." Shang Tao claimed.

"Then why are you here?" Taegrid asked as he stood back up with the relic in hand.

"You have violated my temple. I am here to kill you." Shag Tao answered matter-of-factly. Taegrid felt a sudden fear fall over him. He was so close. What could he do he wondered frantically? Shang Tao rushed towards him and in a blinding flash had his swords drawn.

"No," Taegrid roared and instinctively through the relic at Shang Tao. Shang Tao did not know the power of the relic other than what legend claimed, so he instinctively swung his katana at the marble before it could strike him. A burst of energy blasted him backwards through the gate and wracked his undead body with great pain. The marble flew back towards Taegrid. He tried to grab it, but it was too high, passed over him, and out through the open wall. It did not seem to fall though and simply stopped in mid air. Taegrid ran and leaped out to it, grasping it from the air. He had to leave before the Shang Tao recovered and came back after him, but that meant he had to find another way home. Taegrid had the relic, but he refused to use it for the fear of being transformed into a wraith. Sametria believed that it was her destiny, so Taegrid would take the relic to her if she still lived. The cat man ran across the air as if it was land until he was far away from the Ethereal Temple. It did not take long before the mists of the ethereal plane made it impossible to view the temple, even though he had not gone as far as the mists led him to believe. His side ached and slowed his run a great deal. Taegrid looked around in all directions. It would be very easy to get lost here. The mists made it impossible to see very far and that meant that the local inhabitants could be very close and he would not even know it. He had to be cautious. He was already hurt badly and because he was on an unfamiliar domain, he dared not to take a moment to rest. The denizens would possibly be attracted to his presence. He had to find another way home and fast. Taegrid covered a large amount of terrain in a short while and saw what looked like the walled village of Mordakai ahead of him, but with a shadowy almost silhouette outlines and enshrouded with mists. The wind began to pick up suddenly as Taegrid looked around for some kind of way to return home. He saw a shimmering curtain of white and gray that looked similar to the gate he had passed through to get to the ethereal plane, except that it did not look like a whirlpool. The winds began to get stronger as though some sort of powerful storm of this otherworldly realm was about to occur. Taegrid ran towards the curtain and dove into the shimmering light, vanishing from the ethereal plane. He was back and back at the village of Mordakai.

"Guards," Taegrid called up at the wall guard. The guards looked over the edge to see one of their heroes wounded.

"It's Taegrid and he bleeds," one guard shouted to the others. "Open the gates quickly." Taegrid made his way to the east gate as it opened and passed through to a group of armed guards who promptly helped Taegrid.

"My friends, have they returned?" Taegrid asked.

"No my lord," one of the guards answered.

"It's possible they returned through one of the other gates," another guard pondered.

"No, this is the closest gate to where we had gone. They would surely have returned by this gate." Taegrid said sounding quite worried. What if they were looking for him and something bad happened to them? Then it came to him, the rain of crossbow bolts that were fired down just before he passed through the gate to the ethereal plane.

"What should we do Taegrid?" a guard asked looking to the open gate.

"Rally me a healer and a group of soldiers quickly." Taegrid instructed. He was still wounded and needed attention for himself, but he would not worry about that until he had found his friends. They were his priority now. A guard ran off to rally those Taegrid Prowler needed. Taegrid placed the marble in one of his belt pouches before looking at his wound. It was a bad cut, but alone it would not kill him. Any deeper and it may have hit his liver however and he would have died in agony.

When the guard returned, he had a group of soldiers and two healers with him. They were armed with long swords and shields and wore chain shirts. The healers wore leather armor and wielded spears. They approached the wounded hero of Mordakai.

"Where you lead, we follow Taegrid." The soldier offered. With a nod, Taegrid led them out in search of his friends. The gate closed loudly behind them as they ventured out into the swamps.

"You should let me look at that," one of the healers suggested. Taegrid turned around with a serious expression upon his feline face and halted the group.

"I will receive healing when my friends receive healing." Taegrid growled before turning back around and leading them out. He followed their tracks from earlier for a few miles before they came to a small campsite and Morglum standing ready for battle.

"You are alive," Thortwerg gasped.

"I bring aid. How badly are they wounded?" Taegrid asked as he looked at the bloodied bodies of Gilthanus and Sametria.

"They need the care of a skilled healer," Morglum growled. "What happened to you?" The half-orc asked ever curious about where the cat man went.

"I will explain what happened when Sametria is well enough," Taegrid offered. Morglum through his axes on the ground and stepped forward.

"You will explain now why you left," Morglum barked threateningly.

"We both know that you are physically menacing and I don't stand a chance against you in a fist fight." Taegrid seemed calm as he spoke. His hands did not shake and his voice did not tremble.

"Then you would be wise to start talking," Morglum warned. The soldiers set up a perimeter around the camp and the healers went to work on Sametria and Gilthanus. Sadie and Thortwerg watched the commotion in awe.

"You should tell us something," Thortwerg suggested as he saw Morglum's muscles tightening. He thought that he might have to actually wrestle him to the ground.

"This wound is from the leader swaith named Shang Tao," Taegrid claimed and Morglum relaxed.

"But he never came down the stars," Morglum remembered.

"I know," Taegrid responded. "I was inside."

"I'm sorry I thought you a coward Taegrid." Morglum apologized.

"I am no coward Morglum. If I feel like I am not useful in a fight, I will find a way to be. Know that I would die before I left you guys in battle." Taegrid was sincere and Morglum rushed forward and locked the cat man in a tight bear hug. Thortwerg almost got teary eyed from the whole confrontation. He looked to Sadie.

"I wonder about those two sometimes," Thortwerg whispered to Sadie. Sadie let out a slight whine in response and then looked to Sametria while the healer chanted over her body. The healers checked the wounds beneath the makeshift bandages and made sure they were clean before covering them with healing salves and wrapping them in clean bandages. Morglum felt something warm running down his arm and set Taegrid down immediately. He had accidentally ripped open Taegrid's wound.

"Oh no," Morglum gasped in panic.

"I'm alright," Taegrid said in his calm voice before collapsing. Morglum caught his friend before he could hit the ground and laid him down gently.

"He's hurt bad, hurry!" Morglum called to the healers. They had finished doing all that they could on Sametria and Gilthanus for the moment and rushed over to the fallen cat man.

"I told him he should let me look at his wound, but he said not until we tended his friends." One of the healers complained as she began tending to the wound. "It is not fatal, but he's lost a lot of blood."

"Make sure the stubborn bastard is well," Morglum ordered before returning to his bedroll and leaving the soldiers to act as night watch for them.

They remained at the camp for three days before the healers felt they could move any of the wounded safely. Once they had the wounded heroes back within the safety of the walls of Mordakai, Morglum hid within his house. Thortwerg did the same. Their barbarian prides were eating at them. They had been defeated and they felt that they could not show their faces honorably until they completed their goal. Their strength had been sapped and that was how their pride had been wounded the worst. It would return to them in time according to the healers, but it would be at least a week they were told or at the minimum a few days. Therefore, they sat in their own homes pondering thoughts of revenge while their friends recovered from their wounds. Aleiz had needed some healing attention and remained by the side of his dearest friend Gilthanus even after he was mended.

Taegrid felt renewed with vigor after having his wounds tended to and spending the last week resting peacefully in his own home. He sat in his wooden chair with a simple cushion for padding in front of an open fire and stared at the marble he held in his hand. What would Sametria do with it? If she used it, she would become a wraith according to the legend. Taegrid would not have that. For all she believed and had already sacrificed, there had to be another way. Taegrid put the marble back in his belt pouch and then looked over at the bow he had found and had not yet been able to use. His strength was not good enough to draw back the string, but he had been eating meat and strengthening his muscles since he had found it. The bow crackled constantly with some sort of sparks and Taegrid knew that it was filled with a power with a greater purpose. He wondered if he could finally draw back the string. He had not tried since the day he had first found the bow. Taegrid leaped up from his chair and moved over to the wall where both of his bows leaned. He liked both of them, but as if Sametria's new found scimitar, Taegrid knew there was something more to this bow. Taegrid grasped the crackling bow and took a deep breath as he prepared himself. The cat man took his stance, held the bow out in front of him vertically, and took hold of the crackling string with his other hand. He already felt the tension in the string and knew the great effort it would take to draw it back. Taegrid exhaled and then began drawing back the string of the bow. His muscles did not strain, but he felt the tension as he drew it back and the arch of the bow bent. Taegrid smiled when he realized he had done it and released the string to snap forward.

"This bow could drop a giant," Taegrid whispered with excitement. He pondered a quick thought and then ran out his door with the bow in hand. Taegrid raced over to the home of Gilthanus and knocked loudly at his door.

"Gilthanus open up, it's Taegrid." The excited cat man called. He heard footsteps approaching and then he heard the locking mechanism. The door opened and there stood the elf sorcerer. He looked defeated and depressed.

"I see you are feeling better," Gilthanus balked. Taegrid suddenly remembered that none of them had said a word to one another all week. Only Morglum, Aleiz and Thortwerg knew of where he had gone. Taegrid had hoped that Aleiz would have told Gilthanus, but it was obvious that the vermin-kissed elf had not.

"Aleiz has not spoken to you?" Taegrid asked curiously.

"He remained by my side as I recovered in the healer's temple, but he returned to his home as soon as he saw I was able to return to mine. However, no, we have not really had time to speak. With our failure at the temple, we all just hideaway and await our dooms that we know must be fast approaching. It won't take the wraiths long to find us and destroy everything we have here." Gilthanus rambled with depression.

"If Aleiz had spoken to you, he would have told you that it was not a complete failure. I obtained the relic." Taegrid claimed.

"You did? That would explain where you had gone then, but how?" Gilthanus gasped.

"May I?" Taegrid asked with a gesture of his hand.

"By all means come inside and talk with me," Gilthanus offered as he stepped aside and opened his door wider for the cat man to enter. "I am sorry. I let my depression get the better of me."

"I understand Gilthanus. As I told Morglum, Thortwerg and Aleiz, I felt useless in the battle so I made myself useful." Taegrid began as he entered the home of Gilthanus. The elf sorcerer closed the door behind him and they both moved to his sitting room where they sat in front of a burning fireplace on the floor.

"Can I see it?" Gilthanus asked looking very excited and curious.

"I would wait for that until we are all present. I have come with a different issue." Taegrid admitted. Gilthanus almost looked offended.

"How do I know you tell the truth then?" Gilthanus asked with tension in his voice.

"If I show you it can we move on with other matters first?" Taegrid asked.

"Of course," Gilthanus answered. Taegrid removed the marble from his belt pouch and held out his open hand for the elf sorcerer to look upon. Gilthanus almost became lost in its power as he stared into its very core and saw the unlimited power it contained.

"This is too powerful to exist," Gilthanus gasped. "Put it away quickly before it attracts unwanted company." Taegrid wondered what it was that the sorcerer could see that he could not. Taegrid complied and put the marble back in the pouch hanging from his belt.

"Now my brave friend, tell me why you are here." Gilthanus said keeping his word. Taegrid held out his bow that crackled with energy along the length of its string.

"This, do you remember it?" Taegrid said as he handed it to Gilthanus. Gilthanus took the amazing longbow and looked from it to Taegrid.

"Yes I do remember it. You were angry that you did not have the strength to wield it." Gilthanus recalled.

"I would like to know more about it if you can discover anything as you did for Sametria." Taegrid told his friend.

"Her sword was unique and unlike any magical creations I have ever heard of. It is as though her scimitar grows in power as she does. You think that this omen of crackling energy is like the omen of her scimitar whispering the name Tevlos?" Gilthanus was not sure what Taegrid was looking for other than to see if his bow was enchanted in some way, but that was obvious. It crackled with energy, like a small lightning bolt constantly along its string.

"Would you just find out what you can for me?" Taegrid asked.

"Of course," Gilthanus answered sincerely and stood up with the bow. He walked over to a table and laid it down before gathering some materials from a shelf. Taegrid watched curiously, as the elf sorcerer poured a glass of wine and then dumped some round pearl contents into the glass of wine. He took a feather of an owl and stirred it until the pearl particles were mixed with the wine. Gilthanus looked at his friend as he drank the entire glass of wine and slammed the glass down on the table. He wiped his face and began chanting his divining spell.

*****

Shang Tao paced his dominion of the Ethereal Temple with a great anger that wracked him. He had failed in his duties. In life, he would have been ordered to kill himself for his failure, so the samurai turned swaith tried, but failed. He had plunged his wakazashi through his chest and through his heart, but he did not die. He wanted his honor back. He wanted the heroes to try to raid his temple again so that he could make sure they all died. Shang Tao paced slower now as he realized he could not leave his duties, but he could send the swaiths after them. It had only been a week since his failure. The burst of energy released upon him from the relic was because he was no longer mortal. He knew that and accepted the fact that he was only the guardian of the Ethereal Temple and not the relic. The cat man had only been able to take the relic from the ethereal plane because the Servant of Viscus had destroyed its guardian many years ago. It had never been taken from the ethereal plane before. It had always been used where it was most powerful, that was within the walls of the Ethereal Temple but on the ethereal plane, it was known as the Eye of the Gods. The gods watched over the Ethereal Temple constantly and that was why it had been dubbed as such. However, those times had long passed, and until Armco had told the Servant of Viscus of the relic, no god had watched over the temple in many millennia. Shang Tao realized a second issue. It was possible that Viscus watched the temple on the ethereal plane and knew of the heroes now. His forces could be on their way in an instant and destroy the heroes.

"I cannot let that happen," Shang Tao growled.

"Cannot let what happen, Shang Tao?" one of the swaiths asked.

"I cannot allow Viscus to destroy the trespassers before I do," Shang Tao answered the swaith.

"What would you have us do?" the swaith asked.

"Raid the village of Mordakai to get their attention. Do not kill too many and then return back to the temple." Shang Tao instructed. The swaith acknowledged the guardian of the temple and took his leave with many other swaiths, the large group that had defeated the heroes and nearly killed them, now hunted them to finish the job.

The swaiths tromped through the swamps in search of the trespassers. They were not trackers, but they knew where the settlement of the living was. The swaiths took up their swords and shields as they moved through the marsh, never slowing their pace due to fatigue. They did not tire as the living, but obstacles and the terrain slowed them. When the wall came into their view, the swaiths stopped abruptly. Guards spotted the armed black suited soldiers below and took aim with bows.

"Halt where you stand," the guard in charge commanded.

"We seek a group of six heroes and their wolf," one of the swaiths called up hoping to gain entry.

"You are the sword wraiths of the Ethereal Temple. Go back to your dwelling where you belong." The guard barked. He paid attention to what Morglum and Thortwerg had told them about their encounter at the temple in the swamps. He was no fool and the swaiths were not very inconspicuous about who they were.

"Tell them Shang Tao awaits them and that if they do not return, we will." The swaith directed the others away with him leaving the guards to absorb the message for what it was. It was a threat and a very bold one.

"Should I send word to the heroes?" one guard asked his commanding officer.

"Tell Morglum and Thortwerg. The others still recover from their wounds." The commander instructed and the guard sped off to inform the half-orc and the barbarian of the north.

Chapter Twelve:

Morglum and Thortwerg were dressed and ready for combat a short while after the guard had told them both of what had transpired. The two barbarians marched out together towards the home of Sametria. They had not seen her in a week and figured it was about time that they spoke again. Morglum pounded on her door and nearly knocked it off its hinges in the process. The door opened wide with an angry half-elf woman standing before them.

"What is it Morglum?" Sametria asked as she looked from the half-orc to the barbarian of the north.

"The swaiths have come to the wall and challenged us to return," Morglum answered hoping that a hint of her former hope would return.

"Does it matter? We have failed." Sametria scoffed. Morglum and Thortwerg looked at one another curiously and then back to the half-elf.

"You mean Taegrid has not come to speak with you?" Morglum asked.

"No. I know he turned up at the healers temple with a wound but he was gone before I was ready to come home myself, lucky for him." Sametria growled.

"Sametria, he got the marble." Morglum said suddenly stealing the anger from her face.

"What?" Sametria managed to gasp in shock.

"I was ready to knock his block off when he showed up at our camp with village guards and healers, but he explained to me what had happened to him. Sam he nearly died getting the marble for you. He wanted to wait until you were well enough to tell you." Morglum informed his half elf friend. Sametria looked at her friends with foolishness upon her face. How could she ever think that Taegrid would abandon them after all they had been through?

"We better get over to Taegrid's house then right away." Sametria said as she grabbed her weapon belt and strapped it around her waist before running outside towards Taegrid's personal home. Sadie came charging out and nearly knocked over Morglum and Thortwerg in the process. Morglum pulled her door shut and looked to Thortwerg with a shrug. The two barbarians followed her. When they reached his house, Sametria beat on the door almost as loudly as Morglum, but no one answered.

"Where is he?" Sametria asked as she looked in a window to see that his fireplace burned, but he Taegrid was gone. "Sadie track Taegrid," Sametria barked and the wolf began sniffing. She could have tracked the cat man but her mind was racing and she would have been too distracted to find him right away. The wolf picked up his scent right away and with a howl was off towards the home of Gilthanus. They stepped up to the door and could here Gilthanus chanting. Sametria knew that interrupting complicated spells before they were finished often ruined their effects and would anger the sorcerer. She held her knocking in check.

"What are you waiting for?" Thortwerg asked.

"Gilthanus is casting a spell. I don't want to ruin it and anger him." Sametria responded. "We will wait until he is finished and then I will knock." Aleiz approached looking curious that almost everyone was standing outside of the home of Gilthanus.

"What's going on?" Aleiz asked as he came upon his friends.

"Apparently a lot more than we realized," Thortwerg answered.

"What's that supposed to mean?" Aleiz asked with frustration.

"You already knew that Taegrid had obtained the marble," Sametria accused.

"Yes, I thought he would have told you of all people right away." Aleiz admitted.

"The swaiths threaten the village now," Morglum added.

"We now wait until Gilthanus is finished casting his spell before we knock." Sametria informed the vermin-kissed elf. Aleiz sighed as he pushed by his friends.

"He is quite able to ignore us," Aleiz claimed as he opened the door to the home of Gilthanus without knocking and barged inside. The friends all followed behind the vermin-kissed elf and Taegrid turned to see them all and smiled when he saw Sametria looking quite well after her near death experience. Gilthanus did not lose his concentration or focus as he continued his long casting of the spell that would identify the power if any of the bow and how to unlock it.

The spell took an hour of focusing and chanting until the secrets were revealed to Gilthanus about the bow. He had not gone this extreme with Sametria's sword but now that he saw the hidden power within the bow, he pondered the thought of doing so. There was indeed hidden magic waiting to be unlocked by its wielder. He knew that the bow was called the Arcane Bow of Lightning and that its power was nearly unlimited. Gilthanus focused harder. He realized that it took rituals and rites of passage to unlock the power of the bow. Only the first ritual was revealed to Gilthanus. It needed to be purified with lightning or some sort of electricity. Gilthanus gasped as his spell ended.

"It is done," Gilthanus announced.

"It's about time," Aleiz balked.

"Hello my friends," Gilthanus said with a wide smile.

"It seems we have much to discuss now that we are all gathered." Sametria said to everyone in the house.

"This is true according to Taegrid, I should have been told something important by Aleiz days ago." Gilthanus eyed the vermin-kissed elf curiously. Aleiz shrugged.

"I figured he would tell everyone when we were all gathered," Aleiz said in his defense.

"Enough figuring, what's done is done. The question is what are we doing now?" Thortwerg barked. Taegrid stood up before all of his friends and produced the marble form his belt pouch.

"It was not easy, but I got it." Taegrid said proudly as he held it out for his friends to see. Sametria stepped forward in awe and Aleiz stared intently at the powerful relic that could bring a god to its knees. Sametria looked to all of her friends in sadness one at a time. She ended with Taegrid.

"It would seem that the time has come to part ways," Sametria claimed with sadness in her voice. She reached for the marble, but Taegrid closed his hand and withdrew it quickly.

"No," Taegrid said sternly.

"No?" Sametria asked in utter shock as she looked curiously at her friend. "You of all people know how important this is. I must end this darkness and restore order to our world."

"I agree Sam, but there has to be another way." Taegrid explained. He showed empathy with his emotions, but he was torn. The sadness filled the hearts of the heroes as they had heard the legend of what happens to the mortals who dare to wield the power of the Marble of Godly Doom. Something was said during the silence and sadness that brought renewed hope as Sametria took Taegrid's closed hand and removed the relic, taking it in her own hand.

"Why don't we just destroy it?" Morglum asked. That question was what put hope back into their hearts. The simple question of why they do not just destroy it was as to the point as they needed to be. It would solve the problem of anyone who made similar attempts to grant their deities power that they should not have and it would prevent anyone from becoming a wraith due to the curse of the relic or so they believed. Sametria looked to Gilthanus.

"Is it possible to destroy?" Sametria asked. Gilthanus remembered the legend.

"Only a mortal can wield it, is all the legend ever stated. I imagine that only a mortal should be able to destroy it if at all possible." Gilthanus concluded.

"Then how shall I do it?" Sametria gasped with hope.

"I can research a ritual if you like," Gilthanus offered.

"Do it," Morglum barked before the others could respond.

"I have one more thing to do for Taegrid and then you can all leave me to my research. I will need quiet and no disturbing me for anything." Gilthanus scolded.

"Alright then," Sametria responded and tucked the marble away in her own belt pouch. Gilthanus chanted a spell and his hands crackled to life with the same energy that surged up and down the bow sting. He grasped the bow and discharged the magic into it. The spell crackled with electric energy until at last the spell effects dissipated. Gilthanus handed the bow back to Taegrid.

"It is called the Arcane Bow of Lightning and I have just performed the first ritual for you. It is up to you to discover all of its secrets and unlock them now." Gilthanus explained.

"Thank you," Taegrid said sounding speechless.

"Gilthanus, before you begin your research we have other imposing issues. The swaiths of the Ethereal Temple have threatened the village." Thortwerg informed.

"It is our responsibility to put an end to them if we can," Morglum added, as he looked around the room at all of his friends reactions.

"They nearly killed us Morglum," Gilthanus gasped.

"We were ill prepared, last time. We did not know what to expect." Morglum argued.

"We are responsible if the sword wraiths attack the village," Thortwerg barked.

"We are responsible for a lot of things Thortwerg," Taegrid agreed.

"I agree that we need to end the swaiths," Sametria said suddenly. "But I also agree that we should not rush into battle unprepared. We need to put our heads together and come up with a plan." Thortwerg closed the door to the home of Gilthanus and the companions all took a seat on the floor in front of the burning fireplace. They were all in deep thought of how they could take the swaiths with no losses on their end.

"We don't have much time if they are already threatening the village," Morglum began. "Thortwerg and I know what to expect in combat and except that in order for us to win, we will be sapped of our strength the longer we are in melee."

"The goal is not to enter melee right away then," Sametria added.

"This time let them come to us?" Taegrid asked to see if he understood the plan.

"Exactly," Sametria answered. "We will wait for them to come to us and as they do, we will rain down the thunder and arrows and whatever else Gilthanus can conjure."

"You do remember those nasty crossbows they possess?" Gilthanus reminded his friends. Looks of defeat crossed their faces as they remembered.

"I have learned a spell that will protect us from such attacks for a limited time. I will need the shell of a turtle however." Gilthanus informed his friends restoring their hope.

"So we have to find and kill a single turtle so that we are protected from the crossbows of the swaiths?" Morglum asked as he looked to Sametria and Taegrid for their reactions.

"We need not kill a turtle if we can find one that has already died. Either way, Sadie and I will go and recover what you need for the spell." Sametria decided.

"Also, my arrows did not hurt them." Taegrid reminded his friends. "Or my sickle."

"Try out your knew bow," Gilthanus suggested, "If that fails run for home."

"I'll use my new bow, but I will not run." Taegrid chuckled.

"Then it is decided, Sadie and I will hunt a turtle shell down and return it to Gilthanus. We attack tomorrow." Sametria declared and they all agreed. They dispersed from the home of the elven sorcerer. Sametria and Sadie left to hunt and Taegrid joined her. The rest of the heroes returned to their homes to prepare themselves for tomorrow. Gilthanus locked his door after his friends left. Aleiz had gone as well curiously enough. Gilthanus assumed that the vermin-kissed elf thought as he did. Perhaps the destruction of such a powerful relic was the wrong way to go. They could become gods he pondered. He chuckled at the idea. That would make his life quite dull he thought and shook the idea from his mind. He turned around to return to his desk to study his book but was face to face with his mother.

"Doesn't someone have to summon you here?" Gilthanus asked curiously.

"Not necessarily," Villisca answered. "Your friend has the relic?" She asked him with excitement.

"Yes," Gilthanus asked reluctantly.

"Use it to make me a goddess and my father a god and you will be rewarded beyond your wildest dreams." Villisca offered. Gilthanus looked at his mother with accusation in his eyes.

"You would have me cursed forever as a wraith just for Hell's glory?" Gilthanus gasped

"It is why I created you. It is your soul purpose." Villisca responded heartlessly. Gilthanus glared at her wickedly.

"What you offer is worthless to me if I am cursed as a wraith, especially if the curse is so powerful that not even a god could undo it." Gilthanus complained.

"It is eternal life Gilthanus," Villisca argued the darker point of view.

"If I am to live forever, I would do so in another fashion than as an undead. I hate them all and would rather die than become one of them." Gilthanus barked at his mother.

"I could kill you where you stand Gilthanus," Villisca warned.

"Then do it," Gilthanus said challenging his mother's power. "There has to be another way for you and grandfather to become gods. Why should I sacrifice my eternal soul if there is another means of achieving all of our goals?" Villisca was impressed with his bravery and the way his mind worked.

"There are many ways, but this is the easiest and quickest way at the moment." Villisca responded coldly.

"I will not do it. I will find another way if you give me time." Gilthanus growled defiantly. Villisca glared at him coldly. She wanted to smite him down where he stood for his insolence, but her father had instructed her not to. He had spared her all those centuries ago during her rebellious era. Villisca decided she would show Gilthanus mercy as well and be patient. She knew of the coming storm of wraiths. The only way for them to survive was to restore the sun to its former golden glory before they arrived.

"If Armco defeats and absorbs the power of another god, he will ascend." Villisca finally responded with a way.

"But only Viscus has divine power," Gilthanus remarked.

"And Enamor, but he is imprisoned and they are both far too powerful for either of us to defeat." Villisca admitted.

"I will hurry my research of the destruction ritual then and restore the many gods to power so that you and grandfather can make plans to ascend." Gilthanus vowed.

"He will not be pleased with our decision, but it will have to suffice. Your ritual is simple Gilthanus. Only a mortal can destroy the relic, but before you can do it, each of you must sacrifice a drop of your blood upon the relic. Then and only then, can mortal weapons destroy it. There is one more thing however. Its divine energy that it has stolen from the gods is what now hides you from the forces of Viscus that search for you. Even Viscus himself cannot see who you are or where you now dwell." Villisca informed Gilthanus before she vanished in a flash of flames. Gilthanus smiled. He had found a way to make both parties happy. Gilthanus had plans for himself, but in order to begin achieving his goals he had to fulfill his mother's wishes so he could be rid of her.

*****

Morglum returned to his home to find the boy Gareth standing outside with the dragon bone great sword e had created for him in hands. He stood with the sword held perpendicular to his body. The blade reached high above the boy, but he held it steady due to its lightweight.

"Have you come to train already boy?" Morglum asked with a smile.

"You did promise me," Gareth reminded.

"That I did Gareth, but we have pressing matters right now. I can train you a little today, but tomorrow I have to return to the Ethereal Temple and rid the world of the swaiths that are now threatening your village." Morglum told the boy.

"Today will be fine for now then," Gareth responded and then he came in at Morglum with a heavy and wide swing. It was all too sloppy and Morglum easily stepped to the side without breaking a sweat.

"Your stance is okay, but you over swing your sword." Morglum pointed out to the boy.

"The blade is rather large for me. I probably just lack the skill to swing it as fast or accurate as someone of your size." Gareth thought.

"Nah, when I was your size I could swing a weapon crafted of steel that size easier than you swing that light weight blade." Morglum argued.

"You have orc blood. I'm a human and lack the extra muscle your race possesses." Gareth reminded Morglum.

"That has little to do with it, but I'll give you that point. Why don't you try widening your stance, and squaring up your hips." Morglum suggested.

"Wont that put me lower to the ground?" Gareth asked in confusion.

"Yes, but it will also put more control and power in your swing. At your size striking high isn't as beneficial as striking low and accurately." Morglum instructed. Gareth squared up his stance and widened his hips so that he was lower and the sword was supported easier. Morglum saw that Gareth had followed his instruction well and took out Mar Doldon.

"Now come at me," Morglum commanded. Gareth brought his large blade down at Morglum and in order for him to deflect the strike Morglum had to drop to one knee.

"Wow!" Gareth gasped as he noticed how close he came to actually harming one of his heroes.

"You see boy, that it what I mean." Morglum commended Gareth.

"Maybe next time we will pad our weapons so I don't hurt you by mistake," Gareth suggested.

"That would be a good idea. You did come awful close to hitting me." Morglum agreed with a smile as they relaxed.

"For now, go and practice on the wood striking dummy over there." Morglum pointed to a training dummy he had made in his front yard. Gareth nodded and ran over to the wooden training dummy and began practicing his strikes.

"One strike, one kill." Morglum instructed as he watched Gareth practice.

"One strike, one kill." Gareth repeated repeatedly as he practiced. His sword cut swiftly through the air and more skillfully now than before. He focused on just one single hard strike with his great sword. Morglum watched as the boy practiced. He was determined to become a great swordsman and Morglum wanted to help him.

*****

Villisca returned to her domain on the plane of Hell. Her minions were already cowering in fear from her presence as she set foot in her thrown chamber to sit and ponder her next move. Villisca smiled. She was very intelligent, a genius among devils.

"What have you done Villisca?" a powerful voice asked and Villisca knew right away that it was her father. She spun around to see the all-powerful Armco standing before her.

"He refused to sacrifice himself for us Lord Armco," Villisca responded.

"I know, I watched and listened. Why did you not encourage him more?" Armco asked in frustration.

"No riches or reward could change his mind. I could tell my lord. He has a lot of my rebellious traits in him." Villisca informed Armco.

"Perhaps you should encourage him with your scourge," Armco suggested as he looked to the coiled whip hanging from Villisca's hip.

"No doubt that I would have enjoyed his torture my lord, but he claimed he would die before he would change his mind and I believe him." Villisca explained.

"Then you should bring him before me and I will change his mind for a day," Armco suggested. Villisca knew her father could sway the mightiest of beings with his words. She just was not sure if she should obey this time.

"If the heroes of Mordakai succeed in the destruction of the relic then no mortal could ever bring the gods to their knees again. In restoring the gods it seems we enhance our chances of success more so." Villisca offered a possibility to Armco.

"It is a risk though Villisca. If we are unable to usurp a god and absorb its power, we will forever be damned to Hell. Now keep Gilthanus on our side by whatever means." Armco warned.

Chapter Thirteen:

The wickedest of all wraiths and god of Oblivion, Viscus floated through the corridor of his hidden prison of the gods. He had created the prison on the outer rim of Oblivion's Gates. He sensed the fall of his wraiths at the hands of the heroes. The same heroes seemed to be constantly foiling the plans of his minions on the material world of Athyx. His great power had driven all life into hiding fifty years ago. For fifty years, Viscus' minions have swept across the face of the world, wiping out all life that they came across. The fear of the Servant of Viscus possibly finding existing life kept the denizens of the world in check and no one dared to defy Viscus outright. The closest event to an uprising had been a small band of druids that were wiped out by his minions. The heroes seemed to have risen from the ashes of that event and now someone was helping them hide from Viscus. The only other deity that still had his power was Enamor, but he was Viscus' prisoner. He was bound with powerful, extra-dimensional shackles and surrounded by a constant overpowering negative essence to weaken him and keep the deity from trying anything. Viscus figured that somehow it had to be Enamor aiding the heroes on Athyx. His minions searched for them at that very moment, but they could not see their exact whereabouts in the swamps of Mordakai all of the sudden. The problem with that possibility was that only he and Enamor possessed such power now and Enamor was still in his cell, shackled and weak. Viscus could see him through the bars in the door. Enamor was no sorcerer. He could not summon any sort of illusion and if anyone else had, Viscus would surely see through it. Viscus felt it was time to make new plans. Viscus knew that the heroes could at any time destroy the relic if they possessed it.

"If you are to be restored to power, then I should be the greatest god of darkness, death and despair. No other shall share the power over the undead with me. This is my dominion and I will see that it remains that way." Viscus hissed. Armco appeared before Viscus.

"I may no longer be a god in your eyes Viscus, but I still know many secrets that I have kept for a very long time." The former devil god cackled. Viscus hissed as he circled the devil.

"It was your secret that changed the world Armco, and your secret was what kept you out of my prison." Viscus hissed as he continued to circle the devil. Armco laughed as though even Viscus with all of his power did not threaten him. Viscus relaxed.

"You need my help again," Armco laughed.

"Like I said before Armco, without you I would not have succeeded. You have proven your worth. We should leave here now so that we can devise our next plan." Viscus was direct.

"What is happening with your plans that you need me again?" Armco dared to ask.

"Someone here has summoned powerful heroes to help them. They are so powerful that they are able to hide from my minions scrying pool and my divine sight." Viscus explained to the devil.

"These cells are far too powerful for anyone to use any sort of power they possess even as gods." Armco balked. He knew what Viscus was proposing was an outlandish idea.

"Then there is another god we do not know about helping them. I will create a guard to watch over the prison and a destroyer to vanquish the heroes." Viscus claimed.

"I will discover who is helping them," Armco offered but he already knew. The former devil god followed Viscus down the great corridor of darkness until at last with just the will of Viscus they vanished from the prison.

*****

A great aura of divine energy did blanket the swamps of Mordakai but it was no god that protected the heroes from being discovered by the army of dread wraiths that flew through the skies in search of their whereabouts. It was the relic. Gilthanus had told all of his friends when they had all returned that he had discovered how to destroy the relic, but he had also discovered that the power of the relic was all that hid them from Viscus and his forces. This good, bad scenario sent them into a great debate whether or not they should destroy the relic or sacrifice one of them to restore the gods to power.

"We will decide this after our battle with Shang Tao," Sametria said finally to end the debate and bring focus back to the current problem. The sword wraiths had threatened the village of Mordakai because of them and they needed to destroy that threat. The heroes agreed and returned to their homes to prepare and get some rest. Gilthanus prepared the turtle shell for his protection spell. He would have enough to protect all of his friends so long as they possessed the piece of turtle shell that he would enchant in the morning. He had to break the turtle shell up into enough pieces so that each of them could carry a piece, including Sadie the wolf companion of Sametria. For Sadie Gilthanus had a pouch he would tie leather string around so they could hang it around her muscular neck. After Gilthanus had set out everything, he needed for his spells and his gear for the morning, the elf sorcerer went to sleep. Gilthanus slipped into a deep sleep and began to dream. In his dream the sky, if it could be called a sky was black as night and smoke plumed up from the land. Fireballs streaked through the air and some randomly crashed into mountains, sending sharp rock shrapnel flying in all directions. Lava erupted from volcanoes pluming high into the sky making it seem dark violet in areas where mass eruptions and fireballs existed. He knew it was Hell, a domain located within Oblivion where demons and devils reigned for a time before they were judged and cast through the gates of eternal damnation, known as Oblivion.

His dream showed him great armies of devils marching to war. He wondered what the dream meant if anything. He let his mind take over and the dream ensued. He was suddenly among the army, but not in the front ranks. He marched beside a massive devil standing well over twelve feet tall that barked orders in the language of the devils. They marched through a large gate that took them to Athyx where they met an army of mortals. The battle began and the lands were covered with the blood of devils and mortals alike. Gilthanus watched as the bloods mixed in the ground, creating a thick mud like substance where they warred. He wielded magic in his dream of far greater power than he did in life and held a staff with hellish designs. His magic seemed to disperse the mortals and aid the general of the hoards of Hell. Together, Gilthanus and the devil known as Leb destroyed their foes. The staff he wielded was empowered with magic that Gilthanus had yet to understand. The battle was eventually won and the general looked down to Gilthanus with respect.

"Gordus comes," Leb warned. Gilthanus did not recognize the name and his dream ended suddenly as he was ripped away through gray smoke and then to darkness. He saw a face that resembled a man with the head of a bull, covered in what looked like it might be red skin in the darkness. The silhouette was the last thing he saw before Gilthanus awoke suddenly. It was already morning he knew and roused himself so he could begin his enchanting of the turtle shell pieces. As Gilthanus enchanted, the turtle shell pieces, he thought of his dream. He had dreamed of Hell and whatever plane it was that the war was on. He wondered if he was supposed to go there and help Leb and if so the only gateway he knew of was at the Ethereal Temple. The gate led to the ethereal plane, but it touched many other planes and allowed access through curtain portals if one could be found. Gilthanus suddenly had another reason to defeat the sword wraiths. He wanted to go to Hell and speak with Leb. That journey would take some planning and he had other duties to perform first. His friends arrived shortly after he had finished enchanting the pieces of turtle shells and knocked upon his door. Gilthanus opened his door to see Sametria standing there and went outside to join them.

"Each of you needs to take one of these and keep it on you at all times. So long as their projectile weapons are not enchanted, these should protect you from them." Gilthanus explained as he handed each one of his friends a piece of turtle shell. He hung a small pouch around the neck of Sadie.

"You need one as well," he claimed and Sadie licked his face in response. "They will only last for eight hours so we best get moving." Gilthanus warned.

"Well if these protect us or not, we need to get moving," Taegrid agreed. The heroes made their way to the gate and the guards opened it to allow them to leave. The guards watched their heroes leave to again go and perform the heroic deed of protecting the villagers from foes they could not battle without great losses. The guards wondered if they would ever again see their heroes or if the next faces they saw would be the faces of their enemies.

The companions approached the temple and knew that they were in trouble when they saw the swaiths ready for them. Swaiths lined each terrace as before but there was a smaller amount on them and they did not fire their crossbows.

"Behind us," Sametria warned and the heroes spun about to see a group of swaiths come into view and block their escape route.

"I just want to ensure that you do not escape this time. Let us finish this now." Shang Tao roared. Aleiz, Morglum and Thortwerg rushed forward to meet the swaiths that awaited them on the stairs and left their friends to deal with the group that flanked them. Taegrid put his Arcane Bow of Lightning into action. Each arrow he launched from the bow charged with the shocking power that constantly crackled along the length of the bowstring. The swaiths met their foes in battle. Four surrounded the large wolf and fought it tactically. Aleiz was met with two while Morglum and Thortwerg were faced with three. The swaiths remembered who fell fastest and who had not even done battle during their last confrontation. The wolf, half-orc and barbarian of the north had proven to be the fiercest among the group. The vermin-kissed elf had a trick, but it was limited. He and the swaiths now knew that fact about his cloak. Shang Tao watched to see if he would even have to face off with any of the trespassers. His minions seemed to have them all under control. Morglum cleaved down one of the swaiths with his flurry of axe strikes. The half-orc seemed to roar to life as he focused on nothing but killing the already dead swaiths. Shang Tao wondered if he would be facing the half-orc shortly and stood motionless with his arms crossed over his chest. Sametria watched as Sadie was being overwhelmed and subconsciously enacted a power from her sword. Several images of her appeared and confused the swaiths. Four duplicate images of Sametria now stood to do battle against the single swaith. It looked from each one to the next wondering if they were replicas or illusions. They all struck in unison at the swaith, but it only felt the blade from one. The swaith just had to find out which one it was. The four images surrounded the swaith and they all smiled. Aleiz worked his movements, but still the swaiths forced his cloak into action, making the vermin-kissed elf teleport from where he stood and reappearing where he desired nearby. Aleiz struck hard and fast when he realized the swaiths were trying to force him to expend all of the daily uses of his cloak right away. He cut one down with his enchanted kukri and turned to face his second foe. Thortwerg cut a swaith in half as he roared in his wild rage like Morglum.

"Sametria I need more strength," Taegrid groaned as a swaith cut at him and missed. He felt the strength sapping power of the swaith nipping at his muscles. Aleiz defended as well as he could, but the sword wraiths forced his cloak into action a second time. He knew as they did that the cloak would only protect him once more in that fashion. Sametria's foe struck at her and hit a clean strike, but it was just an image of her. It popped out of existence leaving only three. One of them was the real half-elf. Sadie was brought down by the four savage sword wraiths that teamed up against her. They quickly moved to aid their fellow sword wraiths against the remaining trespassers.

"Sadie!" Sametria cried as she saw he wolf fall. She quickly chanted a spell and touched her friend. The power surged into his body and strengthened his muscles with magic. She chanted the spell a second time imbuing her as well and the swaith she battled thought it might have discovered which one was really her. Taegrid rolled backwards and when he was safely out of reach of the swaith, he put more crackling arrows into its body and dropped it where it stood. Gilthanus leaped back and chanted a quick spell that sent four magical projectiles unerringly into the swaith that he faced. Two more came at him and one more at Taegrid and Sametria. The battle commenced at the bottom of the stairs and Shang Tao watched with great pleasure as the mighty wolf fell at the end of his minions swords. Aleiz leaped back as the swaith came in at him.

Another swaith came towards Taegrid and the cat man sent three crackling arrows into action, but it slapped them away with its shield. Aleiz chuckled as the swaith that had become so cocky due to their smart tactics battling him suddenly discovered that Aleiz had more than one trick up his sleeve. Aleiz turned its sword out wide harmlessly. The swaiths were slowly dwindling down the fierce barbarians in battle. They had not cut a single wound, but every time their weapons seemed to lock, their strength was sapped a little bit more. With two swaiths coming in at her, they stood a greater chance at discovering her. Another image was struck and vanished leaving only Sametria and another image. The second swaith struck true and she was forced to parry. She dismissed the other image seeing how it was distracting her more than it was helping her now. Gilthanus was forced to defend himself with his enchanted long sword and was feeling the drain of his strength as well. He jumped backward as he chanted a spell and encompassed himself within an invisible and impervious sphere as the other two swaiths quickly discovered. Their swords bounced off an invisible field that they could not move or penetrate. Gilthanus smiled wryly as he took out a potion and drank it. Morglum had to take them down faster, but they had already sapped his and Thortwerg's strength back to what it was before they triggered their adrenaline rush and flew into their wild rages of barbaric battle. Sametria chanted a spell and suddenly the grass and roots reached up from the ground, holding the two swaiths she battled where they stood and limited their movement. They struggled to dodge or parry or even swing their swords, but Sametria could move through the spell area as though it did not exist because of her special druidic training and bond with nature. She knew that Sadie was dead and that there was nothing that she could do except avenge the fallen wolf by slaying every one of these undead beings. Aleiz feinted left, but came in on the right to catch the swaith off guard. The swaith was badly wounded, but its body was still able to house the life sapping energy that empowered it. Thortwerg hacked a swaith down where it stood at the bottom of the stairs with his magical battle-axe, Wraith Defiler. He preferred the spears he possessed, but for some reason or another, these swaiths were resistant to them, but not his battle-axe. Taegrid struggled to keep the swaith back far enough to fill it full of arrows. It came in and it came in hard at him. Taegrid spun his bow as if it were a staff to block the swaiths' assault. Gilthanus was safe inside the resilient sphere, but he could not harm the swaiths either. Aleiz slapped his foe's strike aside harmlessly again, and spun around behind the sword wraith as he severed its head clean. Shang Tao thought that he might have to face off with the vermin-kissed elf, but he vanished before the vermin-kissed elf's very eyes.

"Coward," Aleiz spat as he ran up the stairs. Thortwerg backed his foe towards the stairs as he saw Aleiz run up them. Taegrid back flipped away from his opponent and put three arrows into its chest as soon as he landed on his feet. The crackling arrows brought the sword wraith down finally. Taegrid turned his attention to the three that beat at the invisible barrier protecting Gilthanus. His opponent cut Thortwerg across his belly. He roared defiantly to fight away the pain of the wound. Morglum was being backed up towards his friend and away from the stairs like the swaiths were preparing to strike from above and wanted a clear shot at all of the heroes. Even with Sametria's opponents entangled, she still had trouble battling them in melee. She was cut badly across her side and was forced to back off. The wound throbbed, but it was only superficial. Sametria chanted a spell as she called to the thunder and lightning above. It was partially cloudy and not a single storm cloud was overhead, but Sametria did not need there to be. The clouds that were there answered with a loud clap and a flash of lighting struck down near one of her entangled foes. Sametria smiled. It was her turn to show her power off. Last time she had been taken down too fast to really use her spells. This time Sametria was being smarter. Aleiz reached the top of the stairs and looked inside the temple. He saw a flight of stairs on either side and the base of the great stature at the center with burning incense.

"I'm coming for you Shang Tao," Aleiz shouted as he ran towards the stairs to his left. Thortwerg dropped his foe and charged up the stairs after his friend. Taegrid put arrows into motion, but the three sword wraiths around Gilthanus were smart enough to use his impervious sphere as a shield for themselves.

"Damn," Taegrid growled. Morglum was cut once across his belly and once across his arm holding Mar Doldon. The half-orc was even more stubborn than Thortwerg though and growled through the pain. The swaiths held by the roots and grass tried breaking free so they could get to the half-elf and finish her off, but they could not break loose of the grip of nature. Sametria called down a bolt that struck one of her foes and vaporized its body. The armor of the swaith dropped with ash remains of the body that was once inside and smoldered. A swaith rushed up at Taegrid from behind Gilthanus and forced him to drop the Arcane Bow of Lightning. Aleiz reached the first terrace and saw seven swaiths armed with heavy crossbows poised at him. They fired.

Thortwerg ran inside the temple and saw he had two choices of stairs and ran to the right. Taegrid was forced to draw his sickle and do nothing but defend himself. Morglum took down both of his foes with a sudden hack of his enchanted battle-axe to each one. Taegrid worked his feet to keep moving backwards as he defended against the onslaught of the swaith that he could not hope to harm without his Arcane Bow of Lightning. Morglum ran back to help Gilthanus and his other friends.

A swarm of crossbow bolts flew at Aleiz. Panic swept over the vermin-kissed elf and then his cloak wrapped him in shadows for the last time that day. The bolts struck the wall behind where Aleiz once stood. The vermin-kissed elf reappeared closer to the swaiths and engaged them in combat. The swaiths dropped their heavy crossbows and took out their long swords and heavy shields. Thortwerg fell to his knees with fatigue as his adrenaline rush came to a halt. He looked up the stairs and saw that his path was clear now. Taegrid continued to hold his ground and knocked away every strike that the swaith launched at him. Morglum slammed into a sword wraith that continued to bang on the invisible barrier that protected Gilthanus. Sametria brought down another bolt of lightning from the sky and vaporized her other entangled foe before turning her attention towards Gilthanus and the others. A series of twangs were heard and she looked up to see the first terrace of swaiths had fired their crossbows not at them but inward. The third terrace of swaiths did send their bolts down at the exposed heroes.

"Not again," Sametria complained. Of the seven bolts that came down, one struck dangerously close at Sametria's feet in the ground. Another struck Morglum in his back and made the half-orc grimace in pain.

"I guess they have magic weapons," the half-orc grunted through the pain. Taegrid used his opponent as cover from a bolt that came towards him and the rest ricocheted off the invisible barrier around Gilthanus. Sametria chanted a spell and five of the heavy crossbows suddenly bent into a useless shape. Sametria smiled as she brought down another bolt of lightning and vaporized the swaith that had Taegrid on the defense.

"Thank you," Taegrid yelped as he ran over, scoped up the Arcane Bow of Lightning, and slung it over his shoulder. The two remaining crossbow wielding sword wraiths began reloading. Aleiz stabbed his kukri through a swaith and when he pulled it free, the undead being fell from the terrace to the stairs below leading to the temple. He was alone and surrounded by six of the swaiths. Aleiz made a choice and jumped off the terrace while he had a clear path. Aleiz tucked and rolled on the ground next to the bottom of the stairs that led up to the temple some twenty feet below. The impact blasted the wind from his lungs, but

Aleiz came to his feet and caught his breath. With another lightning bolt cracking down along with the swinging of Morglum's axes, the heroes had killed all of the swaiths that remained below. Gilthanus dispersed his spell and the heroes ran up the stair with Aleiz leading the way. A hail of bolts struck down at the stairs after they were safely inside as a warning that this was not going to be as easy as the heroes believed.

"Potions, quickly Gilthanus." Sametria instructed. The elf sorcerer grabbed several vials and tossed them to his friends. Aleiz saw Thortwerg standing to his feet by stairs to their right and ran a potion over to the wounded barbarian. Sametria yanked the crossbow bolt out of Morglum's muscular back before he drank the potion. The potions revitalized the heroes, but many of their wounds remained. Gilthanus made sure his friends wounds were closed before the swaiths began to swarm down the stairs from above. They came from both sides and Shang Tao appeared from the shadows blocking their escape out of the temple.

"I let you drink your potions when I could have easily killed you. I offer you one more gift, a swift death." Shang Tao hissed. The swaiths came in from the right and left and Shang Tao came from their rear. A wall surrounded the temple on the first level, but not on the next two. They had nowhere to go but into battle. Aleiz and Thortwerg blocked the swaiths to the right from coming down all the way and forced the fight to stay on the stairs giving the swaiths even more of an advantage. By giving the swaiths elevated advantage, Aleiz gained a better advantage. Because they were crowding down the stairs, the swaiths were limited on movement and could not move around as defensively as if their fellow swaiths were not right behind them. Thortwerg took a chance and let his adrenaline pump again. He knew it would be hard on his heart, but he had to push himself to the limits if he wanted to survive. The swaiths had stolen so much of his strength already that even while he raged, the barbarian's strength still was not even, what it was normally. Taegrid's strength had been sapped to the point that even with Sametria's spell he could not wield the Arcane Bow of Lightning. He moved with Morglum, which he quickly found to be a mistake. The bold half-orc roared to life as he raged and moved in on Shang Tao. Aleiz parried the swaith easily. It was like a duel, one on one by battling them on the stairs like this. The tactical vermin-kissed elf had to kill these minions as fast as he could and get to Morglum. He knew by the garb Shang Tao wore that he was a skilled samurai. He knew it would take their combined efforts to defeat such a skilled warrior. Four swaiths swarmed around Sametria. She worked with every ounce of speed she possessed to parry their strikes.

Three swaiths surrounded Gilthanus. He moved with precision just so he could deflect their assaults. Taegrid distracted Shan Tao while Morglum came in hard at the samurai turned swaith. The strange armor made Shang Tao even more resistant to their attacks than the other swaiths were. Mar Doldon could not bite through the armor at all. Gilthanus and Sametria struggled as weak as they were in combat. Sametria brought down a bolt of lightning from her spell she summoned that everyone had thought to of dissipated and the blast struck down upon Shang Tao. The samurai staggered, but only for a moment. Shang Tao moved with lightning speed almost as though the lightning bolt had enhanced his movements. His enchanted katana pierced Morglum's chest, dropped the mighty half-orc to his knees, and then cut with blinding movements of his two swords at Taegrid. Taegrid barely managed to deflect the assault. Aleiz knew something bad had happened, but he continued to hold his ground and cut down a swaith from the stairs.

    Thortwerg followed in the vermin-kissed elf's example, leaving only four more to contend with on the stairs. Taegrid focused only on defense now as he saw the mightiest of all his friends cut down with one swift stab from a blade. Morglum had not just felt a mortal wound, but a massive amount of his strength was stolen from him as well. This swaith samurai was far more powerful than any of these other swaiths. At that moment, Morglum realized that he was fighting something far worse than they had even imagined. He looked over at his ranger friend as he frantically deflected the curved blades of the swaith and forced himself to his feet. Morglum roared to life as his blood pumped hard through his veins and though it fueled his strength, it robbed him of life faster. Blood that would normally have ran out of the wound sprayed out as the mighty half-orc hacked at Shang Tao with all the strength he could muster. He left Mar Doldon on the floor and came in with just his enchanted battle-axe. The sight sent chills down the spines of his friends that saw him. His anger was so great that Morglum did not care that he was bleeding out fast through the savage wound that Shang Tao had given him. Gilthanus backed up as he chanted a spell and sent flames fanning out and catching all three of his opponents. They burned, but they did not slow their assault just yet. Sametria spun a half circle and cut one of her opponents. He did not seem to care or even cringe from pain. Undead did not continue to feel physical pain as the living did. She still sensed her spell in effect outside and called down another bolt of lightning that streaked in at Shang Tao. Smoke erupted from the swaith, but he just laughed defiantly.

"I will kill you soon enough if my minions do not," Shang Tao cackled at the half-elf. Shang Tao sensed his body was hurt, but did not feel the pain and slipped into the shadows right before their eyes. It was almost like the cloak that Aleiz wore was taking effect on the swaith in the way he simply merged with the shadows and vanished from view. Aleiz heard the commotion behind him, but he never took his focus from his opponents on the stairs. He hoped he would be fast enough to finish the deadly undead off and then get to his friends. Thortwerg was not sure how long his strength would hold up. Like Morglum, he just pushed himself harder and harder to get the fight won. Taegrid sheathed his sickle and picked up one of the fallen swaith's long swords. He hoped that it would fare better against Shang Tao.

"I need a potion Gilthanus," Morglum beckoned as he staggered and his blood sprayed out like a small fountain of blood crafted upon his chest. The vermin-kissed elf heard the call from the half-orc but kept focus on turning his opponent's attacks out wide so that he could sever the tie between their undead bodies and the plane of Oblivion quickly. Thortwerg managed a parry at the last second and knocked the swaiths shield out wide as the one Aleiz was doing beside him. It was like an artist painting a picture or a master dancer performing his finest piece, they way each weapon was swung or deflected was simply magnificent to watch from either point of view. They were all masters of their own styles. Some of them just seemed to be beyond the level of master swordsman. One such individual was Shang Tao. As Sametria and Gilthanus continued to deflect the attacks of their many foes that kept Gilthanus from grabbing a potion out for Morglum, Shang Tao came back into view. Morglum came in at the samurai fiercely, but Shang Tao caught the heavy battle-axe between his two swords and pushed it out wide away from him. Gilthanus sent out another fan of flames to slow his attackers, but they would not allow him the opportunity to help his friend. When all hope seemed lost to the heroes, Sametria created an opening again after cutting one of her opponents, she summoned down a bolt of lightning that struck home. With a clap of thunder and a flash of light, the husk that once filled the armor and held the devastating daisho set, was gone with smoke emanating from the armor as it collapsed to the floor with the two magnificent swords.

"They have killed Shang Tao," one swaith cried.

"Don't let them live," another swaith roared defiantly. Aleiz silenced one of those swaiths forever as he cut it down from the stairs before it could speak another word of defiance. Thortwerg dropped the one beside him, making the odds now even on the set of stairs. The last two swaiths that came down the stairs at Aleiz and Thortwerg swung their swords hard. Aleiz stepped aside and the sword hit the floor harmlessly. Thortwerg was not quite as finesse as the vermin-kissed elf. He roared as he smacked the sword aside with his enchanted battle-axe. Taegrid and Morglum rushed up to help their friends not just, because they wanted to, but because they had to. If Morglum did not get a potion soon, it was possible that he would bleed out. Gilthanus swept his sword out wide and knocked his opponent's blades away before sending another fan of flames out at them. This time they were fried to a crisp and fell to the floor in cinders. Morglum bled on his opponent as he fought. Gilthanus knew he had to act quickly to save his friend.

Sametria cut down an opponent and moved on to her next. She was furious. Her beloved pet and companion had been savagely killed. Taegrid killed a sword wraith with one of its brethren's own blades before turning to aid Sametria. The heroes were not letting anymore of the swaith's strikes get through. They knew that they had them. It was just a matter of time now. It was almost in unison as Aleiz and Thortwerg dropped the last of the swaiths that swarmed down the stairs. A pile of seven swaiths littered the stairs or around the landing of the terrace around the stairs from their battle. Taegrid severed the shield arm of the swaith Sametria battled and opened up its defenses for her. It still came in at the half-elf defiantly. Sametria stopped the blade with her own sword and turned it up and out wide. With the same momentum, she spun a full circle and plunged her scimitar through the armor and body of the swaith severing its connection to the plane of Oblivion. It fell to the floor when Sametria ripped her blade free. Morglum blocked his opponent's assault with his battle-axe, but not without fatigue and blurry vision. Gilthanus grabbed a vial of the powerful potion from his backpack as he was sprayed with the blood of his friend. Morglum swung his battle-axe parallel with the horizon outside and cut clean, the head from the last swaith. He dropped his battle-axe as he roared defiantly in his rage. He knew he was going to die where he stood as he felt his rage diminishing.

"No wait. Drink this first." Gilthanus called as he handed a vial to Morglum. The half-orc popped the cork with his thumb and drank it as his adrenaline stopped pumping and darkness took him. His friends watched in terror as Morglum fell to the floor motionless.

"Morglum," they all cried. The friends moved toward their fallen comrade slowly with a great and unsettling sadness.

"What?" Morglum's muffled voice responded in question.

"You live," Gilthanus cried happily, as he dropped to the floor and rolled the heavy half-orc over on his back so that Sametria could inspect the wound. Sametria saw the severity of the wound and looked to Gilthanus.

"Those potions are powerful my friend. This wound should have killed the Mighty Morglum." Sametria claimed and the friends looked at one another in awe.

"When do we get our hard earned vacation?" Aleiz chuckled. Sametria looked at the vermin-kissed elf with all seriousness.

"We are heroes my friend, we never go on vacation." Sametria answered before standing back up. She was obviously devastated by the loss of Sadie. The druid left her friends, made her way out of the temple without ever looking back, and didn't stop until she came to Sadie, her powerful wolf that she had cared for and trained. Sadie had become not just a companion, but also a good friend and now she was gone. Sametria leaned against the fur of her fallen friend and sobbed. Sametria finished saying her goodbyes and then began digging a large hole to bury her fallen friend in.

The heroes returned to the walled village of Mordakai. They had discussed the destruction of the relic on their way back home and decided that it was time to perform the ritual. They gathered outside Sametria's home and formed a circle. Sametria pulled out the Marble of Godly Doom and held it out for her friends to see in her open palm.

"We must each shed some of our blood upon it before it can be destroyed," Gilthanus instructed. Aleiz pulled out his enchanted kukri and handed it to Sametria.

"Careful it's sharp," Aleiz warned so no one would accidentally cut too deep. Sametria took the strangely designed weapon. Its blade curved in the opposite direction as a scimitar almost like a half hook. She cut a shallow cut in her palm and made her blood run over the relic as she squeezed it in her closed hand now and lifted it over her head.

"Let this begin the end of our darkness," Sametria said boldly before handing the kukri to Taegrid. The cat man cut his hand first and passed the weapon to Gilthanus before he took the relic with his bloody hand and closed it around the brilliant marble. He felt his blood join with Sametria's and cover the marble. Something was happening and the heroes could all tell as dark clouds began to form overhead. Gilthanus had cut his hand and passed the blade to Thortwerg before he reached out to take the relic from Taegrid. The cat man placed it in the sorcerers open bloody hand. It was Gilthanus that squeezed his hand shut, and felt as the three different blood coatings mixed and weakened the relic. He felt something else, but he could not tell what it was. A clap of thunder echoed overhead shortly after a flash in the dark sky.

"Is this your doing Sametria?" Gilthanus asked as he handed the relic over to Thortwerg. Sametria shook her head in response. After Thortwerg, it was Morglum's turn and then to complete the circle it was Aleiz. When they had finished, Aleiz handed the relic back to Sametria and wiped his kukri clean before sheathing it.

"It is time," Gilthanus said softly as Sametria stared at the blood covered Marble of Godly Doom. She looked on the ground and saw a flat rock. Sametria set the marble relic down on the flat rock and adjusted it so that it would not roll off. Sametria stood up and backed away.

"Morglum," Sametria called and the half-orc smiled. He knew what she wanted and took up Mar Doldon with both hands and rotated it so that the hammer side was forward. Morglum roared as he came forward and dropped it down hard upon the relic. There was a great explosion of powerful energy that sent the heroes flying backwards for several feet and erupted up so high into the sky that the clouds parted and the sky beyond seemed to open up and swallow the energy until it had completely drained from the relic. The sound it emanated was thunderous as the energy roared up from the shattered relic and into the sky. Morglum shook his head free of the daze he was in and saw that the great axe of mithral was destroyed by the power that now erupted into the sky. He was lucky to be alive. The sun did not seem to change color and light up the sky, but the powerful storm that reached out for miles did with every flash of lightning that struck down.

"What's happening?" Sametria shouted to Gilthanus. Gilthanus was not sure. He wondered if his mother had fooled him. He shrugged at Sametria. He had no words to explain what might be happening at that moment. The surge of power that drained into the sky lasted for several moments, but even when it finally ended and the sky closed up, the massive storm continued.

"Everyone, get inside." Sametria ordered as she stood up and ran over to her front door. Her friends stood up and followed her inside. They had to take shelter for several reasons. They mainly could not hear one another over the powerful thunderstorm overhead. After the last of them had entered, the door was closed shut tight and locked.

"Any ideas?" Sametria asked her friends.

"None," Aleiz gasped. They all looked to Gilthanus who stared at the floor looking angry and confused.

"I think we may have started an apocalypse," Gilthanus finally said with great thought.

"So we weren't supposed to destroy the relic?" Sametria asked with surprise.

"It would appear not. But there was nothing in the legend that would have warned us of this." Gilthanus responded in defeat as he plopped to the floor and sat with tears streaming down his face.

"There was no way you could have known Gilthanus," Sametria agreed with a soothing tone but Gilthanus still felt responsible.

"Do you mean we just ended the world?" Morglum asked as though he did not understand what was just said.

"Yeah, that's kind of what apocalypse implies." Taegrid claimed.

"Actually apocalypse means the unveiling of something. The word you are all looking for is cataclysm." Aleiz corrected.

"Thank you for that," Thortwerg growled through clenched teeth.

"You are quite welcome," Aleiz responded with a wry smile. He knew that his correction had not eased anyone's grief, but he tried to entertain them one last time before the world ended. They were his companions. They were his friends. They were family.

"Well if we are going to die, I'm take'n my things and head'n to the ocean." Thortwerg barked before storming over to the door and unlocking it.

"Thortwerg wait," Sametria called. However, he did not stop. The barbarian of the north opened the door and left her home, closing it behind him.

"He seems to have the right idea. Die on your own terms." Aleiz said in the barbarian's defense as he left.

"I think we all need to decide what we want to do with the time that remains," Taegrid said with humility.

"I love you all and whatever you decide, I will always remember you helped me try to restore our world." Sametria fought back her tears.

"We all meant well, but it seems that we actually caused our world's destruction." Gilthanus mentioned before he realized what damage his words would cause. Sametria stormed out of her front room and into her private bedroom sobbing. She had failed. Gilthanus looked to the floor in shame.

"I didn't mean to upset her. I did not think-," Gilthanus tried to explain himself but Taegrid cut him off.

"You did not think before you spoke. If this is our end my friends, I mean to return to the Great Forest where my people once dwelled." Taegrid informed his friends and then took his leave. Sametria was in her room probably crying her heart out. Morglum, Aleiz and Gilthanus stood in her front room.

"Anybody ever wonder how the centaur or satyr was first created?" Morglum asked with hopes of breaking the negative array of emotions. Aleiz and Gilthanus looked at the half-orc curiously. When they failed to say anything Morglum felt the need to finish his morbid humor.

"I had to learn about breeding somehow. My mother always scolded me and said poor goat or poor horse." Morglum boasted and his friends erupted into laughter. If they were to die that day, at least they had each other. Sametria came back out of her room suddenly and interrupted the laughter. She looked very seriously at her friends that remained inside her home. Taegrid was gone now.

"I think we owe Thortwerg his dream. And I think it would be a nice dream to share." Sametria said suddenly.

"The open sea huh?" Morglum pondered for a moment.

"Explore uncharted lands beyond the oceans and find treasure? I'm game." Aleiz said with a smile as a loud crack of thunder echoed outside.

"You know it sounds like fun," Gilthanus said evenly as he looked outside through the window to see the powerful storm raging.

"Ah hell, I'll go." Morglum grumbled.

"Get packed then. We have to make sure that Thortwerg does not get too much of a head start on us. I'll get Taegrid." Sametria instructed before running out her door to find the cat man. Taegrid had not gotten far. He was just leaving his house with his pack when Sametria arrived at his home. He owned very little and could easily fit everything he owned on his person aside from his house.

"I know you mean to return home, but how does the open sea sound instead?" Sametria asked her friend. A wide smile slowly formed upon the cat man's face.

"More adventures eh Sam?" Taegrid said playfully.

"Even in our possible ends my friend." Sametria replied.

Thortwerg ignored the raging storm overhead and tromped his way towards his home. The angry barbarian of the Frozen Wastes, kicked furniture out of his way as he began packing his back pack. He thought of the sea and imagined what it looked like and how it might smell. He longed to see it just once before the world ended. The barbarian of the north left his home with his belongings and did not bother to close his door when he had gone. He pointed himself to the east and walked. He left his friends and the small town of Mordakai behind as he left through the gates. Gate guards waved him off, but Thortwerg ignored them as he focused only on attempting to reach the sea before the world ended.

Epilogue:

The powerful storm struck with energy that seemed to harm even the army of wraiths that searched for the heroes. Many of them were obliterated by the power of the storm as they flew. When they realized the storm could destroy them with a single bolt, the wraiths instinctively tried to fly up through the clouds to get above it. With the constant flashing of lighting within the clouds, it was apparent that the wraiths were being destroyed by this storm. A single dread wraith made it through however and it could only watch from his great height as the flashing of lightning went on and on. It hissed defiantly as though it was meant to win out the night and the storm was not meant to have it as if it had taken its allies. A bolt surged upward at that moment and in a blinding flash, the soul hunting wraith was obliterated. The storm blanketed Athyx in such a manner that anyone out in the vacuum of space could only see the dark flashing storm clouds and no sign of the planet. The storm reached beyond the material realm however and blanketed the planes as well. It seemed to be calling, or beckoning to whomever it was meant to speak to and inviting them to enter the world of Athyx.

*****

Maovolence was only holding the borders against the demon forces without the aid of their goddess. The subterranean realm rocked when the power of the relic was released. No vermin-kissed elf knew what had happened or what exactly had been going on upon the surface of the world. They had been too wrapped up in their personal war with the demons to be bothered. After the quake passed, a divine energy was felt among the priestesses of Na-Dene. Even the vermin-kissed elf that had left to worship Viscus felt the presence of Na-Dene return, but they had already made their choice and could not return to the service if they wanted to. Worshippers of Na-Dene would have them transformed into vermin-kissed horrors for their blasphemy. The vermin-kissed elves that continued the worship of Viscus had formed their own vermin-kissed elf house in seclusion within the wilds of the subterranean realm and hidden from the civil war among the demons and vermin-kissed elf. Na-Dene returned to them, but surprisingly enough, she did not command them to end the war. Both sides regained their power and neither seemed to be out of favor of Na-Dene. Queen Fein'Rauvarra Lirvir spoke with a Mo'Reen of Na-Dene that had remained loyal to the goddess in her absence. The queen of Maovolence sat before Na-Dene's chosen minion, which was only one of three forms it could appear as. It was also the one most vermin-kissed elf preferred to encounter.

"Na-Dene favors neither side. She prefers that you both work out your differences in whatever way you decide so long as both sides remain loyal to her." The chosen minion told the vermin-kissed elf queen.

"Why does she not favor her own people?" Queen Fein'Rauvarra Lirvir questioned the Mo'Reen.

"During her brief absence, many vermin-kissed elves left her and chose to worship Viscus instead. After that, a vermin-kissed elf by the name of Aleiz Alvraloth joined a group of surface dwellers, shattered a great relic of power, and returned the burning sun to its painful and devastating yellow form. He has committed an act that he should not have ever undone." The Mo'Reen explained.

"What else could have been done to release Na-Dene? In my eyes it sounds more like he should be branded a hero." Queen Fein'Rauvarra Lirvir remembered the vermin-kissed elf from her younger years of schooling. She had crossed paths with him once or twice before he graduated and returned to his house to complete his training. Queen Fein'Rauvarra Lirvir was older than Aleiz by only four years, but she still thought he was very handsome when they had met.

"Your house wizards could have led an expedition to raid the prison created by Viscus and freed our goddess." The Mo'Reen responded.

"The chosen minions are divided as well. Why didn't any of you try to do this or even come to any high priestesses and suggest this?" Queen Fein'Rauvarra Lirvir dared to question the Mo'Reen.

"We made similar mistakes, but Na-Dene has chosen to forgive us. Forsake House Alvraloth and let the demon army vanquish them for you. This will bring your house favor in the eyes of Na-Dene. Brand the vermin-kissed elf known as Aleiz Alvraloth a traitor and deserter." The Mo'Reen instructed.

"This will bring my house favor, but will it help end the war between vermin-kissed elves and the vermin-kissed horrors?" Queen Fein'Rauvarra Lirvir asked.

"It will," The Mo'Reen responded with a wry smile before vanishing in a puff of smoke back to the Abyss. The queen smiled at the thought of making the decision that would end this civil war. By exiling the entire vermin-kissed elf house and moving, the borders that the vermin-kissed elf army guarded left it open for extermination by the demon army. It also restored favor to the vermin-kissed elf of the other houses. The queen thought that it was a small price to pay in order to end the war with the children of the house priestesses. She stood up from her throne and marched out of the great chamber to give the command to the other houses and to the army. For that, she had to prepare several documents to be sent out with her royal seal to show that the orders were legitimate.

Memorial to John Bradford:

My fondest memory of dad was a camping trip that we took to fort Stevens for dad's first birthday. We went out in a canoe and fished for blue gill and perch. It was awesome just the two of us. I didn't have to share him. Other than that it was watching him hold Emma and listening to him tell me how proud he was of me. Damn I miss him! – Lisa (Daughter).

His humor was my rock that kept me together. He always had a comeback to whatever someone said. He was my strength, my light of day, my secret hold post to lean on; my best friend. – Katie (Daughter).

One of my fondest memories of John was one of the many times we got together with our group of friends to play Dungeons and Dragons. I barely knew John when we first started playing with him but he grew on all of us through the stories he shared about his past and how he played his unique characters. We never knew what John was going to do or say next. He kept things entertaining and his personality has since been embedded within the characters of my books that were once his Dungeons and Dragons characters. John's legacy outside of his immediate family was the birth of Kid, Gareth, Ladonna, Gelona, Morglum, Fubar, and many other unique characters. He will be missed but never forgotten. His legacy lives on with his family, friends, and through the characters in the Athyxian Chronicles that he brought to life. - Author Kevin C. Davison (Friend).

In loving Memory of John Bradford

8/3/55 – 10/5/12

About the Author:

Kevin C. Davison writes fiction novels in a fantasy-adventure based series as well as other genres. He has survived childhood cancer and conquered his childhood epilepsy as well. In his twenties he met a man named John Bradford who he began hanging out with during social gaming sessions with mutual friends. John Bradford played characters with unique personalities that inspired all present to be more creative with their own characters. Kevin's experiences of gaming and hanging out with his friend John helped enhance his creativity. Kevin already enjoyed writing for his own enjoyment. He feels without his gaming sessions with his good friends he would not have had the inspiration to write the Athyxian Chronicles series. Kevin wanted to remember his friend John Bradford for who he was in life and appreciate all he had done for him. To show his appreciation he asked to release a special edition in memory of John Bradford.

Kevin was born in Portland, Oregon. He still resides there with his family. He is an avid writer and practitioner of martial arts. Kevin has competed in mixed martial arts events over the years and still trains for competitions. His passion for writing runs deep in his veins. He has often made claims that even when he is too old to compete in mixed martial arts events, he will always write.

Books by Author Kevin C. Davison

Athyxian Chronicles: Reign of Viscus
Athyxian Chronicles: Minions of the Servant
Athyxian Chronicles: An Assassins' Revenge
Wrath